The Heart Witch
of
Speckled Hound Hollow

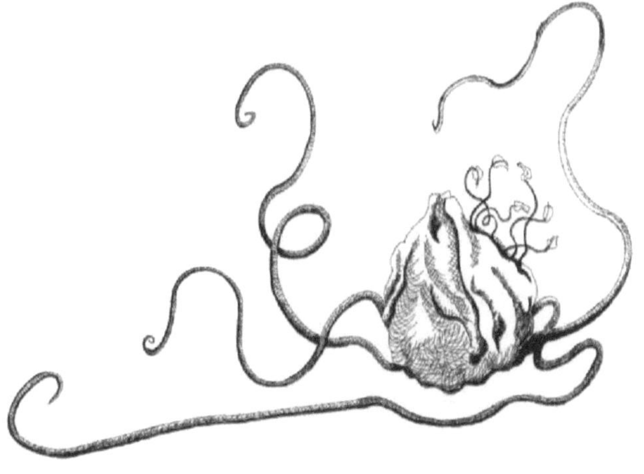

The Heart Witch
of
Speckled Hound Hollow

by Justus Joseph

EYELESS
BARD
BOOKS

Eyeless Bard Books
An imprint of Iza October, LLC
Chicago, Illinois
www.eyelessbardbooks.com

Book Cover Illustration by Tiffany Dae
Book Cover Design by Truborn Design
Map Design by Melissa Nash
First edition 2024

For all of us who belong in the Ceoghast.

Foreword

As I am Justus Joseph's little sister, born exactly 821 days after her, I have prided myself on being her first reader. I have been lucky enough to have a front row seat to her stories, which began as elaborate games in our childhood, morphed into wish fulfilment fiction (mostly about love, horses, and occasionally boy bands) in our preteen years, and have since delved into a seemingly endless well of stories. Justus cultivates worlds with an edge of macabre — and crafts intricate tales of adventure, alienation, and finding your own path in the dark. Whether it is in drawing, sculpture, writing, or even dog training, Justus has delivered her unique, whimsical world view for her whole life, and lives in a constant state of brewing more art and narratives.

This is not Justus's first book, but I am so pleased that this is the first one she chose to share with you. Like many of her protagonists, Justus has similarly needed to carve her own place, and so it seemed so natural (and, of course, unfathomably difficult to me) that her journey led her to not only deliver this beautiful and spooky book, but also originate her own publishing imprint: a place for herself, and maybe others, to find their own place of refuge and belonging.

This story — and the world of the Ceoghast — evokes the chills that only come from eerie autumn evenings, and the warmth that glows from the candles in jack-o-lanterns. For anyone who has ever felt friendless or out-of-step with the world around you, let yourself be drawn into the dark embrace of The Heart Witch of Speckled Hound Hollow. Feel comforted by the knowledge that your author is there with you, alongside Cassia Mooseroot and the many others who will come after her. You are with spirits who are driven by the elusive want to belong, haunted by their imperfections in a way that is so painfully human and ultimately deeply familiar.

If I could suggest a recipe for indulging in this book, it would be this: find a cosy corner (it wouldn't hurt if it was during a thunderstorm), ensure you have a warm beverage, and snuggle in, hopefully under a crocheted afghan. Savour it. I wish I could read this story again for the first time.

Happy Reading,
Moki Milburn

The World

N
W E
S
0 100 200 km
Jack's Patch
Swamp Witch's Home
Speckled Hound Hollow
Rider's Pass
CEOGHAST
Morrow Road
Midt
Crawling Zone
THE BORDERLANDS
Horth
TENET LANDS
Claug
Shivireen
Crepuscular Jungle

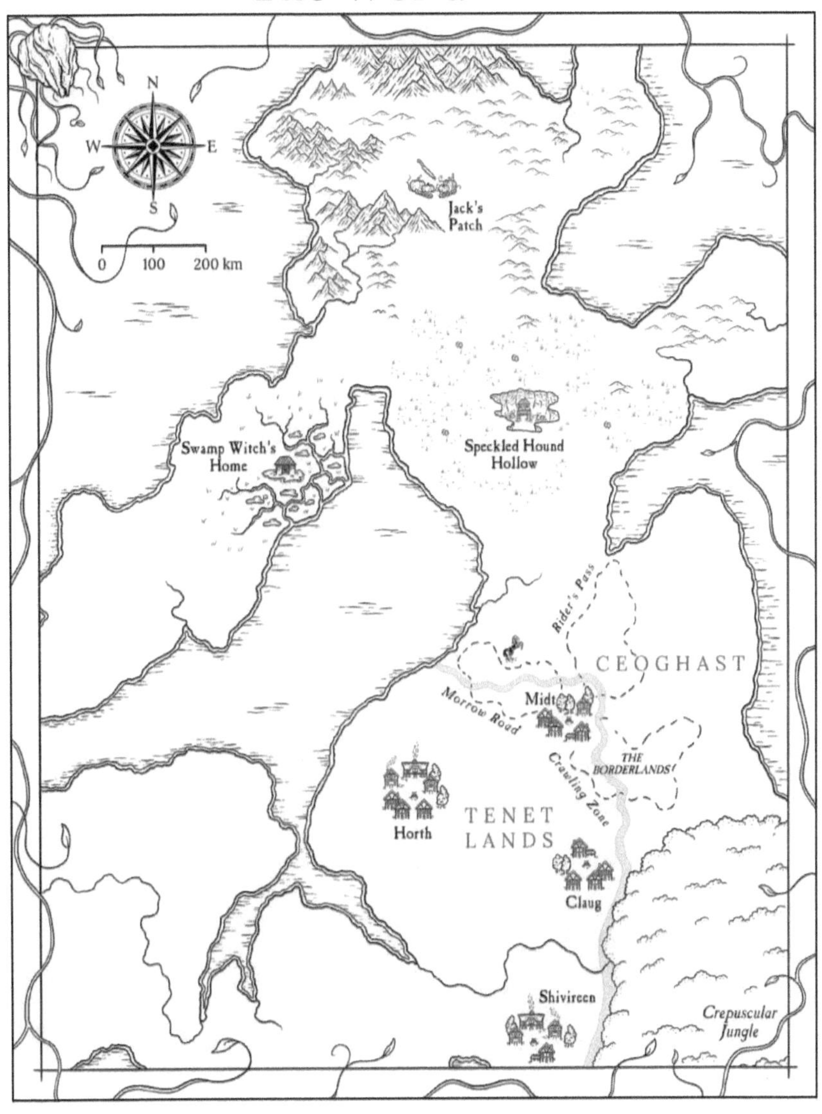

Table of Contents

Chapter 1

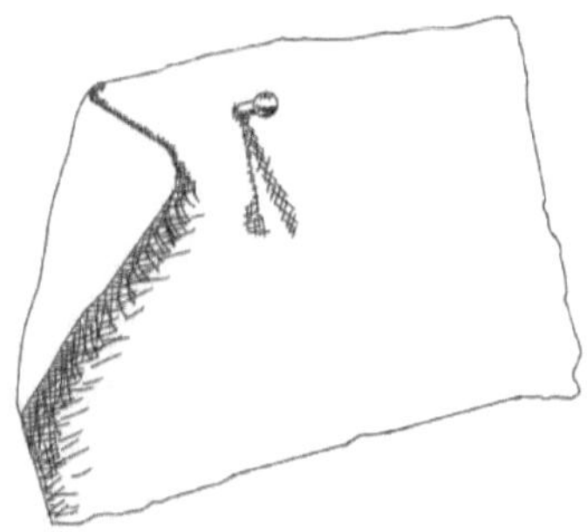

The notice nailed to my front door twists in the wind like a pinned bird, and dread grabs breath from my lungs. I don't need to read the words to know the pristine white sheet is from the town council — no one else in this small border town would have access to such fine paper. If I've attracted their attention, it can't be for anything good.

Feet heavy as stone, I force myself toward my door as my mind races to remember all I've done with my days. What did I do wrong? I've only lived in Midt three weeks, and today, like every other day, has been unremarkable. I wake and go to work at the laundry. I come home and sleep. Even within the privacy of my home, I'm careful to keep the community tenets. No one who observes me could find fault with my routine. I'm a model citizen, which means my actions are not to blame.

My stomach knots, and bile climbs up my throat. This town is supposed to be a fresh start, yet even this far from the central cities, my mother's shadow haunts me still. Do I run? I know no one here, but someone must have sent word to the town council. Why else would this notice be here?

My hand shakes too much to remove the nail, so I tear the page from the door and go inside to read it. While I don't see anyone else about, that doesn't mean I'm not being watched, and I refuse to be a spectacle. I step inside, close the door, and read the letter.

My legs are jelly. I slump to the floor and press the letter to my hammering chest. I'm alright. They haven't found me out. I'm still okay. I take a shuddering breath and rub my face.

"I'm safe here," I say, but caustic fear still runs loose within me. The words don't stick. "I'm safe."

I don't know what I've done if they learned my mother was a witch. I have nowhere else to run. Most of the central cities know the story of my mother's betrayal. People recognize my name. In my hometown, living according to the tenets wasn't enough to make me good. Everyone was waiting for me to turn.

This far away from other villages, those sorts of stories don't matter. Midt is so close to the Ceoghast that everyone here has seen real evil. They live right next to it. One village witch is nothing compared to the daily press of monsters just outside this town. Surely, even if they learned about my mother, they'd be able to see that I'm good. They wouldn't worry that I might be like her.

I haven't made friends yet, and sometimes it seems like the other washers at work only exchange names so they know who to shout at when we have a backlog of clothes, but there are a few people who seem nice. One of the women shared her midday snack with me the other day. Her name is Corna, and I think she could be my first friend.

I stand and smooth out the notice. I'm not sure what a town orientation entails, but I'm determined to make a good first impression. The landlord of my house gave me a brief tour of

Midt's main road and showed me where I was to report to work for the laundry. The town's not so big that I haven't seen the rest of it since then. Perhaps I'm to have a tour of the town hall?

I glance at my work clothes. While washing leaves my hands scoured clean, by the end of the day, my clothes, stained with grease and stiff with soap, are not. I need to change. I abandon the notice on the small table in the main room and go to my mostly empty closet. Most of my clothes are suited for work, and most of those are on the floor awaiting their own washing day, but I keep one blouse and skirt for town gatherings and nicer occasions. Even with the modest embroidery I stitched into the sleeves and hem, the outfit is plain. The tenets shun vanity, and I do all I can to make sure no one ever questions my devotion to the community.

I dress and pick up the notice again. My gaze drifts to the bottom of the page for the address, but what I find is the time. Alarm skitters over my skin, and I rush to the door. I'm late, which means I'm already in trouble. Forget making a good first impression, I've broken the tenet of timeliness. I'll be lucky to escape a formal reprimand. Why didn't I read the whole notice when I first saw it?

I dart down the main road toward Midt's town square on feet that refuse to listen to my head and instead only obey the rapid beat of my heart. The result is an undignified rush, and if anyone is out this close to darkfall, they'll think I lack a sense of propriety. It's not the impression I want to make, but tardiness is worse.

Town hall is square and white and pristine. It's the heart of Midt and the prettiest building in the whole town. Every morning on my way to work, the grounds crawl with caretakers — people who ensure the entire town square remains uncontaminated by the Ceoghast and its encroaching dark magic. With the approach of darkfall, the building is silent, and though the lights remain on in the main hall, it seems abandoned.

I race up the steps and shoulder the front door. I expect resistance, but it swings open so fast I lose my balance. I slam headfirst into a woman in the foyer. She catches me by the arms before I tumble to the floor and helps me to my feet. My face burns with embarrassment.

"I'm so sorry," I say. I smooth my blouse and hope I haven't sweat through the fabric.

The woman's face is as calm and open as a blue sky. She's older than me by a good couple of decades. "Can I help you?" she says. "You seem in an awful rush."

I try to smile through the panic in my chest, but my mouth deflates like a leaky balloon. Why did I barge in here without thinking? I should have taken a moment to collect myself.

"Oh no," I say. "I'm here for my orientation. I'm really so sorry to have run into you like that."

Only after I speak do I notice the people standing behind her. If I'd noticed them sooner, I'm sure I wouldn't have been able to make a squeak. Our ages are not so different, but these people look hard and cruel. Dressed in dark clothes, they carry knives at their hips and crossbows on their backs, and each one of them stares at me with an expression of amusement or anger. I take a step back.

"Cassia Mooseroot?" the woman says. "You're Cassia Mooseroot?"

Wide-eyed as an owl, I shift my gaze back to her. Did she just say my name? My name? Like she knows me or — I clutch my skirt to keep my hands from shaking — like she's been expecting me?

"Yes?"

"What in the ceoguts are you wearing? It's like she wants to be a target," a man in the larger group says. His face twists with glee, and my whole body prickles with fear, the soles of my feet electric in my shoes.

"Shut your mouth, Ealey," the woman says. "Did I say you can speak?"

"No, leader," Ealey says. His smile is gone, but his lips have a mean twist.

"Then be quiet," the woman says. She turns back to me. "You're in the right place, Cassia. I'm Niehe Almadon, leader of this cohort. We've been waiting for you."

"This is orientation?" I say. What sort of orientation requires a group of armed people?

"It is. We're going to teach you how to patrol the border."
Her words are like ice water.

"That can't be right," I say. That's not what orientation means. It can't be. Midt is as close to the border as I want to get. There's no way I'm going into the borderlands.

"It's right," Niehe says. "Everyone in Midt volunteers for border patrol. We have a regular group, but we often need coverage or extra help. When we do, we draw from the town. Everyone gets trained. It's how we stay safe."

"But I can't..." I trail off. The group behind her leers, and I can't think straight. I need to get out of this, but how can I do so without hurting my standing?

Niehe seems to read the fear right off my face. "How long have you been in Midt, Cassia?"

"Three weeks," I say.

"And where are you from?"

"Horth." I regret my automatic answer the moment it rolls off my tongue. I try to avoid telling people where I'm from. What if Niehe or one of her cohort knows someone from Horth? How long would it take to find out about my family?

My head feels so light it could drift away. News travels through every inland community fast, but towns at the edge of civilization — places like Midt — are out of the loop. This is meant to be a fresh start for me.

Niehe speaks, but terror drowns out her words.

"I'm sorry?" I say.

"I said Horth's inland, isn't it? It doesn't border the Ceoghast?"

"That's correct," I say.

"Then I can understand how this might be scary for you."

Scary? Scary doesn't begin to cover the teeth-chattering fear that screams at me every time I think of the Ceoghast. It's so dangerous it can corrupt people as far inland as Horth and beyond.

Which is what happened to my mother. She got the Ceoghast on her and became a witch. She's not the only one it happened to, either. The community hanged her and cast others out — the punishment always depends on how much of the

Ceoghast gets inside. It ate my mother whole, and I don't want to end up like her.

Niehe continues when I don't reply. "It's easy to talk about an evil place when you've never seen it up close. Facing it in person takes courage. But you already moved to Midt — you're already part of the frontline defense against the Ceoghast — so I know you have that bravery in you."

I moved to Midt to escape my past, not save the world. I know better than to share that, but I need to get out of this.

"I'm not brave," I say.

"And she's not dressed right," Ealey says. A few of the others laugh at this.

Shame floods me, and my chin trembles. I suck in a breath and hold back tears. I'd been so careful about my clothes. I'd wanted to make a good impression, but the bright white blouse is the exact opposite of what these people wear, and now everything is going horribly wrong.

"You're brave enough," Niehe says, as though Ealey hadn't said a word. "We go every darkfall, about the same number of us, and we patrol the borderlands in pairs. One of my cohort is out tonight, so we need you to come with us. If you don't, we'll have one group of three, and that means we'll either miss patrolling a section, or we'll have to cover more ground in a limited time. It's sloppy work either way, and if we mess up our patrols, we put the whole community at risk."

Heaviness gathers in my body like Niehe has piled stones into my arms and told me to carry them. I don't want to endanger anyone, but I include myself in that. Going near the Ceoghast, that's too much.

"It's just," I say, but Niehe interrupts me.

"I'm not saying you have to volunteer with us forever. I'm just asking you to be a caring member of the community and give us one night. I'll send you along our safest route. We haven't encountered monsters out there for a few months now, and the last ones we saw were easy to kill. You won't go alone. You'll be safe. More than that, you'll help keep Midt safe."

Monsters? Kill? No one will respect me if I let my fear of the Ceoghast put Midt at risk, but I'm shaking my head before the full rebellion against Niehe's plan settles over me. "I —"

"Let's go without her," Ealey says. "She's obviously not ready for this. Owers, Pansy, and I can team up and cover two sections. We'll take Rider's Pass and the Crawling Zone — they're next to each other anyway."

"No." Niehe's voice is a whip. She levels a gaze at Ealey that would have left me cowering. "Did you not hear a word I said? You've clearly interrupted me enough to not be listening. A double patrol means you're not as careful as you should be because you're rushing to cover ground. I know you want a kill tonight, but putting Midt at risk to get one shows a serious lack of understanding about why we're out here. You're on notice for suggesting we violate a tenet, Ealey, and I'm partnering you with Cassia. Maybe if you walk someone else through the steps, you'll better remember your training."

I choke on a cry. Being on notice for violating a tenet is one step away from having the Ceoghast on you — it means you're open to corruption. I don't want to be near anyone like that.

What if Ealey is corrupt and ends up getting the Ceoghast on me, too?

What can I say that won't sound awful? If I tell Niehe I'm worried about patrolling with Ealey, it means I'm not as committed to the tenets as I should be. Dedication to the tenets keeps a person safe, and I am dedicated, but what if it's not enough?

But then Niehe looks at me and places her hand over mine. "You're saving Midt tonight, Cassia. We couldn't do this without you."

No one has ever looked at me like I can help. Like I'm capable of so much good. I want to be that person — that's why I moved to Midt in the first place. Apprehension tries to stay the words in my throat, but I straighten my back.

"I'm happy to help," I say, and though my voice doesn't waver, it's a little higher than usual.

"I'm so glad," Niehe says. "Head home and change your clothes. Grab a bit of food for the evening, too. We don't get back until daybreak. Ealey will go with you. You two will take Morrow Road."

Morrow Road? The name makes my hand tremble. Niehe brushes past me, and my gaze snags on Ealey. His furious eyes lock on mine as his friends pat him on the back and leave town hall in pairs. Cold rushes through me.

What have I done?

Chapter 2

"Which one?" Ealey asks, hands on his hips as he surveys the three homes shoved next to each other before him.

My body doesn't feel my own as I point at mine. It's the shabbiest and smallest of the gray brick dwellings. Stout and uneven, it slouches toward the house next to it like it needs reassurance. It's not nice or big, but it's all I can afford on my washer's pay, and I was lucky to get it. Ealey doesn't move. He's so far ahead of me he can't see my gesture.

"The third one," I say. Why didn't he let me lead? He's needed directions every step of the way but never thinks to let me walk with him.

"It's filthy," he says, and I cringe. Cleanliness of the home is an important tenet, one I keep. The house is not filthy. It's just gray. Really, endlessly gray.

Ealey marches to the door and throws his shoulder against it as he twists the knob like he expects it to open. "Why do you lock your door? Are you trying to hide something?"

"What? No." My stomach feels heavy with the suggestion. I take a deep breath and remind myself that no one who looks at my rooms will find any sign of the past I want to hide. My mother is gone and dead. I brought no trace of her with me here.

Ealey twists the knob again and throws his weight into the door. It creaks but holds.

"Stop." I hold out the key. "Here."

"If you're not hiding something, why's the door locked?"

"Because I was going to orientation."

"So you don't trust us? You try to keep us out?"

"No, it's not like that," I say. "I always lock my door. It's a good safety practice."

People in Horth lock their doors when they leave. Surely they do the same in Midt. Ealey jams the key in the locks and smiles as he slams my door open. "You know Ceoghast monsters don't use doors, right?" he says as he strides inside. "They just creep in any way they can. The only thing you keep out when you lock your door is your community."

"That's not what I wanted," I say, but my mind is distracted, panicked. Ceoghast monsters? Here? "I thought we were safe here."

"We're only safe so long as we patrol the border, which," he raises his voice, "we're not doing right now because you didn't come prepared."

"I'm sorry."

"This place is a mess."

His words hit hard. I may not have anything in my home to hide, but I didn't prepare for company. Embroidery threads lay scattered on the floor from my late-night stitching. Unwashed dishes from breakfast and lunch pile on the small solitary square of countertop space I have. The door to my sleeping room is thankfully closed. I may not have a spotless home and may not want Ealey here, but I know my obligations to guests. This thought straightens my back.

"May I get you water or tea while you wait?" I say.

"While I wait? I don't have time to wait. Are you not taking this seriously? We need to get out on patrol. Why are you even standing here? Go get changed."

"I'm sorry," I say and back away. "I'll be ready in a minute."

My dinner won't tide me over during the patrol, and I have little food in the house. Actually, all I have to eat is tomorrow's breakfast and lunch. If I bring one of those, it means I'll be hungry, in addition to tired, at work tomorrow. Ealey stalks over to the small, high window and tries to look through it.

"This place is disgusting," he says. "Ugh. I shouldn't have to deal with this."

I want him gone. The way he looks at my space makes me feel like my home is under inspection. Maybe it is. Maybe he wants to find something wrong with me. The thought jolts me into action.

I grab the stew for tomorrow's lunch and pull a bag of dried fallowfoot from the drawer. My father is strict about eating fallowfoot with every meal. When I was little I used to hate its bitterness, but now I like it. The acrid taste cleanses me, and now I know it's a way to outwardly show your inner worth. My father doesn't like a lot of things about me, but he's always been proud of the fact I eat fallowfoot with every meal.

"What in the ceoguts do you think you're doing?"

I freeze, a pinch of fallowfoot squished between my fingers. Ealey's face is a snarl.

"I'm almost done," I say, too scared to move.

He grabs my wrist and I cry out, more in surprise than pain, though his grip hurts. "Drop it," he says.

My fingers spring open, and the fallowfoot falls to the counter. Ealey lets me go and grabs the dried herb. "This is fallowfoot. Why are you putting fallowfoot on your food?"

I don't want to speak or move, certain whatever explanation I offer will be all wrong, but he waits for my answer.

"We put fallowfoot in every meal," I say.

"We who?"

"People who follow the tenets. Everyone in Horth. It's part of the practice. We eat fallowfoot to prove we're committed to our community."

"No," he says. "You stupid inlanders. Do you even know what this does?" He shakes the bag of fallowfoot at me.

"It protects against witches. They can't cast a spell on you if you eat it." I trail off, less certain of the truth in the face of his scorn.

"You stupid ceogot," he says. "You feed it to witches to stop their magic. You don't eat it. They do. We need this to stop them, and you're sitting here wasting it. Is this your whole stash?"

"I have another bag." I gesture at the drawer and Ealey upends the whole of it on the counter. My stew splashes as cutlery and serving spoons fall into it. He grabs the second bag and shoves both into his coat pocket.

"I'm taking this. If I catch you wasting resources like this again, I'll report you for aiding the Ceoghast."

My throat feels tight and raw, and my teeth hurt from being clamped. I don't know what to say to make this better. How can eating fallowfoot, a practice based in the tenets, cast me in so bad a light? It's supposed to show virtue, that I'm committed to the preservation and prosperity of my community. But not in Midt. Here it makes me look like I squander vital resources.

"Take it," I say. Even my father would break this practice to help the community, but I still feel like this choice would disappoint him.

"Get dressed," he says. "How could anyone be this stupid?"

Further scornful mumbles follow me into my sleeping room. A great relief loosens my legs when I close the door. I lean against it, close my eyes, and inhale a deep, chest-swelling breath. I hold it in and let the calm flood me. When I open my eyes, the ease leaves in a rush.

If my common room is disordered, my sleeping room is a mess. What few clothes I have are scattered over the floor and thin rush mat I sleep on. None of them are suitable for border patrol. None of them are the right shape or color. In the corner, my work clothes from earlier today molder in a basket.

My job as a washer is not what I had in mind when I came to Midt, but it was the only place willing to take on an outsider. Once I belong, I'll pick a different trade, one that doesn't burn and crack my skin or leave my back in knots for days. Tonight was supposed to help me move in that direction. Ealey barks a laugh in the other room.

Though they're dirty, my work clothes are the best option I have. The short trousers are wet and the shirt is so stiff with dried soap I have to crack the sleeves to fit my arms inside. The few steps I take toward the door chafe my thighs.

When I reenter the common room, Ealey has my sister's portrait pinched between his fingers. My stomach beats against my skin. That's not his. He shouldn't touch it. He rubs his thumb over the drawing.

"It will smudge," I say, my voice high with alarm. I bolt forward to take it from him.

He lifts it out of my reach. "Who is this?"

"Please give it back. It's my sister."

"Sister? She looks a bit too young for that. Says here this was done a few months ago." Katta looks younger than she is, though she's still only eight. That's fourteen years between us. The tenets say that women are to undergo sterilization if five years pass from the date of the last child they birthed. Closeness in age fosters better sibling relationships, which leads to stronger communities. Katta and I should be only five years apart to call each other sisters. But my father remarried. We don't share a mom.

"Please give it back to me. We need to go. We're already late."

The glee in his eyes reminds me of a dog who steals meat from the table undetected. "You're the one who's made us late," he says. "You know you're putting the whole community at risk. You shouldn't even be coming out."

He hasn't given me the drawing yet. "Please," I say.

"You know I was getting Witch's Watch tonight? It was supposed to be my night. I was going to get a witch. That's what I'm meant to do: hunt witches. But now I'm stuck with you on the baby paths." He tilts his head to study me in a way that makes him seem like a bigger threat than the Ceoghast. I step back.

He drops the drawing of my sister. It drifts to the floor like a discarded leaf. I want to grab it, but his clenched fists scare me. He finally turns to exit the house. "Stay close, but don't get in my way," he says.

I grab an apple, leave the slopped stew on the counter, and dart for the door. But Katta's portrait calls me back. Her cheek, so carefully rendered in charcoal, has a thumb-shaped smear through it. Tears sting my eyes as I scoop it from the floor. I glance at the back where Katta drew the two of us. We aren't supposed to be apart like this. I never wanted to leave. I tuck the drawing it into my soap-hardened shirt and turn to follow Ealey.

14

Chapter 3

Four weeks earlier...

The uneven clomp of too-big boots on the wood floor warns me of Katta's approach. She thinks she's being stealthy when she flies into the room like a sudden blizzard, but by the time she launches herself at my back, I'm ready.

"Got you," I say as I spin to catch her.

Her laughter is a shriek as she crashes into my arms. "But I was so quiet."

"You were not," I say and hug her close. She smells like mud and dandelion milk, and I press my nose to her hair. At eight, she's smaller than most of the other kids her age but has a wiry strength that reminds me of a too-tight spring. Too much energy tamped down about to burst — this is my sister from her head to toes.

"Was so."

"Did you remember to close the front door?"

"Um, yes." She shoves herself back so she can deliver the full weight of her glare. "I'm not a baby."

I think about checking the door — if it's open when father gets home the whole night will be ruined, but then Katta starts to squirm in my arms. "You're my baby sister."

"Still not a baby." She squirms harder, not afraid to push against my stomach and throw her elbows, and I let her go. She begins to shed her book bag, outer wear, and boots like a tree sheds leaves at the first hard frost.

"Put those away. Father will be home soon, and you don't want him to catch those out," I say, but Katta is a whirlwind, already spinning toward the kitchen table.

"I'm so hungry, Cassia." She climbs onto a chair. "Is there snacks?"

"Yes, but pull out your study work. What did your teacher cover today?"

She wrinkles her round nose and smooshes her face into a scowl. "I'm too tired to study more. Let's play instead. But after snacks."

I turn back to the tea I've put together: a cup of mint for her with a pinch of fallowfoot and full fallowfoot for me, along with the bread heel I'd saved from breakfast when our father wasn't looking. "We study first, then we play."

"But not Lightbearer. I don't want to play Lightbearer. Let's be monsters." She leaps to the floor with a growl and stalks about the table, hands cramped into claws.

My stomach twists with unease. If I'd made such a suggestion at her age, our neighbors would've taken it as a sign of corruption. Katta's young enough yet to be beyond reproach — her mother is, after all, not at all like mine — but she's still my sister, which means they'll watch for any indication she's changing.

"No monsters, Katta." My voice snaps and she looks up in surprise. I take a breath and force calm into my tone. "If you don't want to play Lightbearer, we'll pick another game, but only after your studies."

"This is stupid."

"Language," I say. "Words like that aren't okay, especially when you know how important your studies are." I wish she could understand how dangerous her attitude is, but she's like a bird, flitting from one mood to the next with no regard for how she appears to others.

She runs to her bag. "I made a picture."

"Katta." None of the teachers would have given her paper to make a drawing.

"Here," she says as she thrusts it onto the table. "It's for you. See? I made a drawing of us."

If we had more money, I'd buy Katta one of the drawing books from the market, full of once-used papers no longer needed by those with money enough to buy fresh sheets. Sometimes the papers only have a few scratches on them, or a page of finely written numbers easy enough to smudge off. I rub my fingers on the drawing she's handed me, wondering how she came to have such a fine sheet, then flip the page over.

"Katta."

On the opposite side is the charcoal portrait her mother commissioned of her a month ago. This morning it had been where it was supposed to be, in the frame on the parlor table.

"Do you like it?" She wrests it away from me and flips back to her drawing. "It's the two of us. We should've both had a drawing done, so I fixed it. This one's you."

"I can tell," I say, and it's true. In addition to being taller than the spiny drawing of Katta who's mostly rushed straight lines and too many arms, she's captured how I usually stand, each hand holding its opposite elbow, and the length of my hair. Unlike Katta's professional portrait, in which the artist turned her scowl into wistfulness, in her sketch we both have huge grins that take up most of our faces.

"Do you like it?"

"Yes, but Katta, this portrait is important. Your mother commissioned it and…"

"It's better now," she says. "But don't worry. I'll put it back. No one will know."

Except we both know. What would the tenets say? Surely to keep this a secret between us violates one on honesty, or one about respecting both possessions and property? But the thought of her mother's exasperated disappointment, or of Father's rage, makes me wonder if we might get away with this secret.

"Can we have snacks now?" Katta says.

I set the drawing aside. If I can put it back in the frame and all seems well with it, I'll let the matter go. At the thought, panic jolts through my chest. Is this how corruption starts? One small slip in behavior? I shove the thought aside — I'm nothing like my mother.

"What tenet did you talk about today?" I slide her teacup across the table.

"One of the Light ones."

"About inner Light?"

"No, that would've been interesting." She kicks the table leg. "Is there honey?"

"Already in your cup." I settle into my seat beside her.

"Was it about the ground?"

"This is yucky." She shoves her cup away. "I want more honey. I can taste the fallowfoot. You know I don't like it."

In truth, I don't know anyone who likes fallowfoot. "I'll tell you what, you can have my honey portion if you can recite the tenet."

In a rushed monotone she says, "From the ground we pull the poison until our feet are Light and dusty."

I shake my head. "You know that last bit isn't part of it."

"But it's true." She lifts her foot to wiggle at me but frowns when she remembers she'd kicked off her boots. "Everything's dusty."

I slide the honey jar her way but keep my hand over the lid. "And what does the tenet mean?"

"That we're only safe if we walk on the white ground." She pries my fingers from the jar, and I let her have it.

"More than that. If we didn't purify the ground, the Ceoghast could find its way in. Even outside Horth, you could find a screambane or elementrill nestled under ordinary plants. That's why it's not safe. That's why..."

"Cassia." Father's voice snarls from the front entry, and both Katta and I jump. Neither of us heard him arrive home, which means Katta probably left the front door open again.

Katta meets my gaze, her eyes owl-wide, then we rush to pick up her things from the floor.

"We're in the kitchen," I say as I shove Katta's boots next to the hearth.

"Cassia's helping me study," Katta says. She lobs one of her books at the table, upsetting her tea. Before I can stop her, she dabs the puddle with her sleeve.

We scramble into our chairs as Father's heavy feet storm toward us. I notice her drawing still on table and shove it down my shirt. Katta opens her book just as he steps into the room. His gray eyes are winter cold, his cheeks ruddy, and his hair slicked to his head with sweat from his long walk home.

"Hello, Father," I say, my voice a quiet echo of Katta's.

"What do you think you're doing?" This is how so many of our interactions start, and no answer I give is ever correct. Still, he expects one.

"Katta is studying the tenet of…"

"You left the front door wide open, there's mud in the hall, and Katta's still in her school clothes." His fingers twitch at his side, fast as my heartbeat.

"I'm sorry, Father."

"The door was me," Katta says, "and the mud."

His glare doesn't leave my face. "You are a child. Cassia's the one responsible for this. She's meant to be an example for you."

"She was making tea. I did the mess myself."

My hand flutters on her wet sleeve. "Katta, it's fine. I should have checked."

"You know better than this, Cassia," he says. "One slip up and they'll come for you. Have you thought about what would happen to the rest of us then? What they'd do to Katta?"

"I know."

"Then why did you do it?"

This, too, is a routine part of our interactions. I've yet to find an appropriate answer, but if I highlight my failings, we avoid most of his storm. "I wasn't thinking."

"She was making tea. Why aren't you listening?" Katta says.

He finally looks at Katta. "That's enough out of you. You see this, Cassia? This disregard for order? This is what happens when you don't mind yourself. You're harming your sister."

His words are a knife, and I fight the urge to hug Katta and tell her she's safe, that she's still too young to have corruption in her. Not that she needs reassurance — she's unimpressed and unimpressionable when it comes to Father's lectures. I'm the one who's afraid, because I know what awaits her if she ends up like me.

"I'm sorry," I say. When Katta shifts, I place my hand over hers to bring her back to stillness. She's so quick to defend me, even when she doesn't understand the whole of what's going on.

Father shifts from the doorway and comes to loom over the table. His thick, scarred hands creep onto its surface and lay flat in front of us. "I've found you a job, Cassia."

Surprise chokes my next breath. I completed school more than a year ago and am meant to step into a role that helps our community and my family, but no one will have me.

Even during school, my peers refused to speak or work with me more than the exact amount required to meet their obligations. To offer me a job would mean inviting me into a close-knit group, and no one has wanted to risk being around me. I've done all I can to prove I'm a good person, that I'm not like my mother, but the unexpectedness and violence of her deceit casts a long shadow.

"Thank you," I say, all I can manage in this moment where my gratitude has no end. He's saved me, for how long can one go without work before becoming a burden on the community?

Even Katta smiles at the news. "What will she do?"

"You're to work in a laundry," he says. "You start next week, which means you'll have to move sooner."

"Move?"

"I've arranged for you to take a carriage with other workers going east."

"Father." Gratitude drains from me as though from an open wound. "Where am I going?"

"You're moving to Midt."

Midt. My mind scrambles to remember which town that is, but Katta's faster. "And those who keep the borders clean: Midt and Claug and Shivireen. That's right by the Ceoghast," she says. "You can't send Cassia there."

"It's a border town," I say, picturing it now. One of three small towns right against the border that divides all that is good in the world from all the dangers of that vile scar of land.

"You can't send Cassia away," Katta says. She launches herself from her chair, badger-furious, and I grab her into my lap. She fights my arms, but I press her close and murmur all the tenets of calm into her ear.

Father doesn't move. "You'll pack tonight," he says. "I'll buy whatever you need for your new job. The carriage leaves tomorrow evening, so be quick about making your list. I'll have to get to the shops before work."

Katta's body softens, and she begins to cry. She turns and wraps herself around me, but I hardly register her as I press soft, soothing circles into her back. My body doesn't feel my own — the shock of this news too much to hold in so confined a space. I'm losing everything. Who am I if I don't have my family?

"Give her here," Father says, and though Katta tightens her grip around me, when Father walks about the table to take her, neither of us resists him. He takes her to her bedroom, leaving me in the kitchen to think, except all my thoughts are slippery, impossible to catch.

Father returns and sits across from me. "I expected you to be more grateful."

"I am grateful," I say. "It's just… I want to stay here."

"You'll never find work here," he says. "No one's going to take you on when they expect you to be just like your mother. You staying here does more harm than good, especially for Katta. Just look at what she's like. You let her get away with too much, and she keeps trying to protect you. It's no good, Cassia, and I won't have it. She has a real chance here, and if you stay, you take that away from her. The farther away you are, the better."

"Were there jobs closer?"

"None for you," he says, and it's clear he's the one who's barred me from them. Sending me to Midt serves a larger purpose. He doesn't want me here, doesn't want my mother's shadow to hurt any of them, and doesn't care what damage it does to me.

"It'll be a fresh start," he says. "No one knows who you are. To them, you'll just be another worker gone to the border to help hold back the Ceoghast. If you keep your mouth shut, no one needs to know about your mother."

Could that be true? Hope stirs in my chest. If I could just fit in, become a true member of the community, I'd be safe for the first time in my life. My stomach roils at the thought, butterflies and nerves and hope. But to leave Katta…

"Are you listening to me?"

"Can I come back to see Katta?"

"We'll have to see how you do. You get yourself set up well, and we can see. You can write her in the meantime." He sits back and crosses his hands over his stomach. "You have a real opportunity here, Cassia, and I expect you to make the most of it. You stay here, and you'll end up on the rope just like your mother. It's no good, not for you and not for us."

My tongue feels sticky with shame. "Yes, Father."

"Good. Go get packed now. Give me a list of what you need before dinner, and get this mess cleaned up." He gestures at the table with our now cold tea and Katta's book.

I stand to leave for my room and feel Katta's portrait shift under my shirt. A quick glance at my father shows he hasn't noticed, and rebellion roils in my chest. I'm going to keep this portrait. I know it's not in perfect alignment with the tenets on theft, but surely even Katta's mother wouldn't begrudge me this when I have to leave Katta behind. In light of all I'm about to lose, one small comfort doesn't seem too large an ask.

Chapter 4

Ealey doesn't talk as we leave Midt. He rushes ahead on legs that seem to grow longer with every step. The odd shuffle-run I adopt to keep up with him makes me huff for breath. I don't neglect the tenets that pertain to body and health, but I don't observe them with as much enthusiasm as others. Others like Ealey.

He doesn't look back, not once.

What if our whole night is like this? Me chasing after him through places less safe than this? I heave in air and press after him. My thighs chafe against my damp trousers, and my chest burns.

All around me the ground darkens from the bleached white that marks a safe community to a deep, dark brown. The scent of wet earth clogs my nose. Our tenets teach us brown ground is full of rot. While plants grow from it, we may not eat them as it invites corruption into our bodies. Only food grown in water specifically purified and prepared by trained farmers is safe. But not everyone follows this tenet. It's the one broken most often, though the punishment is to lose one's place in the community.

Each step I take falls on softer dirt, like every aspect of the world has gone shifty and unstable. My boots protect me from the poison of such earth, but I still don't like walking upon it.

We reach a crossroad and Ealey stops. Unlike me, he's not the least bit winded. Not that he acknowledges my discomfort. His head is upright the way a sight-hound's is when it finds the trail it wants.

"Are we close to the borderlands now?" I say. Even though I dread getting there, I don't want to travel much farther. My body is heavy and clumsy with fatigue.

"You're in them. Can't you tell the difference?"

"Oh, yes," I say, realizing I should have known the ground indicated the border. Ealey's glare makes panic jump in my chest. My mind shouts at me to say something while also telling me to stop talking. "I didn't know they were so close."

"You didn't think a border town would be on an actual border? Did you learn anything about Midt before you decided to move, or did you just show up like some lookeeloo outsider?"

The insult stings, both because it implies I'm in Midt to judge it and bring gossip back to Horth, but also because even if I wanted to, I never belonged in Horth. No one there would want me back, except Katta.

"This," Ealey says with a flourish at his feet, "is Morrow Road."

"Oh," I say. I don't want to be here.

He then points east. "And that's the Ceoghast."

Unless the Ceoghast is a wall of silvery mist, I don't see it. Before I think too hard about what I'm doing, I move closer to Ealey. One step, then another. It's all cold gray ahead of us until I stand next to Ealey, and then the Ceoghast jumps into view. I cry out and leap back, but now that I've seen it, the vision stays with me.

A dark forest suffused with purple light that hangs like a fog stands before us where moments ago nothing existed. Fiery orange and icy blue lights float between thick, tall trees, flickering in and out of view. Gone is the smell of wet dirt. Instead, a warm sweetness brushes past us, buttery vanilla, and browned sugar with the smoky undertone of autumn bonfires. I inhale deeper to tease out the woodsy, floral scents.

"You smell that, too, do you?" Ealey sounds impressed, but when I look at him his nose is wrinkled in disgust. "You get used to it after a while. It's hard when you first start, but you do it enough and the stink fades into the background. Niehe told me it's like working in a butcher shop: all offal and rot until you adapt. Pinch your nose until you get used to it."

My fingers are stiff as I do what he suggests, but the sweetness is already inside me. I can't stop smelling it, and even though I know it's wrong, even though I'm suddenly so scared my knees shake, I like the scent.

The Ceoghast smells better than the best bakery in Horth, better than anything I've smelled in my entire life.

Is the Ceoghast trying to get me? Is this how corruption starts?

It has to be a Ceoghast trick, but I can't ask Ealey. If he really does think it smells like decay to everyone and I don't fit that pattern, he'll accuse me of being the problem. Who knows what he might do to me then.

Ealey kicks the ground, and in the preternatural silence around us, the rock scatter is deafening.

"Shouldn't we be quiet?" My heart pounds so hard I feel off-balance, like each beat lurches me forward.

"Quiet?" His scorn is back. "They're the ones who should be quiet. We're here to hunt."

The hunters I've known in my life use stealth to find their prey, but I don't point this out to him. Noise seems likely to attract the wrong sort of attention here. Morrow Road is supposed to be the safest path, but I suddenly realize that doesn't mean we'll be safe. "Will Ceoghast creatures attack us?"

Ealey's shoulder droop. "Not likely on this road." He kicks more rocks and shouts, "But I'm ready for you monsters!"

"Don't," I say, both my hands outstretched as though to stop him, a reflex I regret.

"Don't? What do you mean, don't?"

"I'm not... I shouldn't be out here."

"But you are," he says, "and that means you're going to do your job. You had your chance to quit when we were in Midt. This is what you chose. You're going to see it through. I already had to give up Witch's Watch for you. Do you even know how lucky you are to have me? Tonight I'm supposed to kill a witch, or a decomposed groll, or even a leering Jack. I'm not supposed to be standing here on Morrow Road babysitting an outsider with the sense of a ceogot. So I'm going to attract whatever I can to us, and then I'm going to kill it."

He turns down the path and jogs away from me. I rush to catch up. The path is easy now, all downhill momentum. I settle into my stride, and I'm almost level with Ealey when I realize the land isn't sloped. This stops me cold. It's not a downhill momentum that's made my walk easy but a pull toward the Ceoghast.

It's on me, like gentle hands at my back urging me forward, offering to take my weight and walk me right into that evil place. Is that why Ealey goes so fast? Does he feel the pull, too?

But his teeth are clenched, his shoulders hunched. Nothing about the Ceoghast is nice for him. So what's wrong with me? Why is everything I experience so different?

"I'm not ready for this," I say. I'm too scared to stick this out. Even if it means I go back with a tarnished reputation, I need to get away from the Ceoghast. We haven't even encountered a creature yet, but I'm certain I won't survive this. The Ceoghast wants me.

"You're sticking this out," he calls back. "Just defend yourself if you see a Ceoghast creature and stay out of my way."

"I don't know how to defend myself," I say.

I haven't moved to join him. I don't want the Ceoghast's pull to carry me away, to trick my feet into crossing a border I can't come back from. Stories about the Ceoghast road crowd my mind. The road can sneak under your feet, and once you're on its path, there's no way back. You're headed straight for the heart of evil.

"You'll be fine," he says.

"No." I jog to catch up to him. My feet don't want to stay on the path but I keep my course. "I don't know what to do."

"Hit it with your knife," he says with a stabbing motion.

"I don't have a knife."

His glare shrivels me. Awkwardness and shame grip my entire body. My feet hurt, my clothes are wrong. I am inadequate and inept.

Ealey speaks with angry, measured words. "You're walking the edge of the Ceoghast. Why would anyone have to tell you to bring a knife? What did you bring?"

I want to show him that I am prepared, that I have an item on me suitable to be a weapon, but I don't. Instead, I cringe and lift the apple I took from home.

From the moment I stumbled into town square late and unprepared, Ealey and I haven't been on good terms, but the rage that whitens his face now makes me want to run. He grabs a branch from the path and kicks off the dried leaves to give it a smoother grip. He throws it at my feet with such force it hits my shins. I cry out in pain.

"Take that," he says. "If something comes for you, hit it. Can you do that?"

A small drop of blood blooms on the fabric where the branch tore my skin. I press at it with my soap-hardened sleeve as I bend to pick up the makeshift weapon.

"I can do that," I say — but can I? How fast will a Ceoghast creature be? How big? Will I even hear it? What if more than one comes at once? "Ealey?"

He shoves me hard, throwing his entire weight into his shoulder. The branch flies out of my hand as air leaves my body in a rush.

This is it. I've pushed him too far. A triumphant, savage shout rips from his mouth as he raises the crossbow. He fires, and I have no time to react.

The bolt misses me. His shot is so far to the left I finally realize he's aiming for something else.

That's when I see it. A hand skitters across the ground like a spider. Green and vine-like. It's not human, can't possibly be a real body part, but I can't shake the image of a diseased, severed hand. Vines lash at Ealey from its wrist.

It springs at him from too many fingers. I scream.

Ealey's swipe is fast and hard.

"Even the plants out here mean you harm," he says.

The hand, which I now can tell is a plant, falls at his feet. Gone is the angry man who led me here. He looks jubilant. His sudden ease softens his whole body. When he crushes the plant beneath his heel, he even smiles.

"Maybe having you out here is a good thing," he says. "This route's usually dead quiet, but this guy..." He kicks the plant out from beneath his foot, and the plant curls in on itself like a squashed fist before it stills entirely. "...was obviously targeting you. Maybe it sensed your weakness."

The whole world tilts when I stand. Ealey catches my arm. He looks at me with pleasure, and the worry in my stomach starts to dissipate. I still have to ask, "Why is that a good thing?"

"If they think you're helpless, that means more will come for you. When they do, I'll be here to stop them. We might even get something big, a real Ceoghast creature." He squeezes my arm in the way Katta would when she shared news that delighted her. The touch ends as quickly as it came. "It was so stealthy. It's probably killed hundreds of animals it was so good. If anyone else was on patrol with you instead of me, it would've grabbed you before they noticed. They might have managed to get it off you eventually, but it would've done some damage. You're lucky I was here."

I believe him. I am lucky he's here. Even now, with all the terror beating in my stomach, I feel the Ceoghast trying to lure me in.

I will never come out here again. When we get back to Midt I will quit the border patrol and find another way to prove my worth to this community. I don't care if it tarnishes my reputation a little. I can make up for it. If not for Ealey, I could've died tonight, unknown except for my mother's shadow.

I refuse to die before I have a chance to show my community how good and unblemished I am.

Ealey hoots and dances a few steps around the dead plant before kicking it off the path.

I will make it through tonight by sticking close to Ealey. He might be on notice for violating a tenet, one step away from having the Ceoghast on him, but compared to the Ceoghast itself, he's not the threat. I walk up beside him. "Let's keep going," I say.

Chapter 5

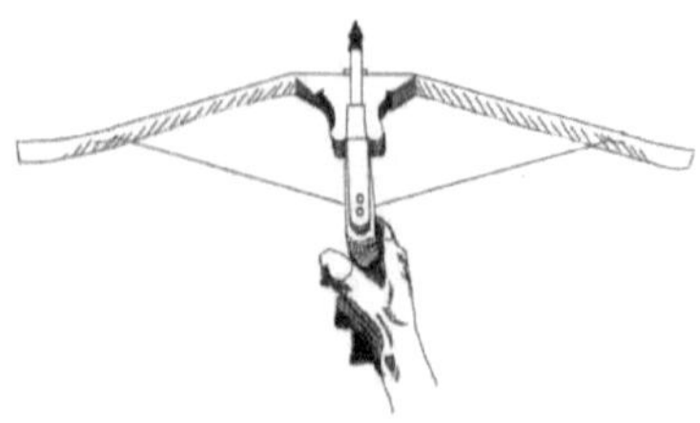

The hours drag, slowed by my expectation of ambush and violence at every step. This night is endless, and in the wraithlike shadows of the Ceoghast's tall trees, every suggestion of movement registers as a threat. I can't shake the shiver between my shoulder blades. We walk with the Ceoghast to our left, but I feel it all around me. Small tugs at my ankles pull my feet from the path. A soft pressure, like an unwanted hug, urges me toward that active darkness.

If I go, if I let the Ceoghast take me, it promises peace and warmth and sleep. To resist takes so much energy, so much effort. I am tense and tired and worry I'll stumble down a path from which I won't be able to come back.

My thighs are chafed, and the blisters that formed at first have popped. Even with the fabric dry and soft now, pain surges into my stomach with every step. I don't think I've ever walked so far or so long.

The orange and purple lights pulse when I look at them, faster and faster, like a predator's excited heartbeat. Bright bright bright bright. I don't mention them to Ealey. He can see them as well as I can, but they don't seem to jump for him.

When we first set out, he was jovial and retold the story of his kill as though I wasn't with him, as though the incompetent partner in his tale was another person all together. But now his storytelling is over. His mood sours. The farther we go along Morrow Road without encountering a Ceoghast creature, the more Ealey's posture grows hunched. The harder he adjusts his grip on the crossbow.

For a time, he makes me call out to entice the monsters he hopes lurk near us. Now he shouts at intervals I can't predict. The strident tones pierce me, but I'm too worn down to jump the way I did at first. Each time he yells I feel like a beaten dog too used to poor treatment to acknowledge any new abuse.

I want to ask for a break. A moment to sit on the dark brown ground and let its softness hold my weight. But what response would that provoke in Ealey? He's determined to find and kill another Ceoghast creature, one bigger than the last.

"This is it," he says, and relief floods my body.

We've come to another branch in the road. If not for his guidance I would have gone astray at the first. Paths that appear to go toward the Ceoghast can end up farther from it, and those that cut away have taken us to its very border. I'm afraid I'll misstep and set foot on the Ceoghast road if I'm not careful.

"Is it okay to sit?" I say.

"Sit?"

"Not for long."

Anger whitens his face, and I raise my apple, bruised from the clench of my fingers, to explain. "Just so I can eat this."

"Eat it standing," he says. "You're headed down that path."

He points to the right and I nod, then bite into my apple. I cringe at the mush that fills my mouth. If Katta could see me she'd squeal in disgust. Neither Katta nor I like bruised fruit, but I would always swap my apple for hers if mine was in better shape.

Ealey starts down the left-hand path. I frown but follow. Is he confused?

"What are you doing?" he says.

"Patrolling with you." I don't mean to make my words sound like a question, but uncertainty shakes every vowel. Is this a trick question?

"I told you to take that path."

I glance in the direction he indicates. "But where are you going?"

"We need to split up here."

My stomach is in free fall. I fumble the half-eaten apple when my hand releases it in shock. "What do you mean?"

He walks back to the crossroad and kicks at the foot of the trail he intends for me to take. "You're going to stay on this road." He moves like a rolling storm as he comes back to me. "And I take this one."

His path points straight toward the Ceoghast. It's so long and dark I can't see its end. For all I know it may go inside. Fatigue dulls my thoughts, makes them thick and slow, but I'm more afraid of being alone out here than I am of walking closer to the Ceoghast with Ealey.

"We need to stay together," I say. I flinch at his look of disgust. "Niehe said we go in pairs."

"We are a pair," he says, "but this is the point where the path splits us up and we walk in parallel. The next time you see a crossroad, you stop and wait for me. That's where our paths meet up again."

His voice is like mine when I teach Katta the tenets. I know more than her and have to find ways to get her to understand. In this he has more experience, but I can't go without him. Deferring to him in this might kill me. What if the Ceoghast notices I'm alone? That he's not around to help me?

"You said the creatures might target me. If you're not there..."

"Do you want the Ceoghast creatures to get into Midt? Because that's what's going to happen if you keep this up."

"No. Of course not." I'm horrified at the suggestion. The whole reason I'm out here is to help the community. I mean to be there when Midt needs me, but I don't think Ealey has this right. Or am I the one in the wrong? Did I misunderstand Niehe?

"If we don't split up here, that leaves one branch of Morrow Road open. That means the Ceoghast creatures won't be scared back to the Ceoghast. They'll take it as an invitation to invade town. The only thing that keeps them back is this border patrol." Frustration makes his voice louder. "If you shout, I'll hear you, so get going."

In this preternatural silence how could he not hear me? Even if we were farther apart than he's implying, my voice will carry. But that doesn't mean he'll be close. That doesn't mean he'll make it back in time to help.

In the corner of my eye, the lights in the Ceoghast dance. They sweep and spin in a way that makes me think they anticipate my abandonment, that they respond to the words Ealey and I exchange.

"What if the Ceoghast gets on me?"

"Who cares about you? You're putting Midt in danger." His words shame me. He's right. No one cares about me, and when Midt's safety's on the line, no one should.

Midt's wellbeing may be our priority, but fear hijacks my mouth. "If I go down that path and a Ceoghast creature attacks me, you won't be able to stop me from becoming a ceogot. You won't get to me in time."

"Do you think I'm your personal guard? When we're out here, we take care of ourselves. We take care of our community."

Chittering swells from the Ceoghast. I startle, every muscle tense, but Ealey continues as though nothing has changed.

"You've wasted enough of our time. You've already put Midt at risk. So these are your choices: follow me and get thrown into the Ceoghast, turn back and good luck not ending up there anyway, or go down the path I've told you and meet me at the crossroads in half an hour."

"Half an hour?" I glance down the path. Can I do that? Be alone for that long? For Midt?

He bucks his crossbow in his hands. "Yes. Now get going."

All around the chattering fades back to the unnatural silence. Is that good or bad?

"Do we have to split up again after that?"

"No."

I don't feel safe or reassured, but I only have one chance to remake my life, and this is it. If anyone found out I'd put my desire ahead of community need, I'd be ostracized. I touch the outline of

Katta's portrait tucked against my chest. She's so much braver than I am. She'd laugh at me for being so afraid.

"I'll do it," I say, "but you need to help me if I call for you."

"I'll be there in seconds," he says. "You know I wouldn't miss killing another creature. See if you can find a good one, something bigger, for me."

This last comment may be a joke, but he delivers his words with a seriousness that makes my skin prickle. I tighten my grip on the apple, like it's all I can do to keep myself together. Ealey walks away with a bounce in his step. The lightness is so different from his earlier moodiness. Will he find me again later, or is this all a trick to get me out of his hair?

I turn to the road meant for me and hold my browning apple to my chest. "Ealey?" I say.

"You're fine," he calls back. "Get moving."

I do what he says, and step by tentative step, continue the border patrol alone.

Chapter 6

Despite what Ealey said about my path being easy to follow, every few steps a new side trail offers a different way to get lost in the borderlands. Each route is thin and uncertain, meant for whatever wildlife dares come this far, but they seem threatening. A creature could crouch under the brush beside such paths and leap at me. I might not see it before it grabs me. I try to look everywhere at once but can't keep track of all I should watch for.

"I shouldn't be out here," I say to myself, not for the first time since Ealey and I separated. This time, my stomach grumbles in response, and I glance at the apple in my clenched hand. I need to eat. I can't be far from the point where my path converges with Ealey's again, and if I don't eat before we regroup, I'm certain I'll not have the chance. Ealey will shout at me if I slow him down.

To my left, a stump offers a modest perch, and I make my way over to it to rest while I eat. My legs can't keep this up for much longer. When I get back to Midt, I'll pay more attention to the tenets of the body. I'll never go on another border patrol, but it would be good not to huff like I do on nicer physical excursions.

When I sit, the relief that washes over me brings fatigue sweeping in like a flood. Exhaustion pours into my limbs like blood, and my arm shakes as I bite into the apple. The mush softens the fruit's crunch, but the sweet coolness is bliss. I bury my teeth into it to suck out the juice. For the first time since we split up, I hope Ealey takes his time.

A rustle from behind freezes me in place. A light crunch, like a foot over leaves, has me slipping from the stump to the ground. Swine make such noise in autumn when they're taken out to uproot Ceoghast plants that grow under the cover of fallen leaves.

No snuffle reassures me that a common creature shares my space. Apple to my mouth, I peek around the stump to find the source.

Foliage puffs into the air a few feet as though thrown. Up and down. The shuffle-crunch sounds precede the launch of more red, gold, and brown leaves into the air.

Not a swine. Not a swine, but maybe a child? A really small child? On the Morrow Road right outside the Ceoghast…

I take a breath to steady myself and choke on the apple's juice. I pull it from my lips and try to silence my cough in my soap-stiff sleeve.

I huddle on the ground. Do I call for Ealey? The thought of inviting his anger when I don't know what's out there squashes the idea. If it's nothing and I interrupt him I don't know what he'll do.

I peek around the stump as another bunch of leaves go up. Whoever, or whatever, this is can't be very big. The leaves aren't thrown far or high, and it's… this is a game I know. When I was a child, I used to play this way with friends as we made our way home from school. We'd charge at autumn piles and toss them into the air so we could spin like dancers under them as they fell.

So what's under the leaves? Do monsters play games? Curiosity prickles under my skin. This is dumb. I'm acting like Katta — and that thought spurs me forward.

I am still too far back to see anything, so I creep from the stump. I don't want to disturb whatever stirs the foliage, and I pick my steps with care. One crunch could give away my approach, and I want to go unnoticed.

Another pile of uplifted leaves obscures my view of its source, but as they fall, a small figure emerges twirling beneath them. The joy of their play surrounds my chest like a hug — when did I last feel free like that?

The figure is about two feet tall, and the bulk of it has the rough, scraped look of a bulbous root vegetable. Long, delicate stamens reach upwards from a small cleft near the top, and unwieldy stalks stretch from the bottom and move in waves along the ground. These stalks gather the leaves into piles and hoist them into the air.

I try to make sense of its body as it plays. The root vegetable portion seems to be a head, and the stamens seem to denote the backside. Its undulous stalks are its limbs. From within the head a hollow grunt-like sound reverberates, like the noise is trapped inside. These grunts have a flat yet musical quality, and I think it might be humming as its plays. Triumphant exclamations punctuate each armload it tosses into the air. It spins and hums and throws leaves, lost in a private delight — one I shared as a child.

Until it sees me.

It freezes in place as though never animated and seems even more plant-like than before. But its vines are halfway in the air with an armload of leaves, and though it doesn't have eyes, it sees me.

A tremor shakes its limbs and it begins to thrash. A high keening fills the air as it tries to scoop itself away from me.

If Ealey hears it, he'll rush over and kill the creature. And if he catches me close to it...

I don't want to imagine what he'd do to me. He'll accuse me of corruption. I can't let him see me with it. I move, but the creature howls louder so I shrink back down.

"Shh," I say. I hold out my hands. "Hush, please. I won't hurt you. You need to be quiet. Please, be quiet."

Its keen continues, and its stalks spasm. My heart hurts to look at it, to see how much I've scared it. Surely Ealey will hear it, and if he comes here, he won't hesitate to kill it. If it can't run away from me, it needs to stop making so much noise.

I hold out what's left of my apple. "Here."

The creature stops mid-flail. The sudden silence rings in my ears.

"It's yours." I hold the apple closer.

The creature bobs toward me on shaky stalks. Its weight shifts forward and back, and its stamens bristle in a way that reminds me of a spooked cat.

"You're okay," I say. "This is yours."

When I speak to it, the stamens soften and sway. One thin stalk reaches for the apple, and I shuffle closer on my knees to bridge the distance between our outstretched limbs.

It touches my palm, soft and quick like the lips of a shy horse. I don't want to frighten it again, so I keep my whole body still. It pokes at the apple a few times, then rests on my palm a moment, as though it needs time to contemplate how to approach the fruit. I wonder if it expects the apple to respond. An ache in my cheeks tells me I'm smiling. I can't remember the last time I smiled with such ease — probably not since I left Katta.

The creature's stalk slides over my skin with the smoothness of a snake. It knocks the apple from my palm and I reach to pick it up, but the creature wraps itself around my wrist before I move a finger's width. Its grip surprises me, not painful but firm.

"Don't," I say.

"Cassia?" Ealey says.

I spin around and am off my knees so fast I feel dizzy. Ealey stomps onto the path from behind a thick bush, loaded crossbow in front of him. I tuck my hand behind my back and try to shake off the vines that continue to encircle my wrist. The creature bounces against the back of my trousers as it dangles. "Why were you making so much noise?" he says.

I'm relieved and horrified that he thinks it was me. He hefts the crossbow, and though it's not aimed at me, anxiety crawls across my skin like ants.

"I was... I got scared," I say. I lower my head to avoid his gaze and slip my other hand behind my back to pry the creature off. I can't let Ealey see me with it. He'll shoot me.

"Did you see a creature? Did something come out of the Ceoghast?" He shifts his focus to the darkness at my back with an eagerness that makes me shudder.

I hesitate. What happens if I tell him? Can I explain the creature attached to my wrist? No. I should have led with the creature if I wanted Ealey to believe my fear. I should have cried for help. Why didn't I?

"Well?" he says when I'm slow to answer.

"No," I say, and my reply startles me. One of the vines tickles the palm of my free hand as I try to untangle the thicker stalks about my wrist, and I think back to the creature playing in the leaves. I don't want Ealey to hurt it, so I can't show him the creature, but to lie outright?

"I was just scared," I say. "I don't like being out here alone."

"Are you kidding me?"

His anger flares bright, and I flinch. "I'm sorry."

"Do you know what your whining's cost me? Nothing big's going to come out if you howl your face off because you're afraid of the dark. We already made that clear. I'm out here on this nothing of a route because of you. I'm supposed to kill a Ceoghast creature tonight because it's my time. My time. Do you know how long I've waited? And now I'm stuck with this?"

His fingers twitch against the crossbow. Branches crack beneath his feet as he steps off the path toward me. The creature drops from my wrist, and I worry Ealey will see it. It stays pressed against the back of my trousers, which means I can't step away from Ealey as he comes in closer.

"My little sister has five kills already," he says, "and if I don't come back tonight with at least one, my family will..."

The creature wraps its vines around one of my ankles as an arrow of green sends Ealey off-balance. He catches himself and whips his head back, glare locked on me. A long line of blood wells across his forehead and spills onto his face like water from a pitcher where the creature hit him.

I open my mouth to scream or explain or apologize, but before I can utter a syllable, the creature peeks around my legs to jabber and hiss at Ealey.

Panic surges in my chest with such upward force I gulp air to keep from vomiting. The apple churns in my throat.

"What in the ceoguts is that?" Ealey says. He wipes blood from his eyes, an action that smears it onto his cheeks and neck. A smile cracks his face open. "Is that your familiar?"

"No," I say, but the creature's empty howls swallow my mousey objection. I stand in horror as it lashes its vines at Ealey, all menace and threat, like it wants to protect me.

Or am I its shield?

"I should have known," Ealey says. He fidgets with his crossbow. "New girl shows up in town by herself and wants to join border patrol? You're not going to poison my town, witch."

"I'm not a witch." My voice is louder, but so is the creature's. I want to explain what happened, but Ealey's jerky movements and too-wide grin tell me he won't listen.

"Maybe I should thank you," he says. "It's not every day a person's first kill is a witch."

He raises the crossbow. I lift a hand to defend the creature then realize midway it's not Ealey's target.

I am.

I step back, but the creature is behind me and has my legs tangled in its vines. I fall. The thunk of the crossbow chills my blood. Did he hit me?

"Ealey, stop!" I say. "I'm not a witch. I'm not evil. This…"

"Shut up," he says. "Shut your ceogot face."

The blood in his eyes makes it difficult for him to fit the next crossbow bolt. He won't listen to me. Whether or not I'm evil doesn't matter to him. All he wants is his first kill, and he thinks I'm it. I need to run. To get back to Midt to explain. I need help.

My attempt to stand fails as I'm still entangled with the creature. It pauses and its bulbous head seems to consider me for a moment before it renews its angry chatter at Ealey.

The bolt clicks into place.

Unable to untangle myself with the speed I need, I grab the creature in my arms. Ealey blocks my access to Morrow Road. I can't reach the path that took me here. At my back, the Ceoghast resumes its gentle pull.

Not that way. I can't go that way.

Ealey winds the crossbow. I hear the telltale snap as the string falls into position. The creature wails and wraps its vine around my waist as Ealey lifts the weapon.

I turn and flee into the Ceoghast.

Chapter 7

Ealey's boots thump hard on the ground behind me and push me to run faster. I can't outrun a crossbow bolt, but Ealey won't have an easy shot so long as I stay in motion. Can I outrun him?

The Ceoghast whips by in blurs of navy accented with wild cerulean and fiery orange. The lights I'd seen at a distance now bob to avoid me as I crash toward them. Helpful as they are, they're also tiny horrors. Within the ethereal spheres, shapes that suggest reedy limbs and broad, flat teeth hang suspended. Never together in the same sphere, each miniature severed body part has its own separate space.

My heart dips and takes my energy with it. I can't do this. He'll get me. He'll catch up. The thought shoves panic into my limbs, and I regain my stride on its electric pulse. The creature holds me tight. Maybe it's the only force that keeps my body from breaking apart to become one of the lost lights. Is this how they happen?

Mad and manic, I can't breathe now. Each breath catches in my throat and can't make it all the way down to where I need it. The air is too thick, and I am too strained.

All at once the Ceoghast lights flare. Blinded, I fall.

Whatever land my feet expected to find before them becomes air. I pitch forward, too winded to scream and too tired to brace my fall. I hug the Ceoghast creature and tuck my face against its cool, smooth head.

My knee hits the ground hard, and I roll onto my hip like a shirt wrapped tight to wring out. My hands fly out, but I don't stop until I hit a hard edge of a solid object. Movement wakes pain throughout my body, but I lift myself into a seated position. The Ceoghast creature unfurls its tendrils from around me and stretches them into the earth. So supported, it swings away from me and nestles into the grass where it settles, so still it looks lifeless.

What felt like an endless hole as I fell is a small, sloped cavity. Moss and grass grow on the soft earth alongside sprouts of unusual mushrooms, and a tall, smooth rock — the object that stopped my roll — rests in the center. The rock is broad enough to sit on, were I so inclined.

I am not so inclined.

Instead, I strain my ears for Ealey, but only soft night noises reach me. The air is still and smells rich with a buttery sweetness. My ragged breaths are the loudest part of the Ceoghast. I try to hold them so I don't draw attention to myself. Who knows what might be out there.

Is Ealey? Did I lose him?

If he could see me, he would've announced himself and shot me. I must have lost him. Or he's turned back to Midt.

Panic runs through me, and I press both my fists to my mouth.

No. He can't get to Midt before me. He'll tell everyone I'm a witch. They won't believe I'm not because they don't know me yet. If he goes back and tells them what he thinks happened, I'll never be able to set foot in Midt or any other town ever again. They'll kill me on sight.

I have to get there first. I have to beat Ealey back to Midt. Which way is it? Which way did I even come from? Each side of this hollow looks like the next. My fall didn't even leave an impression on the springy grass, but I did hit the rock.

I stand and turn to survey it, and the Ceoghast creature stirs. Its stalks move in waves as it regains its animation. The stamens at the back of its head are bright with its own light. It rotates its head one way, then another. When its front faces me, the creature stops, pulls its limbs in close, and begins to hum. Trapped inside its root vegetable head, the sound's sweetness is made discordant by reverberation.

After a few moments its stalks begin to undulate, and then they reach for me. With speed I didn't know I had left, I run from the creature.

I never would've been in this much trouble if I hadn't tried to protect it. Had I gone mad in that moment? I'd lied to Ealey. Surely that wasn't my fault.

I scramble over the edge of the hollow and dart into the woods.

The creature... it must have enchanted me, and now that it has me in the Ceoghast, I don't want to know what it might do to me.

Which way is Midt?

My chafed thighs ache, and sharp pain clicks in my left knee each time I bend it. I must have injured it when I fell. It feels like I have a pointy bone lodged behind my kneecap. Each step hurts more than the last. I push past the pain and run harder. Again, I hear the clomp of boots and alarm strangles the cry I make. I honk like a startled gosling and whirl around.

No one is behind me, and when I stop, the pound of boots stops, too. Laughter turns into a sob when it bubbles up my throat. Did Ealey even follow me into the Ceoghast, or were the boots I ran from this whole time my own? Did he go straight for Midt?

I spin in place but every part of the Ceoghast looks the same, all dark forest and creepy lights. If I stick to one direction, I'll see the sun or the town or some other sight I can use to navigate back to Midt. The tenets don't say anything about how to survive the Ceoghast — only that moral community members should never enter it.

I am good, though. I just didn't have a choice.

I need to get back to Midt.

The hum reaches my ears a moment before the creature comes into view. It is frenzied, all stressed out vines and too bright stamens. I won't let it catch me.

The pain in my knee builds as I run, and on my next footfall it doesn't hold my weight. I fall and skin my palms on rocks and dry twigs that break and jab me. I try to get up, but my legs won't take me any farther.

The hollow hum floats by me. Frantic, I search for a place to hide. That's my only chance to get away from this eyeless creature. The forest doesn't offer much aside from trees, but one of them has a base thicker than the others and there are no odd lights around it. Its branches trail on the ground and provide a bit of cover.

I drag myself over to it and settle against its trunk. It's not a great place to hide — the kind of spot Katta might have picked when I first introduced her to hide-and-seek — but it's all I have. My sister's portrait is still beneath my shirt, still safe. I pretend she's with me and summon the bravery I felt around her.

The creature's hum grows louder. My knee twangs when I shift. I can't run. What can I do if it discovers me? Ealey's voice runs through my mind, "If something comes for you, hit it. Can you do that?"

Shame burns my cheeks, the humiliation still immediate. Hit it. I could hit it.

With the creature closer now, I keep my movements slow and silent. I pull on the exposed roots of the tree in hope one might be a loose branch I can use to protect myself.

Closer. The whip-whip of its stalks brutalize the ground.

The next root I touch pulls free of the forest floor. I pull it to my chest and clutch it with both hands. The hum decreases in volume. Curiosity prickles at me, and I tamp down the urge to take a look. I wait until I can no longer make out its inharmonious notes, then peek around the tree.

The creature is gone.

I sag against the trunk and let the branch fall in my lap. My hands shake. I can do this. I can get out of the Ceoghast. I'll pick a direction and walk until sunrise, then I'll know which way to go. Ealey won't be in Midt yet. He'd have to finish his border patrol. Surely he wouldn't endanger our town. I still have a chance. I've got to.

"You can do this," I say aloud. My voice is choked, but the words give me strength.

I stand and bump into the foliage overhead. I flick the rubbery leaves and wiry branches from my face.

A hand slaps over my mouth.

Others grab me.

I scream, but the hand deadens the noise. The palm is sticky with sap. I twist to fight against the grip, but the hands lift me into the air.

Up, up, up...

Chapter 8

The height paralyzes me. I've never been so far from the ground, so near the top of a tree.

The hand clamped over my mouth is not a hand but a plant like the one Ealey killed earlier this evening. Each branch of the tree ends in a gathering of hand-like protrusions. I don't know how many have grabbed me — enough to cover every part of my body.

I yank at the bindings around my wrists until I realize that whatever holds me might let me fall. The threat stills me. But when I slacken, the vines constrict. Acid burns my exposed skin, and an acrid scent floods my nose. I yell and thrash, and the burn fades as the hands soften their hold.

My chances of escape dwindle with every unsuccessful pull and twist I attempt. Limbs numb with fatigue, my body feels heavier than it's ever been. I don't have much more in me.

I need help.

Even Ealey with his crossbow would be a welcome sight right now. I scream into the plant that covers my mouth again and again until I'm hoarse. I call for Ealey. I call for the Ceoghast creature. I call for anyone who might hear.

No one comes.

I fight and yank and bend until the last of my strength rushes out of me like water down a drain. When the acid starts to eat my skin again, I can only twitch. I sag into the plant hands that hold me, defeated. This is all too much.

With effort my gaze focuses on the ground. My sister's portrait looks up at me from the detritus and grass below.

Katta.

Tears run down my cheeks and drip onto the far away ground. What will Katta hear about me? That I was a witch who fled into the Ceoghast? She won't perform my death rites. My body won't rest within community walls. My soul... I can't think about my soul. If I die here it will be the end of all my good in this life and the one that follows.

I lift my head to resist the plant again, but my strength fails. I flop forward. The vines tighten on me with a hiss. Then the crack of a lash fills the air.

At first, the sound seems part of the tree's movement, but then the little Ceoghast creature charges into the hollow below and flails its stalks at the tree's trunk.

It's come for me. Dread and hope surge through me. I don't know which emotion to grab. The little root is the only one around who might help me, but it may mean me as much harm as this tree.

Its tendrils crack like whips and strip bark from the tree. Compared to the tree's immensity, the attacks are too small to make a difference. But that doesn't mean the tree will let the attack go without challenge. Branches and vines speed past me toward the root creature. The tree flicks the creature's stalks away with the ease I'd use to shoo flies, and the gesture only costs it a few leaves. The creature may not be much given its size, but I shout encouragement. The hand plant over my face presses harder into my mouth to catch the words.

One vine lowers itself behind the tiny root creature and curls its plant hand into a fist. My warning doesn't clear my mouth.

The fist slams into the creature's head at its stamens and sends the creature into the rock. Even surrounded by the shushshush of leaves, the thump is loud enough to reach my ears.

The root creature shudders and tries to lift itself, but its limbs seem overcome with instability and it topples.

More confident now, three hands rush out on long vines and grab the root who makes a hollow shriek in protest. The hands heave the creature out of the clearing, back into the forest.

The ground blurs beneath me.

"Come back," I say, but it's too much for my raw throat to manage. I cough and gasp for breath when the hand over my face shifts. I pull away to keep the long finger-like stalks from covering my nose. Does it meant to suffocate me?

I thrash again to free myself, but now that the root creature is gone, the tree's focus is on me alone. Maybe if I'd thought to fight when it was distracted, I would've had a chance to get away.

The edge of my vision ripples with movement. I fight harder to yank free. I want nothing to do with whatever the tree's prepared for me.

My left arm swings lose. I grab at the vines in panic. "Don't drop me," I want to scream, but the words are muffled.

I look back at the trunk and there, with stalks pointed like knives, is the little root creature. It's scaled the tree. Level with me now, it focuses its attacks on the vines that hold me. With quick thrusts, it severs the hands from their vines. A few cling to me, but without the vine to feed their strength, I shake them off.

The creature frees my legs next, and I dangle from one arm. Hands crawl up my body like spiders with finger-thick legs that dig into my flesh. I kick and swat at myself to get them off and they fall. When the last one drops, giddiness swells in my chest until I can't keep it in and laugh aloud.

I'm going to be free.

That buoyant thought delights me only for a moment before it cuts through me with ice.

"No, wait," I say to the root creature as its stalks dash toward the last of the vines. My voice cracks. The warning doesn't go far. Hands continue to let me go as they're cut away, and within a breath there are too few to keep me in the tree.

I fall.

Handfuls of sap-covered leaves rip from the tree as I try to catch hold of any part of it that might save me. I can't die like this.

This can't happen. My dread seems to drag me down faster.

Vines swathe my arms and wrap around me. A jolt stabs my shoulders as they tighten and slow my descent. They cannot stop my fall, but they soften my landing. Air rushes from me as I hit the ground, but I roll away with bruises, not broken bones. The root creature swings down beside me.

All around us a noise as loud as applause breaks the silence of the Ceoghast. Confused, I look about and see no audience. It's the tree. It sways and shudders. Plant hands slap and grab at one another. A vice squeezes the breath from my chest as the hands tear each other from the tree. The tree's turned on itself, and seeing its strength and fury, I realize that could have been me. If it had touched me like this, it could've torn my body to pieces. But perhaps it was playing with me, because now it's full of purpose.

Hands rain down from the tree and thud to the ground where they twitch like dying insects. The root creature drums on my leg, but the hands hold the whole of my attention. Not until they jump up like spiders and rush for us on green fingers do I look down at the rapping.

The root creature laces its stalks into my hand and yards me away from the clearing. We run, but my knee slows us down. The click-click-click a countdown to contact.

The root creature shoves me forward and throws its stalks out to spear the plants.

I heave myself over the edge of the grassy basin and hobble into the forest. I spot a branch on the ground and grab it. If the plant comes for me, I'll be ready to fight this time. The pop in my knee worsens, and I have to stop. I pause away in a small clearing and do not try to hide.

I wait, each minute thick as the warm air around me, until the root creature lopes into view. No hands follow in its wake, and my knee quivers with relief. I don't want to run again. The creature gives a dulled hoot as it approaches, and I don't move. I don't want to be chased. I don't have it in me. I heave in a breath, hold it, and listen for pursuit.

Nothing.

The creature's stalks curl around my acid-raw fingers and tug at me. I let the breath out. With it comes all the tears I've held in, and I collapse on the ground. Shudders roll through my body along with a bone-deep chill. I curl my knees to my chest and cry. How did my attempt to fit in go so wrong?

I should be in bed by now, exhausted from work I did in a community garden or from conversations with the elderly. To be out here, lost in the Ceoghast, is too much.

I ignore the soft pats atop my head until the patter becomes gentle circles. The root creature nestles closer and brushes my face with its green leaves, reminding me of how Katta wiped away my tears before I left home. Shock runs through my fingers. Katta's portrait. It's still in the basin where it fell.

I shove myself upright. I need to get it back. I can't leave anything of Katta in the Ceoghast. What if a Ceoghast creature finds it and decides to hunt her? What if a Lightbearer finds it and thinks she's a witch?

I'm on my feet and take a few painful steps before the root creature hums and gets my attention. With great care, it pulls my sister's portrait from its head. It had rolled the parchment around one of its slender stamens.

I drop to my knees when it offers the paper to me, and I stare at the drawing until my eyes blur again.

"Thank you," I say and tuck the portrait into my shirt.

I don't know what this creature wants with me, but it's saved my life and recovered my sister's portrait. I'd thank it even if it intends to eat me now.

The creature hums and lifts a tendril. I take the offered limb in my hand and ignore the trill of doubt I feel when it wraps about my wrist.

Right now the Ceoghast is my enemy. This creature may be part of the Ceoghast and just as evil, but it's also the only hope I have to get out of here.

"I need to go home," I say. "To Midt."

A different hum now, and the same bob I fled from earlier. That it's happy is apparent, but what its happiness might mean for me is another matter. Still, when it tugs on my hand, I follow.

Chapter 9

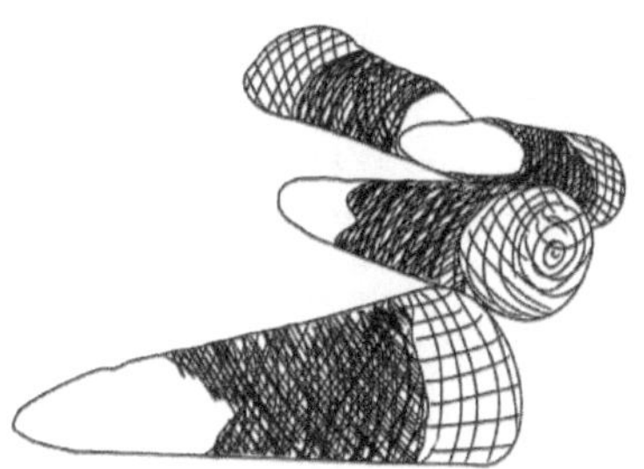

None of the paths are apparent until the root creature steps
onto them. With a single tap of its vines, the route unfurls with
light, the whole length of it clear. The way it opens reminds me of
Horth's winter festival where townspeople line the main street to
the town's center with unlit candles. A Lightbearer lights the
candles farthest from the town square and then walks the path as
the townspeople transfer the flame from one candle to the next.
My family was always farthest from the square, so I could watch
the glow jump up the line. The procession of fire delighted me,
even as our placement in line illuminated my family's shame.

The Ceoghast paths spark with radiance for the creature in
much the same way, though I can see no source. Shudders grip me
each time the paths here appear, and while they're beautiful —
how could light in so dark a place be anything else? — I'm certain
the root calls them into existence through evil means.

All the while, the creature hums, and I begin to think of it
as Hum. Hum the Ceoghast creature. Perhaps its song is what
shapes this place.

To name such a being, even only in my mind, must violate
a tenet. I can't think of which one, for none makes so precise a
restriction. But I'm certain no respectable person would ever be in

a position like this. How will I explain it? To hide this part of my experience is dishonesty. To reveal it would be death. I know I'm good, but how can I go back to Midt and not be found corrupt?

Hum brushes flowers and other plants as we pass. Unlike Hum, they don't appear to have personalities or any other unusual animation, but I no longer trust my impressions. This is not a safe or normal place. I hold my arms close and make myself as small as possible to avoid touching anything.

What if Hum's talking to them? Do plants have conversations? Unless their interactions involve directions to Midt, I don't think any exchange between them would please me.

"Are we going to Midt?" I say. "I need to get home."

Hum waves its stamens in my direction as it bobs its head. I can't begin to guess what the movement might mean, though it confirms the creature heard me. Hum bobs when its happy or pleased, or maybe when it wants me to think all is well.

I need a better answer, even if it's unreasonable to expect one from a Ceoghast creature. Especially one with a root vegetable for a head. How does such a creature even live? Or is this a distortion of life?

I take a huge breath to quell the panic and shove my mind back to the matter at hand. When I'm home, I can consider the perversion of this place as much as I want, but for now I have to make sure I'm actually getting home.

"Wait," I say.

Hum rotates on its many stalks and tugs on my wrist. In this we are clear: Hum wants me to follow.

I want — need — to go home.

Darkness surrounds us still, so I may yet beat Ealey back to Midt, but only if he decided to complete his patrol and even then... I don't know how long our route was supposed to be.

"I need to go home," I say and try to explain by gesture what I mean as I speak. Hum doesn't have eyes but it's managed to find me well enough so perhaps it has other senses. A stab of horror accompanies the thought, so I press on. "I need to go home. I need to go to Midt. Midt is a town. It has lots of houses."

I steeple my fingers together and Hum feeds a tendril through.

"Home," I say. "I need to go to my home."

Hum rests on its stalks and bobs side to side. With each sway I feel my future weighed.

"Please take me to Midt," I say. My hands press my stomach to quiet my nerves.

Hum scurries off the path but is back before I figure out whether it intends for me to follow. It bounces to me and lifts its cupped stalks to my face. Inside its makeshift bowl are small tricolored striped triangles. I stare without understanding. What does this have to do with getting me home? Hum must have interpreted the steeple I'd made to be these triangle pieces.

I push Hum's stalks aside and open my mouth to speak, but Hum scoops up a triangle and angles it at my mouth.

I recoil.

Hum taps the triangle against its root head then offers me the piece again.

"I don't want it," I say.

Hum repeats the gesture.

It wants me to eat. The apple I ate earlier is a distant memory that can't fill the emptiness in my stomach. I've walked and run more this evening than I've ever done in a day, and the stress of my surroundings leaves me lightheaded and anxious.

No matter how hungry I get, I won't eat Ceoghast food. I refuse to invite corruption like that into my body. I eye the triangle. No natural food has such weird colors or stripes.

Hum pushes the triangle close to me again, and I take it, worried the creature may force it into my mouth if I don't. When I bring it close to my face I smell stove-warm butter with vanilla and brown sugar. My stomach growls.

Evil tempts.

I pretend to eat the triangle but palm it and chew on air instead. Hum makes a satisfied chirp and drops the rest of the pieces into my hand. When it resumes its traveling tune and picks its way down the path again, I shove the triangles into the stiff pockets of my trousers and trudge after the creature.

The direction of our route doesn't change, so either Hum has always been taking me home, or has no intention of taking me where I need to go. Whichever the answer, Hum is energetic and uses its tendrils to slap out beats to accompany its song. The result is musically rudimentary but catchy. The rhythm invites me to tap out my own accompaniment.

I won't fall for it. Won't let any part of the Ceoghast seduce me. When my fingers try to twitch in time, I ball my hands into fists and take heavy, off-beat steps to crush out the urge.

"Only the good deserve community. Only the unblemished belong. When we are together no evil shall triumph. The people here know right from wrong," I say under my breath.

The children's rhyme soothes me. Surrounded by darkness, these words are my light. My shoulders relax away from my ears.

The more I recite the rhyme, the more purposeful I feel. I will make it back to Midt. Whether or not I return before Ealey doesn't matter as much as the fact that I will return. I'm new in town, but I've lived an exemplary life in Midt. If people noticed me, they would know my actions there speak for themselves.

But they hadn't noticed me. Hadn't let me in.

"The people here know right from wrong," I say.

They will know the truth when they hear it. Ealey's on notice, which is one step away from having the Ceoghast on you, and while I'm not established, I'm not blemished in Midt.

They'll believe me. Even if Ealey's gone back with a story already, they'll let me back in.

Overhead the sky darkens. I look up and find that Hum has led us under a curved brick bridge. What it spans is a mystery to me, as the land around is flat and even. When we're halfway under most of the light trickles away. Hum reaches for me with a stalk and takes my hand.

Light explodes with the force of a sudden fire on a dark night, and I pull at Hum to escape the sudden shift. The creature holds tight and heaves me out from under the bridge. I blink to clear my vision of the hot white spots.

We're no longer in the forest.

Before us stretches a land of light and horror. Hills twist upwards in uncanny shapes without regard for nature. Trees plump with fiery red and soft lavender leaves sway in a breeze heavy with the scents of woodsmoke and shaved chocolate. Gone are the disembodied lights, replaced instead with slivered silver that blinks from the foliage like eyes or teeth. Each breath burns my throat with the chill of first frost. Worn cobblestones press beneath my feet and branch into five different routes.

Worse even than the unusual twists and turns the ground takes are the flowers that bloom along each route. Evil's Triumph is the only Ceoghast plant I've ever seen outside this terrible place, and seeing it now threatens to drown me in memory.

"Where are we?" My words are choked. This is not the way back home. These roads will not take me to Midt. I'm deeper in the Ceoghast than any decent person should be.

"Why do you have a stunted squash?"

Between the uneven cobblestones and Hum's undulating stalks, I nearly lose my footing as I spin to face the voice. "Who's there?" I say. The voice had sounded human but other creatures in the Ceoghast might have the ability to speak. I should've grabbed another branch, had a weapon of some kind to hand.

A dark shadow steps out from under the bridge, and even the brick is gone, become white stone carved with ornate swoops and whorls. Its majesty stuns me, but pales in comparison to this stranger's beauty.

Tall and lithe, they move with molten grace. Their dark hair stands round and tall atop their head with green and purple thread woven throughout. Their clothes sparkle like sunlight on water and an iridescent green shimmer highlights their cheekbones. They are beautiful in the way that first cherries are: all smooth youth and showy color.

When their gaze meets mine, I forget what they've asked. I open my mouth to ask who they are, or maybe apologize for not answering them, but Hum's enraged growl silences me.

Hum charges at the stranger in the same manner it had attacked the tree. The stranger laughs, a sound of pure light pleasure, and my stomach churns with worry for Hum.

"Hum," I say, but the creature's already reached the stranger, throwing itself into a fight I know it will lose.

The stranger is casual in their rebuttal. They deflect the stalks with a cane and keep the knives strapped to their hip and legs sheathed. Still, I flinch at every crack. Hum's vines must be bruised and broken.

The stranger's face darkens from the joy of novelty to annoyance when Hum refuses to relent.

"Hum," I say to warn the creature, but in its fervor it doesn't acknowledge me.

With a wide swing, the stranger sends Hum flying back in my direction, stalk over stamen. I crouch and gather Hum's disoriented limbs and scowl when the stranger laughs again.

"You could've hurt it." Regret pinches my stomach when I hear my voice, shrill and uncertain.

"And what do you suppose she intended to do to me? I'm not the one who started the fight. You should be thankful I didn't split her head in half."

Her head? I glance at Hum who tenses under my scrutiny. I tighten my arms about her.

"You mocked it — her," I say. "And you came out of nowhere. What do you even want?"

I ache to shove all the words back in my mouth. They sound childish and petulant. A flush crawls up my neck like an ink stain when the stranger laughs again.

"What do I want? Well, I asked you a question, didn't I?" they say. "What are you doing with a stunted squash?"

"Stunted squash?"

"Surely you didn't think you'd made off with a Jack?"

"I don't understand what you're saying, but I didn't make off with anything. I'm not a thief, and I'd never touch anything in the Ceoghast, never mind take it."

The stranger's head tilts and their cat green eyes narrow. "You're an outsider."

"No," I say. I've heard the word too many times to stop my reflexive protest. I hate the word. I'm not an outsider. I belong to a good community.

But I don't belong in the Ceoghast.

"I mean, yes," I say. "I'm not from the Ceoghast."

"And yet here you are using the Eldritch Ways."

"I'm just trying to get home."

Hum begins to untangle herself and makes small hollow growls I know aren't intended for me.

"You're trying to get home, outside — what did you call this? The Ceoghast?"

"Yes," I say. "I need to get home. Now."

The stranger's face lights up and the smile they bestow on me is godlike. Beauty like theirs is unnatural, so perfect and balanced that nature seems flawed and grotesque by comparison. Even the night can't hide the blush that burns my cheeks.

"My name is Knave," they say. The way they shape their name makes me think of butter spread on dry toast, all soft and sweet. "And if you want out of this place, I can help you."

"You can?" My heart thuds hard, and I'm more awake now than I've been all night.

"I'll take you to the borderlands right now, and if you let me know your particular destination, I'll get you as close to it as possible."

My hands shake, and Ealey's voice chatters in my mind. I can't tell a ceogot where I'm from. What if they want to know so they can invade it?

"Why? Why would you help me? What do you want?" My voice is strong this time. I won't fail to protect my community.

"I want a favor," Knave says, mouth warm with a grin. "One favor."

"What is it?"

"I don't know yet, but it won't be big. Maybe a bit of food for the road, or a place to sleep for a night or two."

"Here?" I say.

"Oh no. Outside. Away from this place. You have nothing to offer me here. But out there? One favor. One small favor that will put you at no risk and cost barely a thing," they say. "For that favor in the future, you can have your freedom now."

Refusal sits on my tongue. I hold it there while I consider the cost. This is a trick. Maybe Knave and Hum are in this together and trying to fool me somehow, but if it means I can leave the Ceoghast?

"If I promise to grant you a favor once I'm back home, you'll take me to the borderlands near my village now? Tonight?"

"This very moment," Knave says.

"And you won't follow me in? You won't invade or hurt anyone?"

Knave laughs and sweeps a hand along their body. I blush and study the buckles on their shoes. "Do I look dressed for an invasion? That's not really my style."

I almost ask what their style is, but I need to get the details of this agreement straight. "And your favor won't hurt me — or anyone else in my community — in any way?"

Once I'm home there's no way I'll deal with this ceogot, but in case they do show up, I need to be sure we'll all be safe.

"I'll hurt no one, and I'll come alone. I'll make sure no one else ever knows I've come. What other assurances do you need? The night wears out. Dawn approaches. It seems to me you need to be somewhere in a hurry."

I don't know what to do, and Hum's no help. Her growls have faded to occasional irritated grunts. How long will I wander the Ceoghast if I don't have a real guide? This place is huge, bigger than I want to think about, and I don't know where I am within it.

Even the brightest of Lightbearers can't stave off the corruption of this place for more than a month, and I'm not so good or holy. I need to get out of here as fast as possible.

Knave's smile widens when I meet their gaze. "One small favor in the future that doesn't harm or endanger me or anyone else, and you lead me to the borderlands now," I say.

"And to which part of the borderlands shall I take you to?"

The lump in my throat makes me quiet, but I force the words out. "Midt. I need to get back to a town called Midt."

"Consider it done," Knave says and extends their gloved hand.

Had I not just made a bargain with a ceogot, the thought of touching one would've filled me with horror. But the handshake is a lesser evil than being stuck here. I'll go through every ritual of obedience and purification I know. I won't get the Ceoghast on me.

My whole arm quivers as I take Knave's hand to seal the bargain. Their grip is firm and quick.

"Done," they say. "Grab your stunted squash friend and we'll be off."

"I can't take Hum with me." There's no way I'm walking out of the Ceoghast with one of its creatures.

"Oh, you're not. She'll come with me back to the patch. I'm sure Knife's been looking for her."

"Knife?"

Knave's expression loses its ethereal lightness. "My sister, of a sort. I don't recommend you seek her out."

"But you're taking Hum to her?" I want no claim to the creature, but to hand her over to someone called Knife feels wrong. It hurts the tentative trust that's grown between us.

I shake my head. It doesn't matter. Hum's part of the Ceoghast. Hum's evil. I need to get home.

"Never mind," I say and scoop Hum into my arms. "Let's go."

Chapter 10

The trail is as unsteady as water beneath my too tired legs. Like a toddler, I try to understand my balance with every step. Hum touches her stalks to trees and other landmarks to keep us on the path and prevent the tumble I'm likely to take.

Knave's long strides carry them with ease. In their wake leaves stir in small whirlwinds that flatten by the time I reach the same spot. We walk uphill, and the summit isn't far, but right now it feels impossible.

Knave's at the top and glances back at me and Hum. "This is it," they say.

When I reach the ridge, my chest twists. A tree-lined path winds its way down the hill to the borderlands. Beyond that barren place is Midt. The ordinary yellow glow of night torches along the main road in the distance fills me with a rush of warmth. Tears blur my vision.

Home.

I'm nearly home.

Overhead the moon shines bright and all the stars remain. Morning hasn't lightened the horizon. I still have time. Maybe I can even beat Ealey back. Even if I can't, no one in Midt's awake yet. They won't all be against me.

I take a step toward the tree-lined path.

"I'll see you soon," Knave says.

A shiver rolls over my shoulders and leaves me cold. This close to Midt, the evil around me feels worse. The threat of corruption heavier.

Hum protests when I unwrap her vines from my body. I shove her on the ground to keep her from grabbing me again. She lifts her head toward me, and I push her back.

"No," I say, "I'm leaving."

I want to shout at her not to touch me. She's as wrong as the rest of the Ceoghast. My skin crawls with it. I need to escape before that wrongness gets in.

I step onto the trail, but Hum wraps her stalks about my boots. The cry she makes would be a wail if she had a mouth.

"Here," Knave says. They scoop Hum up and tug her stalks off me. "Time to say goodbye. I'll see you soon." A threat leveled in a saccharine voice.

However tired my legs are, they're with me now as I go down the path toward home. Downhill is easier, but my knee still hurts, my thighs now raw. Midt's not far. I can see it now, and it's almost as good as seeing Katta.

At the foot of the hill, a woman on horseback rides onto the trail and stops. The intention behind her movement is clear. She blocks my path, though neither she nor the horse acknowledges me.

I stop.

"Hello?" I say.

The horse shifts and snorts, then the woman turns. Shadows slide off her body, and I scream.

She is made of cobwebs and dust. The left side of her face is mottled flesh, and in every shadow cast on her by the trees overhead I see long-legged, round-bodied gray spiders.

Hum is by my side in an instant. She wraps herself around both my legs and snarls at the woman. The woman nods at Hum as though the growls are pleasantries. Knave is nowhere to be seen.

"Please get out of my way," I say.

"I ain't going to stop you," the woman says. Her mouth is a shadow that crawls over her face when she speaks. "You're free as anyone to come and go as you like."

"Then will you please move?"

"Now you're an eager little thing. I ain't done. As I was saying, you're free to come this way if you like, but if you do come this way and I'm here, you ain't going to be alive much long after."

The threat is delivered with such warmth and friendliness I doubt my ears. "Did you just tell me you'll kill me if I try to get by you?"

"Oh no. I ain't so much for the killing. You'll be killing yourself if you walk on by," she says. She arches her back and releases a series of chattering cracks before she resettles on her horse.

Bone and cobwebs. She's made of bone and cobwebs.

"What you have here is a choice, one I'm letting you in on," she says. "So, if you walk by me now, you've decided to end your life. Wait a spell, come back when I ain't here, and you'll be just fine."

I glance around. I could get off the path and keep going. I know where Midt is well enough now. I don't need this path.

The woman sighs. "If you think you'll get by tonight by picking some other path, let me spare you the trouble. I'm at every edge of this border. There's no way out that don't go by me first."

I grip one of Hum's tendrils, hoping my world will stop spinning. "I need to get home."

"I'm not saying that you can't go home. All I'm saying is you'll want to rethink your timing."

"I need to get back now." A whine builds in my throat, shrills my words. Why is she doing this to me?

"You're welcome to it. You know the cost."

"What do you want?" All I have of value is Katta's portrait and no one else would have an interest in it but me. "Why are you doing this to me? I have no money. I'm not anyone important. I just need to get home." The anger in my voice makes me flinch when it booms.

The woman's laugh skitters out her open throat. "Ain't nothing personal about it. I'm just doing my job best as I'm able.

You're pretty lucky to even have a choice. Most people just fall right into me with no warning at all."

The woman turns her head away from me. She waits for me to choose. Even if I walk back in the Ceoghast, she'll wait for me here. She'll block my way home.

I back away from her, and Hum retreats with me. When I'm sure the woman doesn't mean to follow us, I return to the summit. Knave sits on a rock at the top, arms on their knees.

"I need another path," I say.

They shake their head. "You heard what she said. If you try to get to the borderlands, you'll find her first."

"She can't be at every path." Heat pitches in my chest. I need to get home.

"She can, and she will. You're lucky she warned you."

"Lucky? Nothing about this is lucky," I say. "No. This is it. I'm going home."

Knave grabs my shoulder. Their hand is warm and brings me back to my body. I'm heavy and sore and the thought of my bed at home makes me want to cry like an overtired child.

I shove their hand off me. "Don't touch me," I say. "I need to leave this place."

Ealey's probably already back there, and if I don't go before everyone else wakes up... Would they even let me speak? Even if they don't believe Ealey's claim I'm a witch, I've been in the Ceoghast. What if it's on me?

"If I can't explain what really happened," I say. Rocks tumble in my stomach. I clench my teeth hard to still the quiver in my chin. Hum taps my cheek, and I shove her away. "Get off me!"

Hum wilts and her vines slide from me. She gathers them around herself as though she wants to hide. Her withdraw is so complete she appears inanimate, an odd vegetable wrapped in its own greenery.

Shame burns me, but it's better this way. I don't want a Ceoghast creature to touch me.

Knave watches me without expression.

"How do I leave?" I say.

"If you go that way, you'll die. There's nothing you or I can do to change that fact, so you need a new plan."

"This isn't a plan. It's my life, and if I don't get back now, I won't have one in Midt at all."

No emotion touches Knave's face. Our conversation could be about the weather. Their neutrality gets under my skin. This doesn't matter to anyone else. I'm the only one who cares whether I get home or not.

"Our bargain is done if you don't get me home."

They shrug. "You can't honor the deal if you're dead, so you're going to have to wait. You try to go home now and life's over for you."

"If you don't help me, you'll never get your favor," I say, "so you need to figure out how I can get past her."

"I can't. She won't listen to me. I'm not important. I don't have the right magic." Bitterness as strong as dried fallowfoot coats their voice. "But I know who can help you, and I'll take you to her. She knows how to influence hearts."

"What do you mean 'influence hearts?'" Could this person corrupt mine?

The smile Knave flashes is all teeth. "Worried about your own? She's doesn't meddle for fun. You explain your situation, ask her to be your intermediary, and offer an appropriate payment."

"But she could? If she wanted to?"

"Could she what?"

"Influence my heart."

Knave snorts. "You have to want to change."

"I don't," I say. If that's what it takes, she probably won't be able to help with the cobweb woman, either.

"Well, no one's asking you to," they say. "Now, shall I take you?"

"Will I owe you more?"

"You'll still owe me a favor, and I'll take you right back here when we're done. Nothing extra owed."

"Okay," I say. They probably mean to trick me, but I'm too tired to care. I take what they offer at face value. It's not like I mean to see them again once I leave the Ceoghast.

"Let's go then. We have a fair distance to travel."

Tears wet my cheeks. "How long will it take to find this person?"

"Another hour or so of walking. Lucky for you, we'll be heading downhill. We'll get there just as the glows start to sleep."

"The glows?"

"Those irritating orbs — the ones full of light and faery bits? Have you seen them yet? You'll see plenty where we're going." Knave adjusts their hair. "Grab that stunted squash, will you? I'll need to deal with it once we're done."

I touch Hum's outer stalks but she does not stir. "Hum?" I say.

A harrumph echoes in her head like a groan.

"Please, Hum? I'm tired and I can't do this. I can't carry you."

Whatever animated Hum before has left her. Maybe I extinguished it myself. That should have felt like a triumph, but faced with the prospect of carrying her, all I feel is defeat.

Chapter 11

Without Hum's levity, the Ceoghast is more sinister. When I followed her before, I'd been distracted by her antics and worried about whether she communicated with the plants she touched. I'd not looked around then as I do now. I jostle her in my arms and try to get her to stir, but she remains lifeless.

Knave leads me down a path of gray ash speckled with white shards that make me think of ground up bones. The way sinks into the earth until walls as tall as my hips frame either side. Knave saunters down it like it's town square on Lights Day.

"Can we not walk on the grass?" I ask when I have to step over what looks like a large avian mandible, though the teeth lodged in it are needle-thin and as long as my fingers.

"That's not grass," Knave says.

I look again at the embankment on either side of this bone road. The green shoots are oily and move in startled stabs in our direction. I hug Hum closer. If the greenery comes at me, I could hide behind Hum's root head. In the distance, plant hands scuttle over the oily grass. I jump. Are they following us? I trot to catch up to Knave and clutch Hum tighter to keep from grabbing Knave's hand. Bone shards press into my soles and threaten to roll my ankles.

"Who are we seeing?" I say. I need Knave to talk. I need to keep my eyes on them and not our surroundings.

"The Heart Witch, as I said."

My toes kick up ash as what Knave said ricochets in my head. "You're taking me to a witch?"

"Who else do you think could help you?"

"No," I say. What stupidity had driven me to trust a ceogot? To think Knave's solution involves a witch — as though that's not somehow a million times worse than a woman made of cobwebs. Even in my exhaustion I should have suspected their offer to help.

I stop walking and put Hum down. "You can't take me to a witch."

I'd never recover from the corruption. No one but a Lightbearer could. I was a child when my mother turned against me, and even though children are wholly innocent and incorruptible, all of Horth worried I had the Ceoghast on me. Not even years of obedience to the tenets could heal the blemish.

If I see a witch as an adult, I'll have no protection from the corruption.

I'll get the Ceoghast on me.

"You were fine with the thought a moment ago."

"No. Not a witch," I say. "There has to be another person who can help me."

"There's not. Definitely not. Did you not see what blocks your path back home?"

"Are you just trying to keep me here?" Is this all a trick to corrupt me?

Knave snorts. "I suggest you consider what I get out of having you stay here when I need you out there. Is it the word itself that has you all tied up in knots? Think of her as a person who influences the hearts of others, if that helps you. We don't have to call her a witch."

"Why would that be better?" I say.

"You seem uncomfortable with the word witch."

"Witches are evil." They're evil and want to corrupt the innocent, the good, the obedient. They destroy communities.

"Ah. She's not what you're thinking," they say.

"You don't know what I'm thinking."

At this, Knave bares their teeth. I don't know if it's a smile or a threat, but either way it mocks me. They lean against the bone wall. "Don't I, though? You're from a little village called Midt. You call this place the Ceoghast. You're not from here, so what could you know of witches? The ideas you have come from stories — superstition meant to scare and titillate." They drag out the last word and my cheeks burn.

"We have real witches," I say. My mind fills with my mother's face as I last saw it. She was thin, more bone than flesh, and her hand — the one she raised to cast her curse on me — was raw and chapped.

Evil rots a person inside and out.

Knave's voice cuts through the haze of memory. Their voice is bitter. "Well you don't have one like Emathi. She's a nice old lady who happens to be persuasive when it comes to matters of the heart. She's exactly what you need if you want to clear your path home."

Rain begins to fall all around us. I cover my head only to realize no water falls from the sky. I only hear the noise.

"We best get going. Your choice which way you'd like to go," Knave says. Their gaze shifts from one side of the embankment to the other.

"What's out there?"

"Just a bit of blood rain, no doubt," they say. "Not nice stuff if it decides to fall on you. Wreck a perfectly good, well, everything really. There's no getting blood rain out. Not for months. So, what'll it be? Death or help?"

Death or help? In this case, Knave's help seems a slower way to the same end.

"Do you want to go home or not?" they say. Impatience curls over their shoulders.

"I need to get home."

"Then your path still lies this way." They take off at a brisk walk.

I lift Hum into my arms and this time she wraps her stalks around me. I inhale a big breath to stave off my tears. I'm glad she's back. Not only because she's lighter now, but because she makes me less afraid.

I watch Knave's back disappear around a corner and I rush forward. Bad enough to need comfort from a Ceoghast creature, I now follow a ceogot to meet a witch.

The tenets teach that it's better to die in dutifulness than allow any corruption into one's soul. The idea was so clear to me before I ended up here, but now the line of observance blurs. Does a witch corrupt on sight? None of the tenets specify when corruption takes root. Children have protection. A Lightbearer could get help from a witch without becoming blemished. I could have time. I might get away without harm.

If I walk past that woman on horseback, that won't be the case.

"Are you coming?" Knave says.

I round the corner and find them stopped. "Yes," I say.

They shake their head, and the threads woven in their hair catch the starlight. "You don't have to be so scared," they say as they continue to walk. "She lives alone, so there's no one else to frighten you, and she keeps a neat cottage. Think of her as a grandmother or old auntie or something."

I had an old auntie, one who knit and sat me on her knee and told me stories, but like most old people, the Ceoghast got her.

"She used to be a real good baker. I think she's mostly given it up now. There was an incident with her stove. Her mind's starting to go a bit."

If Knave means to reassure me, they need to not tell me about the habits of a half-mad witch.

"Speckled Hound Hollow is a nice place. Too quiet for me, but I'm sure someone like you will find it appropriately paced."

"I don't like dogs," I say. Hounds especially. Horth kept a pack that could scent corruption. Every week they'd wander through the crowd gathered for the recital of the tenets. Even now the idea they'd stop by me makes me shake. I can't walk into a place full of them.

"I really don't like dogs," I say.

Knave laughs. "I wouldn't worry about dogs if I were you."

"What would you worry about?" I want to take the words back the moment they're out of my mouth. I don't want to know what they'd worry about. I have worry enough without them sharing additional fears I ought to have.

"Nothing now," they say. They charge up the wall and drop down the other side. "Come along."

Neither the strength nor grace is with me to climb the wall. It's not so tall, but I am so tired. Hum extends her stalks, and with her help, we ease over the edge and drop down to the other side.

The grassy ground here slopes toward a round depression in the earth in which sits a small cottage on stilts. Hum perks up and begins to sing, and as she does, my gaze sorts out the odd bumps in the landscape. Speckled Hound Hollow is covered in pale orange pumpkins with green highlights that ooze from their stems over the sides in drip-like patterns.

Tiny white lights like frozen stars hang in the air all around us. They fade out of sight when I move toward them and wink back into existence once I've passed. They're so bright I can't see the body parts inside them, if there are any. Hum reaches for the pumpkins and for the lights. I squeeze her tight and hope her song elicits no response.

Knave strides toward the wood cottage. It's squat and square with a narrow purple door painted with blue leaves and a window so overrun by the window box plants only slivers of the silver glass are visible. The pottery fragments gathered under the ladder and rain barrel tucked against the side give the home a familiar, safe look. If not for the setting and colorful ornamentation, the cottage could be an ordinary homestead in one of the smaller settlements.

A woman opens the door and steps onto the small porch. Her appearance makes me want to hide behind one of the large pumpkins.

Few of our villages boast an elderly population. People that live long often stay at home and are seldom seen within the community, so I've never seen a person so old.

Her face hangs off her bones, and her eyes are rheumy. She is bent at the hips and were it not for the curve of her spine, her upper body would be parallel to the ground.

"Is that you, Knave?" she says, voice soft with surprise.

"Yes, Emathi," they say. "I've brought friends."

"Oh, I like friends. Will they be my friends? Are they witches like me?" This old woman sounds more like a child.

"We need a place to stay for the night, Emathi," Knave says. "We've been many places tonight and need a spot to rest for a while. Will you let us inside?"

"Inside? I haven't cleaned up, and what was I supposed to do today? Do you remember? Something inside the house. Maybe with the jars? I had jars. Do you know where the jars are?"

I am not that close to the cottage, but I take a step back. Her confusion sends alarm through my veins.

"I'll help you look," Knave says. Their voice is calm and smooth and wraps around me like a blanket. Emathi's hands drop from their fretful circles.

"Come look," Emathi says. She disappears into the cottage and leaves the door open.

Knave watches the door, then turns to me. "She'll be better come morning. Her mind leaves her at darkfall."

"She's being punished," I say. This is why we do not have many elderly. They become corruptible.

"It's an illness," they say. The snap in their voice can't touch me. I know better. I've seen it happen.

When you're old and don't follow the tenets, bad things happen to your body and mind. Corruption finds you. If you're good and obedient you don't fall apart like that.

Knave holds the door open. "Come on."

I might leave this house as withered and poisoned as the witch. No community would take me in.

Hum begins to drone a familiar tune — the children's tenets I recited to myself earlier. I'm a moral, unblemished person. I belong in a virtuous community. If I want to get home again, I have to do this. This is how I get past the cobweb woman without dying.

I take a deep breath, begin to chant the tenets in my mind, and step into the witch's cottage.

Chapter 12

The cottage is taller on the inside than it looks from without. The layout is unusual, too — five rooms circle a central hearth. The Heart Witch leads us in the circle until we reach the room next to the foyer where we entered. I don't know why she took us the long route when she could have stepped left from the front door. Perhaps she means to confuse or disarm, but if so, it's a meager attempt.

I won't let my guard down, and I won't fall for her tricks. I straighten my shoulders, only to have fatigue tug me back into a hunch. My legs hurt, Hum feels heavy in my arms, and for all I have to protect myself, all I really want to do is sleep.

"You can have the loft," she says. She raps a ladder that hangs on the wall. "Move it back when you're done."

Knave sets the ladder against the loft's lip and holds it for me as I climb, knee popping with each bend. My boots feel clumsy on the rungs. The wood is rough but new. Bent as she is, the Heart Witch probably doesn't make this ascent.

I expect dust and clutter at the top, but the small loft is neat and arranged for a guest. The air smells like rosemary and rhubarb with a hint of watered-down anise. The bed roll appears

fluffed, and towels sit on the corner along with a navy nightdress.
The small table holds a water basin and brush.

Hum leaps from my back to splash in the basin. Steam rises
from the bowl, and my face aches beneath the layers of grime and
sweat and acid-peeled skin.

Hours ago, I'd washed with great care and spent too long
deliberating about what to wear to impress my neighbors. The
version of myself who'd taken extra time to embroider an old
brown skirt for a nice occasion is a stranger to me now.

In the last few hours I've become an animal desperate to
survive. The washbasin, this reminder of normalcy, hurts like a
slap. It's out of place in the Ceoghast — too ordinary for the evil
around me. But whether it's a trap or cursed doesn't matter in light
of my filth and fatigue.

I strip off my clothes and set Katta's portrait aside. Hum
has dirtied the water with her play, but not enough that I won't use
it. The first swipe of the cloth across my face is an excavation. It
feels so nice I leave the cloth on my cheek a moment to absorb the
warmth. The tension in my shoulders and spine begins to unknit.

The Heart Witch's nonsense chatter and noisy rummaging
filters into the loft. Knave's footsteps track her with the regularity
of a clock's tick. Knave makes a chesty noise of assent whenever
the Heart Witch pauses.

By the time I've scrubbed most of my body, the water is
black and oily. Now that I've washed, the grime on my clothes is
more evident. My trousers hadn't been clean when I threw them
on earlier, and after a night in the Ceoghast they reek.

I touch and smell the navy nightgown that's been set out
on the bed. If there's a curse or other evil on it, I can't tell. Only
Lightbearers learn such skills. It seems only an ordinary clean
nightgown.

I slip it over my head and hold my breath, but its only soft
comfort, the kindest sensation I've felt since this whole awful night
began. Hum sings a contented note and curls on the pillow, her
stalks still dripping from her water play.

Alone with Hum in the loft, I almost feel safe. Well, maybe
not safe, but I feel like the Ceoghast can't touch me. Like I'm
strong enough to keep out the corruption. If, like Knave, I had to

spend time with the Heart Witch downstairs, that might not be the case.

I crawl into the bedroll and stretch out. Now that I'm still, every muscle in my body protests.

"But the jars," the Heart Witch says from the room below me.

"They're in the cupboards, Emathi," Knave says.

"But who moved them? What if the nyxies got in? What if they did it?"

"That's impossible, Emathi. You set the charms against them yourself."

"I'm the only one who knows." A note of pride strengthens her words. "I figured out where they belong."

To this Knave makes no reply, but they both shuffle about the room below. After a while, the witch says, "Did you find my jars?"

Their conversation repeats with little variation. The witch seems to recall none of it.

What will she be like come daybreak? Knave said she loses her mind at night and recovers in the morning. It's hard to believe the old woman could be a threat when her mind is soft with rot, but if she's coherent when I wake, what danger will she be?

I begin to drift off to sleep when a new inquiry startles me back awake. "Did you trap me here?"

My body tenses again at Emathi's plaintive tone. "No, Emathi."

"But I can't get out. No matter what I try, I can't get out. There's a barrier," she says. "I know you put it there. You're trying to trap me."

Alarm forces me to sit up. Why would Knave want to trap the Heart Witch? What if they brought me here to trap me, too?

"I have no such magic," Knave says. They sound bored. "That spell is there to protect you. You put it up yourself."

"It's not mine," she says. "It doesn't respond to me."

"This will be better in the morning," they say.

"You need to take it down. We need to find the jars. If we throw them at the barrier, we can get through."

My mind snatches at the instruction in case I need to escape. I push my legs out of the bedroll.

"Where would you go, Emathi?" they say, but the witch has lost the conversation again. She begins to mutter about her jars and moves to another room.

My stomach growls, and Hum perks up. She taps her stalks to her head where her mouth might be, and I remember the tricolor triangles she gave me earlier. Maybe she wasn't tricked into thinking I ate them then.

I could eat them now.

Hum wouldn't give me harmful food, not if she knew they were bad. If she intended to hurt me, she could have already done so in more ways than I want to consider. I could eat them.

Not certain of the wisdom but guided by appetite, I grab my trousers from the floor and dig in the pockets. The ripe scent of sweat and earth that rises from them turns my stomach, but my hunger is stronger.

My fingers close around the four triangles and something sharp pierces my thumb. I yank my hand out and study the pinprick of blood that oozes down my skin, then stare at the food in my palm. The colorful triangles are no longer simple shapes. They have legs and arms — too many of both — and eyes and teeth.

Such teeth.

For a few seconds we stare in surprise at each other. They recover from their shock faster than I do, and all four grab hold of my fingers and bite down hard.

I scream.

Hum leaps to action and flails her stalks about, but she can't hit the tiny triangles as I fling my arm like I want to shake my whole hand loose — I'd be just like that demon tree right now if I could. My hip hits the washbasin and dirty water spills over the loft's edge.

I reach out to catch the basin from tumbling, and Hum takes the moment to land a blow flat across my palm that sends the triangles flying. All four would have gone over the edge if not for Knave's sudden appearance at the top of the ladder.

They fly straight into Knave's face.

The look Knave gives me chills my entire body. They pluck the triangles off one at a time, and with each removal, small bites blossom red on Knave's cheeks and chin and forehead. Knave sweeps them into an embroidered handkerchief and wraps them inside.

"I know you're not from around here," they say, "but surely even you know better than to keep candy corn."

"Candy corn?"

Knave sets the tied handkerchief on the floor and pounds it with a fist until the fabric is flat and unmoving. "If you're desperate enough to grab candy corn off the forest floor, you need to follow the rules. They're simple," they say. With each statement, they hold up a finger. "One: eat them right away and leave no trace you were there. The last thing you need is to create a scent trail for more candy corn to follow."

"More?" I envision an angry, toothed swarm.

"They're like ants. You know what ants are, right?"

"Yes."

"So they follow each other. If you don't want that to happen, you eat the candy corn you've grabbed right away. Then you don't have a problem," they say. I understand what they tell me, but my mind is stuck trying to figure out how food became vengeful creatures.

"Okay," I say.

"But if you're dumb and you decide to save them for later..."

"I didn't know," I say. "Hum gave them to me."

At this, Hum growls and launches herself over the loft's edge. She hangs off Knave and climbs down them to the ladder below.

"Two," Knave says as though they didn't notice Hum leave, "if you save them for later, you don't carry them past the witching hour because that's when they wake up. If they wake, they try to eat you."

At this, they gesture at their face where the blood begins to dry. I glance at my own hand where tiny sets of teeth marks reinforce Knave's warning.

"If they wake up, they start to call their friends. A handful of these tinies might not do much damage, but an ear? An ear of candy corn numbers in the thousands, and I promise that they won't have any problems eating you."

"Please stop," I say. I don't want to hear more. The bites burn in my hand and I imagine the pain spreading to the rest of my body. I eye the flattened handkerchief and hope the triangles — the candy corn — are dead.

"The third rule is that you squish every one that wakes up as quick as you can," they say.

"Did you kill them?" I want Hum to come back. Was she angry I told Knave she'd been the one who'd given me the candy?

"Did you see any escape?" they say.

I can't remember how many Hum handed me. Did I only pull four from my pocket? Was that how many Knave caught?

"Can you send Hum back up?" If any of the candy corn did escape, Hum can get them, or keep them away from me.

"Did you hear anything I just said about...?"

"Why is there a stunted squash in my house?" the witch says from below. A bang like the collapse of crockery stacked high shakes the loft floor.

Knave closes their eyes, clearly gathering patience, before they swing down the ladder. Their expression so familiar to me, I can only stare after them — how many times did I call upon the same well of peace to address one of Katta's outbursts?

Hum's guttural chirps are hard to hear above the crash of dishes, and I peek over the edge. Hum skitters into the room below, burlap fabric caught in her stalks. She bounds about Knave's legs a few times before they catch her and toss her up the ladder. I reach my arms out to help her, but she scales the rungs with ease and swings onto the floor beside me.

"Why is a stunted squash in my house? Did you get it? Is it gone?" The witch storms into the room below. She wields a broom like an axe.

Hum fusses behind me, and I hush her.

"It's gone now, Emathi," Knave says.

"Why was it here?" she says. Her voice drops to a hiss. "What if Knife finds out? She'd come here. It'd be the end of us."

"Knife doesn't leave the patch, Emathi, and the stunted squash is gone. There's nothing to worry about."

"I'm not worried," she says.

"Come on. Let's storm the kettle before bed."

"Are you staying the night?" Confusion weakens her voice, and as the two of them go to the kitchen, she begins to speak of her jars again.

I shimmy back from the edge to find Hum surrounded by odd bits of food she's pulled from the burlap sack. She trills a smug note of satisfaction at my expression.

"Hum," I say, but the disapproval I expect in my tone is absent. I'm too hungry to pretend I won't eat what she's brought, and as she reveals her catch, I can't help but be impressed. She's grabbed half a loaf of bread speckled with olives and onion slices, strawberry preserves, a bright green apple, a slab of uncooked meat, a handful of dried tea leaves, and a metal dustpan.

Hum corkscrews her stalks and bounces around the spread, effuse with pleasure. I open the preserves and use my fingers to spread it on torn pieces of bread. The flavors are odd companions, but I'm so hungry it doesn't matter. Hum puts the bread and tea leaves on the dustpan and offers the arrangement to me like a plate. It's gross, but I take it and continue to eat.

Downstairs Knave tells the witch her jars are fine. Her confusion makes it hard to fear her now, but I may face a real witch in the morning. The thought turns the bread into a rock in my gut.

Fatigue rolls over like a heavy blanket and drags me down. I shove the food aside and curl into the bedroll.

Tomorrow I need to fight against corruption when I bargain with the witch. If Knave's tricked me and this is a trap, I'll need to get out. Either way, I need to be rested.

"A good community consists of people who are unblemished. By their selfless acts, they are incorruptible." The tenets roll from my sleepy tongue as I drift off to sleep. Each one reminds me of my need to return to Midt.

Hum tucks herself on the floor beside me and goes still. If I end up in trouble, Hum might help me. I don't know why she looks out for me, but she's the only one here I can trust even a little.

Chapter 13

Scents of warm bacon and fresh torn mint pull me toward wakefulness like stretched taffy. Not since I left Horth has anything so pleasant greeted my nose in the morning. In Midt my work at the laundry means my home smells like lye and clothes still wet with dirty wash water.

Midt.

The Ceoghast.

With a snap, my memories of the previous night flood my body. I am in the Ceoghast, in a witch's house.

I throw off the soft, warm covers and look about the loft but fail to find Hum. In this part of the cottage, I am alone. But not if I go downstairs.

From one of the other rooms I hear the soft clatter of cutlery, its rhythm too intentional to be Hum's impulsive play. I peek over the loft's edge to see if she's below.

"I know you're awake, so let's not have all this mousing," the Heart Witch says. Her voice sends ice through my chest. Last night she sounded uncertain. This morning her words crackle with strength, and the command makes me feel trapped.

"I've got breakfast and a bargain for you," she says. "Your little friend is already down here. If she tries to steal food for you one more time this morning, I'll cut off her stalks, so you best hurry."

I glance around the loft. My clothes are gone, but my boots and Katta's portrait are where I left them. To meet the witch barefoot seems foolish — what if I have to run? — so I pull the boots on and tuck the portrait against my ankle. I have everything I need to go. The nightgown may not be practical, but it's enough.

I'm about to leave the loft when the memory of Ealey's voice hisses in my head. Despite the reminder, nothing around me would be any use as a weapon. Besides, if this witch can truly change hearts, I doubt I'd have a chance to use one against her anyway.

"It's rude to tarry, dear," the witch says.

My knees knock on every rung as I descend the ladder.

When I walk into the kitchen, the witch is bent over a cauldron, and Hum sprawls over one of the table's wood chairs. She sings a few notes when I enter. The witch turns from her cauldron and shoves a bowl of what looks like wet mashed potatoes with chopped bacon into my hands.

"It's hardly hot now, seeing as you wasted your morning in bed," she says. "Have a seat."

In any other setting, this might pass for hospitality, but here the gestures seem like threats. The food could be poison. The table might collapse. I set the bowl down and sit next to Hum who pets my head with her stalks when I settle. It takes me a moment to realize she's trying to tidy my hair, and I shoo her away.

"Where's Knave?" I say.

The witch fusses with her kettle. It's so large I'm surprised she can tip the boiling water into the mugs she's set out.

"That's not how this conversation starts," she says. "They said you came to make a bargain, and we'll get to that. First, we begin with introductions. You'll state your name and explain what you're doing in my house."

Did Knave leave me here? Our agreement mattered to them. Surely they wouldn't have abandoned me.

"You're crossing the line into rudeness now. I suggest you change your course and tell me your name and business. No more mousing," she says. She places two mugs on the table before she eases her crooked body into a chair.

"My name is Cassia Mooseroot," I say. The tenets teach us our good name protects us from evil. I hope it's enough to keep her poison at bay.

"And your purpose?" she says.

Hum scoops food from the bowl with her stalk and presses it to my lips. I shove her way, but she makes a noise of protest and tries to feed me with another stalk.

"Stop. I'll eat," I say. I spoon a small scoop of the food into my mouth. Despite what the witch said, it's still hot. A mix of cinnamon, bacon, and tart apple burns my tongue. Hum settles back down with a satisfied harrumph.

"Well, that explains a bit," the witch says. I don't know if she means my name or Hum's behavior. "But not your purpose, so onto it."

"A thing... it looks a bit like a person, blocks my way home," I say. Even in daylight, the memory of cobweb skin makes me shudder. Urgency forces my words out. "I have to get home as soon as possible."

Already I've been here too long. I won't be embraced when I return, but if I'm fast enough and get out of the Ceoghast before it corrupts me, I can earn my way back into the community.

Hum rouses to fuss with my bowl so I eat another spoonful.

"If that's what you want, it doesn't explain why you're here, or why you were sleeping in my loft."

My cheeks flush red with embarrassment. "Knave said you could help me. They said you're the only one who can."

The Heart Witch leans forward and narrows her eyes. "Who did you see on the road that Knave thinks you'd need me?"

Her intensity alarms me. I lean away. "I don't know. She rides a black horse, but neither of them looks..." Looks what? Normal? A Ceoghast witch won't share my understanding of normal. "They don't look alive, but they act like it. Sort of. She moves and talks."

I cringe at my inaccuracy even though I have no better way to describe the creature that threatens me.

"And the precise problem she presents? How is your way barred?"

"She threatens death," I say. "And is always before me no matter what path I take back home."

The witch sits back in the chair, curled as an autumn leaf. "You'd do better to give up."

Anger hits me like a lightning bolt. "I can't just give up," I say. Hum startles beside me, but I'm too jumpy to quiet down. "I need to go home. Now. You need to help me."

"Help you renegotiate your death?"

"No. I don't want to die. I want to go home. You need to change that thing's heart so I can leave."

"Need," she says. "Such a strong word. Is that what you've come for, then? You want me to change this creature's heart so you can pass by unharmed?"

"Yes," I say. I exhale the tension in my shoulders. With the bargain in the open, I feel closer to Midt.

"And what do you offer in exchange for such a complicated service?"

Katta's portrait presses against my ankle. It's the most valuable item I have, but it would mean nothing to the witch. Like a fledging tossed from its nest, I flounder to find my balance and try to think of a worthy exchange. I haven't considered what I could offer her, and I doubt I can skip payment like I plan to do with Knave.

"What do you want?" I say.

"I want nothing. I certainly didn't ask for you to be here," she says. "You brought me this request so it's up to you to define the exchange. Tempt me."

Her gaze moves to Hum.

"Do you want her?" I say. Hum's not mine to give but the answer may give me an idea of what she'd like.

"I didn't understand the relationship between you and that stunted squash at first."

My mind stumbles over this shift in conversation. "What?"

"They're not this developed usually, these off-shoots, and they certainly never make it out of the patch. I thought you might have stolen it."

"Her," I say. My spine bristles at the witch's tone. "Her name is Hum, and I didn't steal anything."

Not even in the Ceoghast would I steal, even if it meant I did harm to the evil here.

"All to my point," the witch says. "She's an anomaly and quite attached to you. But she doesn't consider you her master, which is the way of proper Jacks. I am convinced, in fact, she rather considers you offspring."

Revulsion crawls over my arms at the suggestion. The revelation casts me in a piteous light, and as though the act might proclaim my independence, I spoon more food into my mouth before Hum can prompt me.

"All that aside," she says, "she has to go back to the patch. If you do that, if you take her back, I'll consider it half your payment made."

Discomfort prickles my back, but the thought of Midt makes me nod. "Okay," I say. "Where does she have to go back to?"

"Jack's Patch," she says. I wait for more, but she sips her tea and seems to think the name is enough.

"I'm not from here. I don't know where that is."

"I'll give you directions when you're ready to leave. It's not far."

I'm ready to leave now, but then I glance at Hum. She's grown still beside me. "And I just leave her there?"

"Knife will take her."

I've heard that name before, but I can't remember what Knave said about her. I have a sense she's no good. "Who's Knife?"

Hum growls, and the Heart Witch raps her gnarled knuckles on the table to silence the noise. "Knife is the keeper and carver of Jack's Patch," she says.

"I don't understand."

"Do you know what a stunted squash is, Cassia?"

I hate that she says my name, and her tone makes clear a stunted squash is undesirable. A need to defend Hum rises in me.

"No," I say.

She straightens and looks down her nose at me. "A stunted squash is stolen magic. The patch is full of spells to bring the Jacks to life, and that is not a Jack." She jabs a finger in Hum's direction, and Hum flicks a stalk at her for the trouble. The witch is so unperturbed by Hum's outburst I wonder if she noticed it. "A stunted squash shouldn't have magic. It should never have life beyond what any other plant might have, but sometimes the spells seep in."

Her words carve terrible images into my mind. I walked through a dark forest to come to this place and now wonder how many errant spells tried to grab me. This is how a person gets the Ceoghast on them, I'm sure of it.

I should run. I should shout the tenets at this witch to protect myself. She speaks of magic, of evil, in a tone so casual it would be better suited to discussions of gardening or the forecast.

If spells can seep in, can they creep out? I shift away from the table. Hum and the witch might both be able to infect me. "Those spells need to go back to the earth and find their way to a proper Jack."

"What's a Jack?" My imagination creates nightmares, and not knowing seems worse now than having the truth.

"It's like your stunted squash there, but bigger and less..." She waves a hand at Hum and I flinch, worried she casts magic. "They're proper creatures, not scattered whimsy."

The food I ate churns in my stomach. "What happens to Hum?"

"What do you mean?"

"If the..." The word magic sticks in my throat. I don't want it to be real. "After what she has goes back to the Jacks, what happens to her?"

"There's no separating her from the spells," the witch says. "She goes back into the ground. Once she decomposes, the magic goes back to the ground and finds its way to a real Jack."

"You're going to bury her. Alive."

"I'm doing nothing of the sort," she says. She doesn't meet my gaze. "That's Knife's purview."

"But if I want your help, I need to take her there? That's
your deal?" My anger's driven me back to the table, and I lean
closer to the witch. Her expression remains friendly.

"Yes. If you want me to help you get home, this is what I
require." She sips her tea then daps a napkin to her wrinkled lips.

"I can't take her somewhere to die." Hum might be a
Ceoghast creature, but she also saved my life.

"You can if you want my help. You brought a stunted
squash into my home without my consent. Perhaps you're ignorant
of the danger you invite, but that doesn't free you from the
consequences."

She rises, and even though she's stooped in half, she looms
over us. Hum squawks and slips under my chair. Her vines wrap
around my legs and eliminate any chance of a quick escape.

The witch points a finger in my face, and I close my eyes. If
she's going to curse me, I don't want to see it happen.

"You need to get that thing back to the patch before Knife
hunts you down. She won't care that you didn't know, or that it
followed you. The fact is you stole that squash because you have
it."

She slaps the table and my eyes spring open. Hum lashes a
tendril against the table's corner before she retreats to cower again.
"Pay attention and stop your mousing," the witch says. "You're
lucky I'm taking this as part of your payment at all." She snatches
my bowl and mug away and tosses them in the sink.

"If you head out now, you'll be back before darkfall and we
can go negotiate safe passage past your problem. You can be home
for dinner."

Home. Midt. I could be home tonight.

Hum crawls out from under the chair and arranges herself
in my lap. I keep my gaze on the witch and fix my mind on home.

"We'd go tonight," I say.

"I don't see why not if you're quick about it." She glances
at us and her shoulders sag. "And I can do something about that."

Before I can ask what she means, Hum wilts in my arms.
Her stalks soften and her stamens curl in.

"There," she says. "You'll get no protests or obstinate behavior from that one now. It'll follow you there and let you return alone."

Is that how easy it is for her to turn hearts? No outside indication or warning — just a terrible and sudden change?

My heart thrashes in my chest. She will not have it. She will not touch it. I will not change. I close my eyes and focus on my goal. I need to get back to Midt. If I want to go home, this is my path.

I gather Hum in my arms and stand. "Show me the way."

Chapter 14

I leave Speckled Hound Hollow with four items: my clothes, washed and dried; Katta's portrait, tucked into my shirt; directions to the patch, which I doubt but have to follow; and Hum.

"Go straight out the way you came," the Heart Witch says, "and stick to the dirt path. It will take you direct."

If travel in the Ceoghast were so easy, I'd never have gotten so lost in the first place, and didn't Knave take us by the dirt path on our way here?

Still, I go the way she says and find the path wide and clear. Hum is deadweight in my arms. Her stalks trail limp and undone. I try to loop them over my shoulders, but my knee has me walking off-kilter, and they slip no matter how I arrange them.

We are not long on the road when the path crests upwards. I want to cry at the stiffness in my thighs but push myself onward, each step a penance for finding my way into the Ceoghast in the first place.

When I reach the summit, I stutter to a halt. The valley below burns orange with wide swathes of fire that run down the low hillside and through the middle of the valley. The whole area is aflame, and my path leads down its center. How can we get around it and not lose our way?

But as I search for a different route, more details filter in: the stillness, the lack of smoke. The air smells like rich woods and zesty sweetness, nothing burning.

This is no fire. This is our destination.

Jack's Patch is a scar of orange in the middle of the lush green ground. At this distance, the wild colors mimic an uncontrolled blaze.

I carry Hum into the valley, relieved to be going downhill, and as we near the patch, a low wall of gray and green stones comes into view. The wall snakes around smooth, vibrant pumpkins and seems to mark the boundaries of this place. At the valley's belly, scents of wood smoke and cedar hang in the air, and green and purple lights twinkle about the heavy vines that lie draped from one pumpkin to another like arms tossed around a friend's shoulder. Though we've come in daylight, the patch is clothed in the valley's shadow. Cool air nibbles at my skin and leaves goose bumps in its wake.

The path leads to an opening in the stone wall. Wind hisses through the gap, its voice a shriek of terror and glee wrapped in a single discordant note. The remains of a black gate rusted by the elements and time rests deep in the overgrown grass. My skin crawls as I contemplate the opening. I don't want to walk into the patch. It's bad enough to have crossed into the Ceoghast — I don't want to know what will happen if I cross this boundary.

I place Hum at my feet and carefully wrap her stalks about her. We're here. This is my task complete. All I had to do was take Hum to Jack's Patch. I can leave now. I'm done.

Except I don't move. My skin ripples like a monster's gaze rests on me. If I turn and walk away now, I'm certain I'll feel its teeth in my back.

Hums moves and I leap away startled. She breaks the silence with a low groan and pulls through the opening in the wall on stalks stiff and boxy. I watch her go. She collapses on the other side, as though whatever had created the movement was not of her.

Not once has she looked at me. Whatever the witch did to her, it's buried Hum's playful and generous heart.

Which should make it easier for me to leave. I twist my hands in my shirt and feel Katta's portrait, once again tucked close, shift against my chest. My courage is as scattered as autumn leaves, but Katta's never was. I can be brave like her. I take a deep breath and step into the patch.

A shudder rolls through the pumpkin vines. The lashing begins at my feet and stretches out in every direction away from me, like a great wave. For a moment the fields roll like the sea, but then, as one, the vines stiffen and drift back to the ground to resume their heavy slumber. Hum offers no indication as to how I might interpret the movement. She remains collapsed on the ground, strangled by the witch's spell.

Minutes pass, and no one comes to greet us. I've done what I've said I would. Hum is in Jack's Patch. I can leave. I don't look at her as I shift to walk backwards…except I can't back away. My feet are stuck to the ground. Distracted by the vine's undulations, I'd not noticed the tendrils that wrapped about my boots.

I bend to claw at them, but they're like too tight laces and I can't get a grip.

"Oh, I loves a panicker. They make everything so sweet." The voice seems to come from all around me, rough and low yet effuse with pleasure. Ahead of me, a diminutive woman comes into view. Her grin reminds me of Ealey's when he fought the plant hand, all malice and triumph.

"What do you wants?" she says. She pulls a wide silver knife from her belt. "Have you comes to play a game?"

Her blond curls fall in frayed strands from a pink bonnet with dirty white lace better suited in style to an infant. She's no taller than a five-year-old, but her round face is lined by sun and age. She twists the double-edged knife, one side smooth, the other jagged.

"No," I say. "I'm here to... the Heart Witch sent me to bring this back."

The woman follows my gesture with indifference until her gaze alights on Hum. "That. You brings me that? Stupid stunted squash." She plods closer to us. The heavy black muck boots she wears look too big for her feet. "Did you thinks you could walks away and that I wouldn't finds you? That I don't haves people everywhere?"

"Is that it, then?" I say. The vines are still about my boots, but softer now, like they've fallen asleep. I work my heel back and begin to pull free.

"We could plays a game. We calls it Cuts and Hides. You see, we cuts," she says and slashes her knife at me. My feet are not as free as I thought and when I try to leap back, they slap my feet back down. I right myself before I fall. "And then you hides. Or we hides the knife and whoever finds it gets to cuts next."

She speaks without malice, her voice full of a kind patience, like this might be a desirable invitation.

"No, thank you," I say. The polite decline slips out of me, and I cringe. A firm no would broker no further interaction, but the social nicety sounds like I might capitulate to her if pressed.

"Then you should leaves," she says, "so we can plays Cuts and Cuts with the thiefs."

"What are you going to do to her?" I can't stop myself. I need to ask even though the witch already told me. Part of me hopes the witch is wrong, that Hum will have to stay here, but will also live.

"Stupid stunted squash," she says. "Thoughts it could runs away, so we'll cuts off its stalks, and shave its stolen stamens, and stabs its stupid head. We'll chops it into so many pieces we won't needs the compost."

"Don't," I say. Hum quivers beneath whatever binding the witch placed on her. My nerve runs out my legs when the woman turns back to me.

"Do you wants to plays a game?" she says.

"No."

"Then you better leaves. We're busy."

The vines at my feet roll away until only one stalk remains stretched toward me. It's one of Hum's.

"What do I have to do to get you to let Hum live?" I say. My words trip over my tongue in their rush to get out.

"Hum lives? Hum lives. What's a Hum?"

I point at Hum's collapsed form. "That's Hum. Her name is Hum."

"Stunted squash haves no names. You can calls them thief." Her tone is conversational, as though she relays facts to a child.

"How can she live?" I say.

"No. No lives for that one. She stoles spells and the Jacks needs them. No one comes and seeks stunted squash." She bares her teeth at me and all niceness flees from her. "They wants real Jacks."

"What if I want her?" I say. I don't want her. I can't. She's a Ceoghast creature. But I can't let her die.

The smile that splits the woman's face in half has shivers racing over my shoulders. I'm a mouse in a cat's paw, this is a trap. "Well, that would takes a games," she says.

"What sort of game?" My mouth is dry. I clutch my clammy hands together to stop the tremor.

"Nots my favorite," she says. Disappointment drags her vowels down. "But ifs you do it wrong, then we plays my game."

"Do what wrong? What's the game?"

The woman turns and motions toward the fields of orange pumpkins. "People comes here for Jacks. If you wants the stunted squash, you goes through the same," she says. "Maybe the stunted squash is for you. Maybe it's nots. You finds it, you keeps it. You fails and we keeps you to water the fields."

"So I have to find Hum? You hide her in the patch?"

"In the piles," she says. She gestures behind her but all I see are fields.

"What piles?"

"I stacks the Jacks," she says. "You walks round three times to finds the one you wants."

"And if I find Hum?"

The woman wrinkles her nose the way a dog does when it growls. "You takes her."

"But if I don't see her?" I want to bite my own tongue. I need to stop this. This isn't a game I'll play.

She claps her hands. The knife clangs against her silver rings. "Then you waters the fields."

Her delight tells me I don't understand the whole of her meaning. "For how long?" I won't risk indentured servitude.

"For how long?" she says. Her face twists in confusion, and she tugs at her bonnet. "We cuts your throat and catches your bloods and waters the fields."

My stomach heaves. The little mash I'd eaten for breakfast at the witch's cottage burns my throat, and I take a deep breath to keep from vomiting.

"Takes maybe two hours," she says, level with reason, as though this is a rational response. "Then it's backs to works until someone else comes to plays."

"No," I say. "I can't do this."

"We cuts either way, but you should go if you're nots here to plays."

Hum's stalk flutters at my feet. My throat tightens. I did my job. I kept my bargain, and I'm not here to make more deals.

I slide my foot back. The vines don't stop me. "Please don't..." Don't what? Hurt Hum? She's spelled out the terms of Hum's destruction. To ask for mercy is a waste of my breath.

Go. Leave now. The witch will take you home, and you can forget about all of this.

"I just need to find her in your pile, and we can both leave? You'll let both of us go and won't come after Hum again?"

"She says she won't plays but she still asks about the games." Her hands clench and unclench on her knife. "Come sees, then. Come sees and decides."

She turns and strides up a hill. Pumpkins roll away from her feet and leave a clear but narrow path. I lift Hum's limp form and follow her.

Each step is a battle against my better reason. To join this woman's game is madness. The risk is too great, and I have nothing to gain. Hum is not worth my entrapment in the Ceoghast or my life.

The valley tumbles into another lowland on its far side, and within the bowl of earth, three great piles of pumpkins at least twice my height are visible. The woman waves her blade at them.

"That's the games. You finds the stunted squash in one of those. Three times rounds you can looks. Finds it, you grabs it, you leaves. All safey-safe and nice."

Even at this distance, the pumpkins in the pile look different from Hum. They're bigger, most are bright orange, and they have a uniformity Hum doesn't possess.

I can do this.

"So you add her to one of those piles. I wouldn't have to dig for her? I'd be able to see her?"

"No digs and no touches. You touches to pick your Jack." She spits. "Or stunted squash."

We walk closer. The piles are tall, but I can see each pumpkin in them. None of them look like Hum. If this is all it takes to save Hum, we can both leave this awful place.

"You gives us the stunted squash and closes your eyes. You opens them before we says and we cuts them out, so no peekings."

She studies my eyes as though to figure out how best to remove them from my head.

"I won't peek," I say. With such a threat, I'd be foolish to risk it. To wander the Ceoghast blind would be a terrible, shortlived fate.

Go back, go back, go back.

Sour saliva fills my mouth.

"I want to play." Even as I shape the words, I think they must have come from someone else. I am not this dumb or desperate.

"Have you comes here as a seeker?" she says.

"Yes," I say. A ripple reels through the vines.

"Your names?"

"Cassia Mooseroot."

"We are Knife, Keeper and Carver of Jack's Patch. My sibling said you'd comes."

"Sibling?"

"Knave," she says. She growls their name like a curse. Then she grins at me. "Time to plays." I close my eyes.

At first the roar of my heart as it pounds out a frantic protest drowns out all other noise, but then the woman's grunts and noisy movement filter in. The sounds she emits seem dramatic, more for show and distraction than actual exertion. Her volume fluctuates as she moves around all the piles, and in the end I can't guess which one of them might hold Hum. But I don't need to guess. I just need to walk around until I see Hum.

"Cassia Mooseroot, Seeker of Jack, the games begins. Finds your stunted squash."

I open my eyes. The pumpkin towers stand before me, more real now than they seemed before.

"Remembers," Knife says, "you may goes round three times. If you don't finds your Jack, the games ends and we takes all."

The threat pierces my determination, and my first step toward the pile is a weak-kneed stumble. I keep my chin up and study the first tower.

Each gourd is distinct and unique, even among its like fellows. I scan up and down the height of them to locate Hum's mottled skin. The air is cool against my face as I search, and away from Knife's gaze, ease relaxes my tense muscles.

I will find Hum, then she and I will leave here, and the witch will help me get home. Knife's leer when I finish my first circle of the piles feels like ice water on a cold day.

The shock startles me from my daydreams.

I've missed Hum.

I wheel back to study the piles again. The orange heads blur together, one Jack indistinct from the next, and a pull at my belly button drags me toward them. I take three big steps before I recognize the pressure.

The Ceoghast calls me. Like it had in the borderlands, it tugs on me now and tells me to reach out and touch a Jack.

Just one.

Any one.

It wants me to fail.

I rock back on my heels to stop my forward momentum. The pile looms so far above me now its top disappears into the clouds. Voices begin to seep from it.

Pick me.

I'll bring you such power.

For such a seeker, what would I not do?

I know the way home.

I barge past the pile and run into Knife. She shoves me back and flicks her blade at me.

"One more times," she says.

I stumble past her. My head wants to float away it feels so light, and the ground seems to tilt beneath my feet. The pumpkins leer at me with faces cut from shadow and sunlight. None of them look like Hum.

If I go past Knife again, my life is forfeit.

What if she lied? What if she buried Hum or didn't add her to a pile at all?

I drag my feet, but the Ceoghast pulls me past the first of the three piles. Orange and green blurs swirl by my eyes and I shut them to block out the confusion.

With my eyes closed, the Ceoghast doesn't have so firm a grip on me, and my heart slows from its race. Tears wet my cheeks.

"Hum," I say, more mournful plea than name.

How long can I stay like this? At what point will Knife prod me along? I glance at the piles, but they've only grown madder. Uncertain colors and unsteady forms replace the once approachable stacks, so I focus inward again.

Can I find a makeshift weapon and defend myself from Knife? Laughter bubbles at my mouth at the ludicrous suggestion. I haven't a chance against her. My only hope is Hum.

And that's when the discordant strain, three notes groaned without melody, reaches my ears. My eyes fly open, but the chaos of Jack's Patch threatens to drown all my senses now. I retreat inside myself and try to better hear.

There.

I step to the right and make my hesitant walk toward the familiar, messy hum. Every time I look around, the world grows more volatile, so I make my way blind and hope Hum's broken song is enough to guide me.

When my toes bump against a low barrier, I listen for a moment more and position my head in the right direction before I look.

The pile is mad as a painter's wet palette, but there, solid and misshapen and dusty, is Hum.

I grab her from the pile. Her stalks wrap around my wrists and together we free her. I hold her so tight I think she might break but I can't let her go.

"We almost died," I say. This feels truer now than at any other point of my time in the Ceoghast. No one else was here to save me. Not even Hum. Not at first. Without her help, though, we'd both be dead.

Our survival does not please Knife who storms around the tower of pumpkins with a snarl.

"I have her," I say. "You have to let us go."

"Stupid thiefs," she says. Deep breaths heave her shoulders up and down. I don't know if they calm or rile her. "Fine. You can goes."

"Both of us," I say. An electric energy courses through me and makes my tongue bold.

"Thems the rules," she says.

My knees clatter together so hard it's like they want to applaud Knife's verdict.

"We takes your payment."

"Payment?" I don't remember her saying anything about a need to pay.

"You thinks Jacks has no price?" she says. She holds out a hand, palm up. "Your hand."

"My hand?"

"We gives it back," she says. Before I can respond, she snatches my wrist and slices my palm with her blade. I pull back hard, and she lets me go, but not before she grabs Hum.

Off-balance, I fall. My cry comes out a huff of air as I hit the ground.

Knife stabs Hum's head over and over and over.

"No!" I say. I scramble to my feet, but the field is awake again and the vines hold me in place.

"Leave her alone. You said you'd let us go."

But Knife doesn't stop, and each wet slosh hurts me so much it's like she strikes me and not Hum.

"There," she says. She drops Hum.

I expect Hum to fall into a thousand pieces, but instead she lands on her springy stalks and bounds over to me.

Knife has carved a nightmare into Hum's face. Hum's three eyes are obsidian diamonds above a double triangle nose. Her smile starts at the corners of the outer two eyes and dives low across her face to meet in a serrated center reminiscent of teeth.

Her once-muffled hum is now clear, no longer locked inside her bulbous head, but still off-key and inharmonious.

She rushes at me, and I expect her to attack — what else could she do with a face like that? — but she launches herself into my arms and cuddles close.

"It's times to go," Knife says, and she's right, but I should have gone before now. I shouldn't have played her game.

With Hum pressed close, I can pretend she hasn't changed, but the memory of her face stays with me. I know what she is now. I see the Ceoghast in her. How could I have forgotten what she is? Where she's from?

When I leave Jack's Patch, I do so with a monster in my arms.

Chapter 15

What daylight penetrates the Ceoghast begins to fade when Hum and I return to Speckled Hound Hollow. The Heart Witch walks about her smaller patch and wipes dirt from the speckled pumpkins with a thick blue cloth. Her back is so bent she doesn't need to reach far to clean them.

Hum trills a note of greeting, and the witch narrows her eyes at Hum. Before I can stop her, Hum flounces by the Heart Witch with her stalks above her head.

"Hum," I say, but she's too enamored of her victory lap to pay me any mind.

The witch allows Hum to parade by a few times and then swats at her with the cloth. Hum evades the hit with playful ease and prances back to me.

"You half listened," the witch says.

"We went to the patch like you said," I say. "I took her there."

"And played one of Knife's games."

"You didn't say I couldn't." For the first time it occurs to me the witch might try to get out of her side of the bargain. "All you told me to do was take Hum to Jack's Patch, and I did that. Now you have to get me out of here."

"So I do."

Her admission feels like I've won an out-of-reach prize.

"Will it be the two of you now?" she says.

"What? No." I can't go back to Midt with a Ceoghast creature in tow. If anyone saw me with Hum, they'd kill me as a witch. "I'm going home. Hum stays here. It's where she belongs."

"So it is," the witch says. "But she also belongs to you now. What do you think she'll do if you leave her?"

"Hum belongs to no one. She's her own..." I gesture at her but don't have the right word. "I'm going home — that's all that matters. You need to take me."

"That's all fine," the Heart Witch says. "We'll go find your problem first thing in the morning."

She moves to polish another pumpkin.

"No." That's not the deal. I need to leave this place now. It's a gift of Light that the Ceoghast hasn't gotten me yet. "I need to get home."

"I understand," she says. "But you've come back too late. I can't leave this close to darkfall."

"You can't add arbitrary conditions. I won't stay here. Do you know how hard it'll be for me to go back if I stay here longer?" A Lightbearer on a mission might spend such time in the Ceoghast, but the newcomer who ran away from their border patrol partner? The townspeople won't believe I'm good. They'll see corruption in me.

"I will take you," the witch says. "And I am sorry to delay you more. I know it makes your homecoming harder."

Her words hold all the sincerity in the world. Is this her magic? Does she mean to twist my heart to believe her?

"You're trying to keep me here to corrupt me," I say. Unlike her words, mine ring false, so when she disagrees with me, I feel like a child caught in a lie.

"I'm not," she says. "The truth is I can't travel after darkfall. If I'm not safe at home, I'm not safe at all."

I remember the confused woman I met last night, a scared and distracted version of the woman who stands in front of me now.

"It's not far," I say. "You could get back in time."

"Even you, new as you are, know that's not true. The nearest border is an hour from here if you go as a feryot flies."

I have no idea what a feryot is and don't want to. The thought of Ceoghast creatures with flight is too much.

The witch stretches out to brush dirt from another pumpkin. "That's two hours of travel when the sun's got less than an hour left," she says.

"But I can't stay," I say.

One night in the Ceoghast I can explain: I was lost; monsters tried to eat me; it took me a while to find my way back home. But two nights? How can I explain such a delay? What can I say to my community members that will convince them I didn't loiter here?

And even if I justify my prolonged absence, how will I keep the Ceoghast off while I'm here?

"It was hard for me to accept my confinement after darkfall at first," the witch says. "Like you, I had obligations that did not allow me to stay in one place. They needed me to be elsewhere. But the truth is I don't have the ability to see my duties through at night. Who and what I am leaves in the dark." She surveys the pumpkins.

"That's why I can't take you until morning," she says. "I won't know my way around and certainly wouldn't be able to make any deals on your behalf. We'd both end up dead, or worse."

If I were still in Midt, I'd have no idea what might be worse than death, but the Ceoghast revises the possibilities.

To wait may not be my first choice, but in light of my options, it's the best chance I have to get home. I wouldn't trust the woman I met last night to lead me around her yard, never mind the Ceoghast.

"Are we settled then?" she says. "I'll take you out first thing in the morning?"

"Yes," I say. I feel like an energetic animal shoved in a box that doesn't fit, but I have no other option. I need her to take me.

"Head inside then and make yourself useful. Storm the kettle over the fire and dice the potato on the counter."

"I'm not your servant," I say.

"Nor are you my invited guest," she says.

My cheeks grow so hot I lift my hands to hide them. The witch waves her cloth in the direction of the house.

"That's the last time I'll mention it if you lend a hand where it's needed," she says. "Now get going. I have to set the barrier."

Curiosity crawls up my spine and turns my head to watch her, but the thought of being near whatever spell she casts hastens me into the cottage. Hum bounds along beside me. When we enter the kitchen, she leaps into a chair at the table and slaps out a tune on its surface.

I swing the kettle over the fire and take the potato in hand. She's not left me a knife, so I open the drawers to find one. Hum launches herself onto the counter and watches my search with her obsidian gaze. When I pull out a knife, she chatters at me and her lips curl toward her eyes.

"This isn't for you," I say. The thought churns my stomach.

The knife is sharp, the potato a little soft, and Hum loses interest in my work. She turns and opens a cupboard door.

"Stay out of there," I say, but like a puppy starved for attention, my scolding prompts more play.

Hum's stalks pull at drawer handles and cupboard knobs. I abandon the potato to shoo her away. But now it's all play to her, and she jumps about the tiny room on coiled stalks.

"Hum. Stop," I say.

The kitchen looks ransacked. If the witch returns now she'll think I meant to snoop. Hum finds a drawer of cutlery and snatches up the spoons in delight. She shoves them into her carved face. My eyes feel as big as my open mouth. Hum glances my way and squeals in delight at my abhorrence.

"That's enough," I say. "Put those back."

Hum preens and adjusts the spoons.

"You know they don't make you look good," I say.

A short croon lets me know she doesn't share my opinion.

The front door creaks open. I grab for Hum but she dances out of my reach. A yarn basket tumbles to the floor. The witch's shuffle grows louder.

Let Hum keep the spoons. I shut every drawer and cupboard and gather up the yarn. I don't have time to rewind the unspooled balls. They go into the basket a tangled mess. I step back to the potato as the witch enters the room.

"Did you finish?" she says.

I pick up the knife. "Just finishing."

"Good." She takes a pan down from a wall hanger and scoops the diced potato into it. She takes the knife and cuts a dollop of grease to help it cook. The thick scent of warm lard fills the air, and my stomach grumbles.

"I have cold cuts in that box," she says. She waves a knife at a wooden box by the door. "Fetch them out and get them on this plate. We don't have much time before I go, and we need to go over a few things."

I open the box and recoil at the cold air that blasts out. It's like she's trapped winter in the tiny space. I'm hesitant to reach inside, uncertain about what the cold might do to me, but then Hum comes along. In her current mood, she's liable to grab the meat and throw it about. I take out the cold cuts and close the box.

"Leave it," I say to Hum as she drums her stalks against the box.

"Does your friend mean to give me back my spoons?" the witch says.

Hum still has the cutlery jammed in her face. "I don't know," I say as I set the cold cuts on the plate.

"See if you can get one for the tea," she says.

Hum takes a spoon out. My stomach twists at the small glob of orange goo on it. Who knows what that might be. Spit? Boogers? Brains?

I motion for Hum to give it to the witch. I don't want to touch it.

"I have rules if you mean to stay past darkfall," the witch says. She takes the spoon from Hum and wipes it on her apron. "I won't be myself, so you're pretty much on your own if you do something stupid or dangerous."

My life these past few days seems a series of stupid and dangerous decisions. "I'll do whatever gets me home safe," I say. I mean it to reassure her I'll behave, but the twist of her thin lips tells me she takes it as a defiant challenge.

"You'll stay in the house and not touch my belongings. And don't open the front door."

I feel the walls tighten around me with this command. However open the accommodation, it is still a cage.

"I won't recognize you, won't know why you're here," she says. "My name is Emathi. Use my name when you speak to me and it'll smooth things out between us. Only people in my closer acquaintance use my name."

She motions for me to sit at the table and brings two mugs of tea, then sets a plate of vegetables fried in the lard next to it. We begin to eat. Hum sneaks a round slice of meat from the plate and spindles it on her stalk. She shoves it in her carved mouth but part of it catches on her serrated teeth and hangs out. The song she hums suggests she is either unaware of the error or delighted with the result.

"I like talking about simple subjects at night. You can hand me my knitting if I get agitated, and I'll quiet down to work. Don't aggravate me," she says. "You wouldn't like the results of any trouble you cause, and I'd have an awful mess to clean up in the morning."

Interpretations of what she might mean by "mess" run through my mind. Most speculations end in curses and blood, or painful transformations.

"I'll be kind," I say. "Maybe I can just stay in the loft?"

"And let me suspect an intruder? No. You stay and introduce yourself and get me settled before you think of going to bed."

We eat in silence after that, and as the sun lowers, the witch — Emathi — begins to frown. Her shoulders curl inwards, and her hands clutch at her sleeves.

"Who are you?" she says. "Are we having dinner now?"

Gone is the power of presence that the Heart Witch possesses during daylight hours.

"My name is Cassia, Emathi," I say. "We finished dinner already, but you still have tea. Would you like to drink it?"

Emathi's nervousness is childlike. Her gaze searches the room as though she hopes to find a missing parent or someone else who might help her make sense of what's going on.

"Why are you here? Who are you?"

I won't tell this version of the Heart Witch my purpose — who knows what that might trigger.

"I came to visit you, Emathi," I say. To make it believable, I add, "We have a mutual friend, Emathi. Knave brought me to meet you."

"Is Knave here?" She begins to stand.

"No," I say. I have no idea where Knave is but feel certain we'll see them tomorrow when I leave. They'll want their bargain.

"It's just the two of us," I say.

"Did you move the jars?" Her tone is both plaintive and accusatory. The shift leaves me on edge.

"Would you like to knit?" I say. I fetch the yarn and needles for her and hope it's an adequate distraction.

"Oh, this wool is nice," she says. She runs her knobby hands over the skein. "Would you like me to knit you something?"

I shake my head. What sort of darkness would she weave into her pattern if given a chance?

"You make something for yourself," I say. "I should go to bed."

"You're staying the night?"

"Yes. You told me to take the loft," I say.

"Don't touch my bed," she says.

Her voice is such a match for Katta's haughty child's commands for a moment I can't breathe.

"Or my jars," she says.

"I won't. Goodnight, Emathi."

Hum lopes over to me and slings herself into my arms. Emathi's eyes go wide.

"You have a Jack," she says. "But what's wrong with it? Why's it so small?"

I remember well Emathi's shouts about the stunted squash in her house. I don't want a similar episode to happen tonight. Even Knave had a hard time calming her.

"It's a new variety Knife's made," I say.

"Don't say that name," Emathi says. "What if she comes here? She'll cut us to ribbons."

With my mind full of that nightmare image, it's hard for me to reply with reason. "Knife won't leave the patch, Emathi. You're safe, and you have knitting to do."

Emathi picks up the skein like she hadn't noticed it before. "Oh, this is lovely yarn," she says. "I'll make a hat. A good witch needs a good hat."

I slip away while she's distracted and climb the ladder to the loft. Warm water puffs in the basin, and Hum darts over to it like the steam is a siren's song. The bed pallet is made and fresh. Even the navy nightgown I wore last night feels and smells laundered.

I want to scream at all the unnatural world that surrounds me, but even Hum's biggest splashes in the basin wouldn't hide such a noise. I grit my teeth instead.

Tomorrow I leave this place for good.

Chapter 16

That night, my old dreams come back to me.

My friend Rasmo and I run down the creek-side road behind all the fine family homes in Horth. We swoop down on piles of crispy orange leaves like they're flocks of birds we can scatter into flight. Rasmo's cheeks are red from our games, and a sweet heaviness sits in my limbs. After a day stuck at our school desks hunched over tenets, I need to jump and run until I feel alive again. So we race each other and laugh and crow with delight.

Enamored of our sport, I don't recognize the voice that calls my name.

Dread lifts me from sleep for a moment, but my exhaustion is too strong, and I slip back into the childhood I've long left behind.

Hands full of leaves, I turn, afraid Rasmo and I are in trouble. Were we too loud? Is playing with leaves not okay?

A woman stands in the middle of the path. I know her, but I don't remember why she's familiar. I take a few steps toward her to make sense of her features. Her hair is shorn to her scalp, her cheekbones stark.

And then she smiles.

"Mom?" I say. Then everything clicks. I see her and she makes sense! "Mom!"

She throws her hands out wide and I drop all the leaves I meant to throw at Rasmo and run to my mom. It's been almost a year — a whole year — since she left and I know she hasn't been visiting a sick friend all that time because she would've written if that were true.

I've imagined seeing her again for so long and practiced all my anger, but now that she's really here all I feel is joy. I'm so light I could fly. Am I even breathing? I run faster, swelling with elation, and everything is gold and bright and happy like me.

But then my mom's face goes all wrong and her hands shoot out toward me, and Rasmo starts screaming.

I turn back to Rasmo, but I'm running too fast and my feet don't know which way to go. I trip. My shoulder hits the ground first and I skid along until I ram into something rock hard. Rasmo's still screaming but the high pitch dulls to a background buzz when I see what I've hit.

The black flower stalk is nearly as round as my arm and heavy purple flowers shaped like bulbous hearts droop toward me. My whole body clenches with fear. I know this flower. Everyone does, and it wasn't here a second ago. They never grow this close to good communities.

I shove myself away from it, but my back slams into another, and when I scramble to my feet, I see them all around me: the Ceoghast flower called Evil's Triumph.

"Mom!" I need her to help me, but when I look at her she's standing with her arms limp at her sides, her head down. She doesn't meet my gaze. Behind me Rasmo's cries have become a single word yelped over and over and over again.

"Witch! Witch! Witch!"

"Mom?" I say. I want all this to stop. I need her to grab me and scoop me into her arms like she's supposed to. I want us to talk over each other when we say how much we missed each other and how much we love each other still. We can go home — just the two of us — and hold hands all the way and wait for Father to get back. We'll all have dinner together and the community will burn the flowers and raze the ground and everything will be okay.

They won't hurt us. The flowers can't reach us at home. Not when we're all together again.

"Cassia!" Rasmo says. "Get away from her. She's trying to kill you!"

I look up sharply at that, and see my mom's face twisted into a snarl I don't recognize or understand. She looks angry. I'm so focused on her I don't see the baker charging out of his house until he tackles her. Her head bounces against the ground hard, and I'm trying to understand who's screaming when Rasmo yells again and cuts me off.

"Get away from the flowers! They'll put the Ceoghast on you! She's trying to kill you!"

I stumble out of the patch of Evil's Triumph and land hard in a pile of leaves. I watch more people come from the houses. There's so many of them I can't see my mom. A few of the adults start to jog over to us. Rasmo, breathing in short hard breaths, runs up to me and leans over her knees. "I thought you'd be dead. She started calling them up all around you and I thought she'd kill you for sure."

"That's my mom," I say. None of this makes sense. She's good. She's not a witch. She belongs in the community.

"She's a witch. She tried to kill you! It's no wonder your father sent her away," Rasmo says.

Sent her away? I don't understand what's happening, and then the adults rush over and make everything worse. Their words are quick and concerned, but I can't answer any of their questions. Did my father send Mom away? Did he know she was evil? Did she get the Ceoghast on her?

I glance at the flowers, unnaturally tall and strong and rooted deep in our community's good soil. Those flowers can only grow in the Ceoghast. Those flowers can only grow in places where evil lives, and my mom called them here. She forced them to grow around me.

Everything tilts. I turn my head to the leaves and vomit.

"Cassia," one of the adults says. She puts a hand on my back. "Was she touched? Did the flowers touch her? She might have the Ceoghast on her."

"She's fine," Rasmo says in response. She must have gotten a look because she follows up with a meeker explanation. "She got out of there fast."

"I ran into a stem," I say. Speaking makes me feel sicker and I heave again but nothing comes up. I feel empty, like I have nothing left inside my tummy or mind. "But I got out. I don't have the Ceoghast. I'd know, wouldn't I? You can tell?" I turn to the woman rubbing my back.

"We sent someone to get your father," the woman says. I don't know her well but she works in town. She pats my back a few times then pulls away. Without her touching me I feel cut out, like I'm not okay. It feels like floating in all the wrong ways.

I touch her knee, my fingers grabbing at her pants even though I don't mean to clutch at her. "I'm good," I say. "I follow the tenets. I didn't touch my... I didn't touch her. My dad sent her away, but I didn't know. I didn't know she was bad. I thought she was... she was my mom." My throat is thick and breathing is hard. How long have I been crying? "But I'm good. I'm not evil. I promise I'm good."

I keep whispering that I'm good even after the woman leaves to help the group. They're pulling my mom away. I can't watch. Rasmo lifts a hand to touch my arm but drops it before she touches me. I know I'm good. I know I don't have the Ceoghast on me, but I need to prove it. I need to show the community that I deserve to be here, that I'm not like my mom...

I wake covered in sweat, still mumbling "I'm good." But as the darkness of the Ceoghast presses in around me and sleep tries to reel me in again, I wonder how long that will be true.

Chapter 17

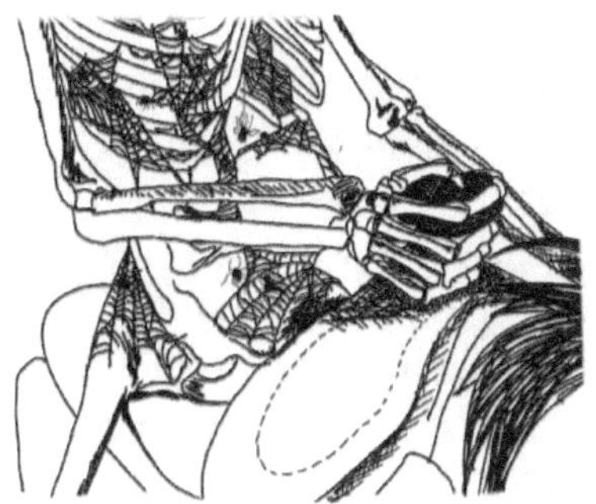

True to her word, Emathi wakes me after daybreak to take to me to the borderlands. The morning is all rough edges as I throw myself together and hurry out the door. My knee aches. My palm throbs, and my thighs are raw, and my heart leaps in my chest like a trapped rabbit. I am not at my best, and even Hum is sloppy with fatigue. But I'm going home.

This thought keeps my pace steady as I follow Emathi down the road. Other thoughts threaten to stop me cold.

I'm not sure how my return will go. No one really knows me, and Ealey will have spread his story about me being a witch. On top of that, I've been in the Ceoghast two days. If my home were still in Horth, the people there would hang me for a witch upon my return. They've watched me my whole life because of my mom, and this jaunt into the Ceoghast would be all the proof they'd need to kill me.

In Midt, I'm still a stranger. No one will speak against me based on my past, but no one will speak for me based on my present. Horth is worse, but that doesn't mean Midt will be better in the ways I need it to be. I'd still choose to be in either place if it meant I wasn't in the Ceoghast anymore. Even with those consequences.

Ahead of us, the tree-lined path down the borderlands comes into view. A figure steps out, and I tense, but it's not the cobweb woman.

It takes me a moment to recognize Knave. When we met, Knave cut a dashing figure, part gentleman, part rogue. Today they are elegance embodied. They walk over to us, their long, billowy skirt covered in a million tiny flowers that seem plucked from the earth itself. Gone are the green and purple threads in their hair. Today they wear a halo of dusty pink roses and miniature fivepetaled orange flowers. Knave's softness is ethereal. Next to them I lumber like an expectant cow.

"Hello, Emathi. Hello, Cassia," they say.

"I wondered if you'd show up here," Emathi says. "It's not like you to take an interest in matters that don't benefit you."

"I think we can all agree that seeing this woman home benefits all of us," Knave says. "We don't need wanderers running about."

Hum hisses at Knave who studies her new face and laughs. "I see you've gone out of your way to improve yourself, my stunted friend," they say. "Knife must be furious to lose so much magic like this."

"I presume you have some purpose and won't continue to delay us in ours," Emathi says.

Knave sweeps a hand toward the road. "I've come to see Cassia Mooseroot, woman of Midt, through the borderlands," they say. "Once you clear her path, that is."

I glare at Knave. Why should I keep that bargain when I've had to make a second one with the witch?

"Where is your problem?" Emathi says.

The path before us is clear, but fear keeps my heart heavy. "I don't see her," I say.

"Best walk out slow and find out where your problem's hiding, then," Emathi says.

My hands shake at her instructions, so I bury them in my trouser pockets and begin my walk out of the Ceoghast. Five steps in, the cobweb woman urges her horse onto the path. I stop.

Hum's stalks slap the ground as she rushes to me. She growls and yips at the woman, then wraps me in her stalks and pulls me back.

I don't resist. In daylight the woman's bones protrude through her cobweb skin and a ball of shadows and spiders churns in her abdomen.

Behind me, Emathi barks a laugh. She marches past us. Her muddy boots squeak with every step and give the impression she's more mad woman than witch. Perhaps she is. No one sane would go near that monster.

"What are you doing here?" she says. Her words split the air like a crack of thunder. "Have you forgotten your actual job, or is this one of your adolescent fits come back?"

"Does she know that woman?" I say.

Knave shrugs, the motion smooth as falling water. "Emathi knows a lot of us," they say.

The cobweb woman seems unperturbed by Emathi's outburst. She smiles down at the witch. Spiders run from her mouth into her eyes.

I look away, but the image remains burned in my mind. Hum watches with interest, and I worry she may learn such a trick.

My whole body is tense. I'm ready to run. Hum's only got one stalk on me now, and I'm pretty sure if I take off, she won't try to stop me.

While the conversation began at great volume, whatever Emathi says now doesn't carry to us. The hunched witch gesticulates with wide, quick movements that threaten to unbalance her. The cobweb woman replies with ease. She's as neutral as she was the night she threatened me. But she shakes her head a lot. She does it so often, I worry Emathi's powers aren't working.

The spider-stuffed stomach runs through my mind. What if she doesn't have a heart? Does Emathi need an actual heart to influence others?

"She doesn't belong here. She needs to go home," Emathi says. "What difference does waiting make?"

The woman's reply doesn't reach our ears, but Emathi's attempt to reason with her deflates my hope.

Knave said Emathi would help, that she could change this creature's heart. Instead, it sounds like she's run out of ways to advocate for me and now whines on my behalf.

"This isn't working," I say.

"Seems this is bigger than we thought," Knave says.

A note of awe widens their words. They shift closer to me and the heady scent of roses fills my nose. A blush burns my cheeks as they lean in.

"What did you do to deserve this kind of attention, Miss Mooseroot?" they say.

For a moment their interest is a warm glow that fills me from tip to toes. But when Knave leans back and the air no longer smells of roses, the sensation turns to ice. What did I do to deserve this kind of attention? What if it's not me at all but my mother? Did her touch poison me in a way this monster recognizes?

Emathi stomps back to us. Beyond her, the woman remains seated on her horse in the center of the path. She waves her skeletal fingers at me.

"She won't be swayed," Emathi says.

Blood rushes from my head. I reach out to keep from falling, and Hum's stalks coil about my hand. I ease myself to the ground.

"I did my best," Emathi says. "But she'll not leave. Not for two weeks or so. That's as good as I got. You can try again then."

"Two weeks?" I say.

Emathi nods. "Something may have changed by then. That's the best I could do."

"That's not okay," I say. "I need to go home. I can't stay here."

Hum begins to chatter beside me and twists her stalks together to loom over Knave and Emathi. I stand and take a step toward the cobweb woman.

"You can't keep me here," I say.

The cobweb woman turns her head. Her black gaze sends shivers down my back. "Ain't no one keeping you here, honey. You're free to go anytime you want," she says. "It's just that you ain't going to go so far before you die if you leave while I'm here. But that's still a choice. Ain't no one put you in a box."

"You're trying to put me in a coffin," I say.

"Only if you pass by. Ain't nothing personal about it. I'm just stating facts."

I hate her. I know hate goes against the tenets, but right now I feel like there should be an exception if what you hate is evil.

Overnight is long enough, but two weeks? Even if I manage to keep my soul intact and keep the Ceoghast off me, no one in Midt will welcome me back. They'll kill me on sight. No one but a Lightbearer can survive that kind of exposure.

"You can stay with me," Emathi says. "You'll have to help around the house, but nothing's going to hurt you there."

I wheel on her. Rage rises like a flood. "Did you not hear what I said? I need to go home."

What scraps of composure I have leave me, and I sob until my face hurts and my breath jerks in my throat. Hum sidles next to me and murmurs a soft melody in my ear. My energy abandons me. I slump to the ground. Even my anger loses its edge.

"They won't take me back," I say. "If I'm gone too long, that's it for me."

"This is it for you, too, if you try to go home now. It's best you wait, even if it's not what you want to do," Emathi says. "You'll have time enough to figure out how to get home."

"I'll have two weeks," I say. It feels like a sentence a judge would pass: two weeks in the Ceoghast. A euphemism for certain death.

Anger pricks me.

"I'm going to wait here," I say. "Whenever she leaves, I'm going."

"Where? Here?" Knave says. "You can come back daily if you need. Staying out here, the way you are... You wouldn't need to walk by your problem to find your end."

A shout leaps to my tongue, but Emathi touches my wrist with one papery hand.

"Knave will bring you here every day, Cassia," she says. "But you should stay at Speckled Hound Hollow."

I wait for words of protests that don't rise in me. My emotions are flat as a pond.

"They won't take me back," I say. The statement, gutted of my fear, rings empty. So empty is feels unimportant, like it's not a life changing.

"Come along now," Emathi says as she tugs at my wrist. I stand. Hum no longer sings.

"I'll come back." My tongue is thick, like I'm half-asleep.

"I'll swing by to get you every day," Knave says.

"Every day," I say. The promise reassures me. It encircles me like a fire-warmed blanket.

"Back we go," Emathi says. "There's a girl."

Chapter 18

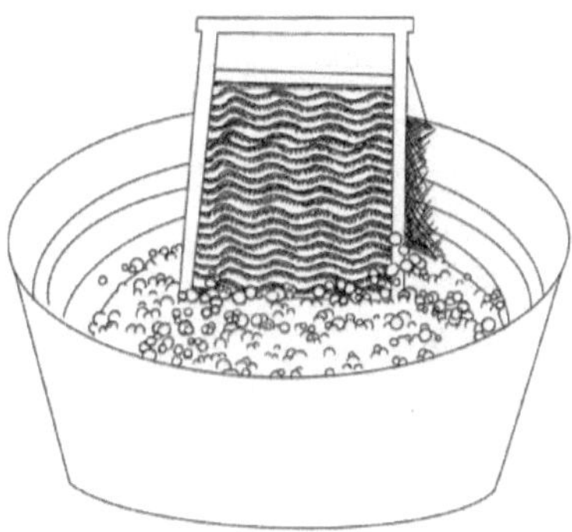

The blue blouse in my hands isn't mine, and I don't know where it came from. It's wet from the washbasin at my feet. I don't remember washing it, or why I'm washing anything at all. But I dunk it again and run it along the washboard. Soapy water sloshes onto my trousers as I lift the shirt out.

I pause.

What am I doing?

My head is muzzy. These clothes aren't mine. I lift my head, but my surroundings blur. Only the washbasin is clear. I wring out the shirt, then drop it back into the tub.

"That took longer than I expected," Emathi says.

I look up from the sudsy gray water and find her seated on one of the larger green pumpkins not far from me. We are in her yard close to the small porch.

"Didn't feel like facing reality again so soon?" she says.

"What do you mean?" I say. My thoughts move like water in a clogged sink.

"You've been out here for nearly two hours. I was afraid you'd wear a hole in my shirt."

That slaps the confusion right out of me.

We'd been on the path with the cobweb woman. I had planned to stay.

"You used your magic on me." Shivers run down my back and over my arms as though to chase away whatever dredges of her magic remain in my skin.

"I gave your heart a small push," she says. "You couldn't stay there."

"Why? Because you need a mindless slave to do your laundry?" I upend the basin and kick away the stool I sat on. Bright pink pain lights up my big toe. "You poisoned me."

"It's not a poison, just a push." Emathi eyes the water that runs over the ground. "If you keep this up, I might do it again."

"You are not allowed to use magic on me." Tears choke what I want to say next. If I force through them, my rage will drown us both.

Emathi folds her gnarled hands on her lap. Her face is placid with the forced patience a parent might employ when faced with a child's tantrum. It makes me feel small even though I'm not in the wrong.

"Don't you ever try to change my heart again, or cast any other spells around me." I spit each syllable.

"I think we both need to set a few ground rules." She shifts on her pumpkin and pulls a small book and pencil stump from her apron pocket. "We'll make it formal so there's no misunderstandings between us."

Anger fizzes in my chest and makes me bold. "Then take mine first: no magic on or around me." This woman could turn my heart from my interests on a whim, but I stand tall, arms crossed in defiance the way Katta does when she doesn't get her way. Emathi stares at me and I meet her gaze with a steadiness that surprises me.

She waves the notebook in my direction. "Here. You take the notes. You can read and write, I presume?"

The question seems more an attempt to insult me than a serious inquiry. I write my rule at the top of a clean page with all the emphasis I feel it deserves, then I add another.

"You're not allowed to hurt me, or trick me, or corrupt me."

She arches an eyebrow at the last, and I wonder if I need to be more specific.

"Why don't you write down that you're to remain safe and unharmed while you're in my care? That you should be so protected from any such harm that you leave here in the exact state you are now?" she says.

If she's hidden a trick in that suggestion, I can't see it. I add it to the page. Once it's written, I feel better.

"You also can't ask or hire another person to hurt me or do anything bad to me for you." I pause. "Or creature."

"You certainly have a low opinion of me."

I write down my additional condition. I won't take any chances. Each rule makes me feel I can survive this intact. That I won't get the Ceoghast on me.

Unless she already put it on me when she changed my heart.

"Is it my turn now?" she says.

All the reassurance I felt flees me. Suspicion crowds in. "Okay."

"Let's start with the basics, then. You are welcome to stay here as a guest so long as you follow the night rules I've set out and earn your keep." She squints at me. "You do remember my nighttime rules?"

"Do what I can to soothe you. Say your name a lot. Don't go outside."

"And don't touch my things." Her triumphant verbal pounce leaves me shame-faced.

"It's not like I'm going to take anything and go anywhere," I say.

She flicks a hand at me. "Write it down."

I add the nighttime rules. When I get to the last one, the pencil tip breaks from the pressure I apply.

"Careful now. Wouldn't want to have to find the blade to sharpen it and interrupt our nice chat. That could delay negotiations, you know."

"It's fine." The tip is dull but I can still write with it.

She snorts and rocks back on her pumpkin.

Anger rises in me again, all sharp and jumpy. "Are you enjoying this?"

"This? No. What's to enjoy about this?" Her uneven smile reminds me of the faces in Knife's Jack piles. "But now we move onto the good part — how you plan to earn your keep."

The upended laundry tub feels like a third presence. Soap stains the dirt gray.

"What do you want?" Laundry isn't so bad a task — it's how I earn money in Midt — but it leaves me exhausted. Not that Emathi would have that much wash to do.

"I'm old and tired and stiff. You may have noticed I don't get along very well." This seems more an attempt to insult my powers of observation than personal disclosure. "You will complete tasks I find burdensome given my limitations."

"Like laundry?"

"You chose that yourself. I gave you options."

Without memory of this, I can't confirm her assertion, but it feels true. Laundry is safe and familiar and ordinary — who knows what other choices she presented.

"What do you find burdensome?"

"A friend of mine is out of town and left the care of her homestead to me. It's too much with all the work I have to do here."

She gestures at her pumpkin-covered lawn as though what's to be done is obvious. All I can think of is the pumpkins she polished with her blue cloth, which doesn't seem an important task.

"It's basic enough," she says. "Keep the home clean and tend her creatures."

"Creatures?" Not pets or animals or livestock. Creatures. My stomach twists like the shirt I'd wrung out.

"A couple of hens and a kelpie. They don't take long to tend, but the kelpie needs the right approach. The way I move these days, I don't have it." Her rheumy eyes wrinkle at the corners. "You shouldn't have a problem. With all your mistrust, you'll be smart enough to avoid its tricks."

I have no idea what a kelpie is but can tell by her amusement I won't like it. Emathi pokes fun at me and insults me

— she could throw a creature like the kelpie at me just to watch my discomfort.

"Is a kelpie dangerous?"

"Only to people with less sense than a gourd. For all your foolishness, I think you'll be fine. It's currently a bit like a horse."

The cobweb woman comes to mind. If it's like her horse, I won't go near it. I want to ask if it will corrupt me, if its proximity might be a poison to my goodness, but the witch won't understand my concern. I don't want her to mock my ignorance again.

"You agreed to keep me safe."

"I know what you've scratched down there, and we'll both stick to it. It's not like I'd send you alone. I'll go with you the first time." She studies my face. "And the second time, if you need."

I look at the agreement in hopes it might buoy my confidence, but even with the whole of my unfortunate stay laid out, I don't feel safe.

"I get to watch you do everything first." It's a small protection from whatever harm might await me at her friend's house, but when she nods, I'm reassured. "And I get to say no if it's not safe."

"That's fine, but the other tasks I have for you if you refuse this one aren't half as pleasant or easy." She smacks the pumpkin beneath her and stands. Noisy pops run the length of her spine and knees.

"We have to sign," I say.

I scratch my name below the rules and hold the pencil out for her to do the same. She struggles to hold the pencil in her twisted hands. Her signature quivers across the page without a single discernible letter. She opens her hand, and the pencil falls to the ground.

"Grab that basket by the door," she says. "It's time to earn your keep."

Chapter 19

Emathi leads me down the same path Hum and I took to Jack's Patch, but it delivers us to a different place. I want to believe I missed a turn, but the marks along the trail are the same. I remember the bush shaped like a bear, the bone-white trees whose branches stretch toward each other like children holding hands, and the way the path pitches over the small slopes.

The two of us do not speak. Her silence seems one of focus. Her feet twist on the uneven ground, and her hands startle like birds as she catches her balance again and again. My silence, on the other hand, keeps my screams inside. Magic must surround me, but I don't know how to avoid it or protect myself from its taint. I clench my teeth, keep firm hold of the basket, and chant the tenets in my mind.

The once fresh and crisp breeze becomes heavy with the scent of wet earth mixed with a sour, noxious undertone. Beneath our feet, the walkway softens and begins to suck at my soles.

"Almost there," Emathi says. She wheezes and is so unsteady on this new ground I almost reach out to help her. The thought that her evil might contaminate me if I do holds me in place.

We come upon a footpath of hand-hewn planks. They bow and whine with our weight, and I worry they may not support us. The stench of vegetation in decay burns my nose. Trees draped in long, dark moss block our view of the sky, and on either side of us, still and dark water rises.

When we come upon the homestead, its dilapidated state surprises me. The Heart Witch keeps a neat home, and I'd presumed any acquaintance of hers would do the same. I find it hard to believe anyone would inhabit such a ramshackle space.

"This is it," she says. She eases onto a stump and curls into herself, her breathing labored.

The house is a plain square constructed with long, thin boards now warped and peeling. Forest detritus covers the flat roof, and the only way in or out of the shack appears to be a single tall door. The home abuts a stationery green body of water from which the sulfurous smell seems to emanate. Wood railings and longer slats from a deck rot in the water and look like they fell many years ago.

The more I look at it, the more I suspect Emathi's created busy work for me. This can't be a person's home.

"Someone lives here?" I say.

"Not for a while."

Is Emathi responsible for this place's ruin? How long has her friend been gone? I almost ask, but the glare on her face stops my tongue.

"I don't expect you to go about trying to repair the outside," she says. "That is what it is. The inside needs minor upkeep. You can dust, sweep, and such, but I expect you to devote most of your time here to the care of her creatures."

"The kelpie."

"And a few others," she says. "You manage your little Jack well enough, so you shouldn't have much trouble."

Who knows where Hum is now. I'm not sure whether I'd feel more or less worried had she come with us here. I trust her to look out for me, but she is also full of mischief. What would she make of the kelpie?

"What others?" I say. "The hens?"

Emathi eases herself from the stump. "Come along. I'll show you. It all depends on what's still here. I haven't made it out in a few days. The lot may have moved on."

"Lot of what?"

"Creatures," she says. "Are you trying to be difficult?"

"Are you trying to be obtuse?" The barb is meant for Emathi, but I feel its burn. I've never spoken to another person with so little respect in my life. If I were home, I'd be whipped for my tone, then again for my words.

I wait for the witch's face to whiten, for her lips to tighten, for a reply that puts me in my place. Instead, she laughs.

"You are feisty for a beggar," she says. "No one else around to help you, but you try to take me to task. What an attitude."

"I don't have an attitude." Katta's the one who's always told to watch her attitude. If I'd ever made critical comments, or failed to be kind and obedient, I'd be put on notice.

Or accused of being a ceogot.

What if I am one? What if this is how it starts? The idea sits like ice in my stomach.

"You do," Emathi says. "I like it more than the mousing you usually try. Now come along and meet the pets."

Pets is a nicer term, but I'm not dumb enough to think whatever we're about to meet is safe.

I follow Emathi down a path of raised dirt. Swamp water presses against either side of it, close enough that any misstep would be an unpleasant — and smelly — mistake.

"Mind you don't touch any of them until I go over what you can and can't do," she says.

"I'm not a fool," I say, but I wonder if that's true. I'm stuck in the Ceoghast. I've agreed to work for a witch. In a few moments I'm to meet evil creatures. None of this speaks to intelligence. Shame and despair dig within me and leave a hole so big I think it might swallow all I am.

This isn't my fault. I didn't choose this path. I block out the hopelessness, and I hold to the tenets like a light in the dark.

Emathi takes me to the hen house, which is neat and ordinary. Three typical farm hens peck at the ground and fill me with delight. They remind me of home, of the people in my community, of my normal life.

"These ones are easy," Emathi says. "Feed them and keep their house and yard clean."

It's obvious Emathi's only managed to feed them for a while. The stink of manure fills my nose. "They're not strange?" I eye them for surprise monster teeth or hidden double heads.

"Boring as they come and too old now for any use. Your job is to keep them clean, fed, and comfortable."

She shows me where the food is kept and what supplies I can use to tidy their area. It's easy enough, though I've not cared for animals before. My father never allowed us to have pets back home. Any odd or inappropriate behavior could've cast suspicion on my character. I never questioned his decision, but Katta threw frequent tantrums every time he and his wife denied her request for a cat.

Homesickness hits me on a wave that threatens to bowl me over.

When I go home now, it means I go to Midt. Even if I wanted, I can't go back to Horth. Not if I want to keep Katta untouched by the potential corruption that surrounds me. Emathi shuts the chicken shed, scattering my thoughts, and takes me further into the homestead.

I nearly run into her when she stops in front of a large clearing. A quick sidestep allows me to avoid the collision, though my knee protests. I rub it and take in the scene. The ground is trampled flat, but not a single animal is in sight.

Emathi sighs, a sound part relief, part exasperation. "Just as well," she says. "If any come back, I'll go over their care then. No sense in wasting our time now. Let's go see his horseness."

She must mean the kelpie. "It can't be anything dangerous," I say. "We agreed."

"Don't start mousing again. Where's your courage?" She takes a path that dips toward the greater swamp waters. "I know what we agreed, and I mean to stick to it, but you've also got work to do."

"I'm not mousing."

"It'll not be so unlike caring for your Hum. The kelpie's a pet, of a sort. At the moment. Only dangerous if you don't keep your head about you."

I don't know what it means to keep my head about me in the Ceoghast. I'm certain most inhabitants would take my head right off if given the opportunity.

Emathi walks straight to the water's edge and stands with her toes in the muck. "You want to get his attention like this," she says. "Just your toes, mind. Go in up to your ankles and you'll be gone before you see a single ripple."

She's made herself bait and expects me to do the same. I stand well clear of the water.

"Keep a sharp eye for... there." A few ripples and bubbles disturb the mirror-like surface. "Give it another bit after you see that, then step back."

She demonstrates what she means and hobbles back onto the soft ground. The water churns faster and harder. My legs rattle with the desire to flee.

Pointed, webbed ears breach the surface, and with a thrash, a horse-like head emerges. The kelpie is all sharp angles and too long limbs. It has an equine shape and grace but seems more skeletal. Its skin is dark and green like algae and draped in what looks like swamp grass. It throws its head as it trots toward Emathi, and the long oily strands whip about it. Not swamp grass, then, but a sort of hair covering.

Emathi wipes her apron over her face to clean off the spray. "Alright. That's enough of that," she says.

The kelpie snorts and shakes itself again.

"Does it understand you?" I say.

"Quiet," she says.

The kelpie turns to study me. Its eyes are feline, predatory. Emathi flaps her apron and draws its attention back.

"He understands enough to know I don't appreciate getting wet." She studies him. "We're going to cut the corrosion from his mane and tail. You see those gooey bits?

The dark spots stand out. "Yes."

"We cut just above them."

"I don't want to touch it."

"And you best not. Don't put a hand on him." She looks at me like I might not understand how serious she is. "I'm going to get him out of the water — you can lure him with a snack — then we'll get to the grooming."

I dig around in the basket and remove an apple. "Is this the snack?" The kelpie shrieks and whips its head at me. The slimy mane slaps my face and knocks me over.

I fall in the water. The mane drives me deeper. I tear at it, but my fingers can't grip the seaweed slick hair. I fight to the surface in time to see Emathi slam her palm against the kelpie's narrow chest.

"You don't want to do this," she says.

The kelpie bares its stone-like teeth and laughs. He has a human laugh, dark and full of malice. He tries to pull me back under.

"You don't want to hurt her. You will let her go."

Even I feel the command. My hands spring open in obedience.

All at once, the kelpie lets me go. I scramble back to the bank and crawl away from the water.

I want Hum. Why didn't I try to find Hum? I trust her to keep me safe more than anyone. What if Emathi can't hold the creature?

"Stay," Emathi says. The kelpie freezes. When the witch turns to me, her face is flush with rage.

"You stupid woman. Why did you wave food in its face like that?"

"You said to lure it with a snack."

"I said that's something you'd be able to do. Did you forget you're supposed to watch me and learn?"

I hadn't forgotten. Not really. I'd thought she'd given me an instruction.

She snatches the basket from where I'd dropped it and takes one of her blue cloths out. She returns to the kelpie and flutters the blue cloth near its muzzle. "Follow me," she says.

The kelpie's ears perk forward.

"This is how you lure him," she says. "Don't touch him and don't offer him food. He's a fey creature. The only thing he wants to eat in our world is flesh, and you don't want to offer him that."

"This is too dangerous. I want nothing to do with him."

"It's not if you pay attention and stick to the agreement you were so fussed about. Watch and learn."

"I just want to go home."

Tension coils about Emathi and pulls her tight. Her hand shoots out at the kelpie's face. "Stay."

Perhaps she meant to command both of us. When she turns to me, face in a snarl, I'm rooted in place.

"Cross the border and deal with the consequences or stay here and do the work. Whining at me about what you want isn't on the table." She jabs my shoulder. "I don't mind keeping you. I'll help you as much as I'm able. But you will earn your way, and crying about what you can't have isn't part of it. Do you understand me?"

In the last three days I've had more low spots than I've experienced over the course of my entire life. Not since my mother's hanging have I felt so lost and alone.

This lecture reopens the hole that gapes within me, and I have no anger left to fill it. Is this even worth it? I work for a witch. I'm to deal with creatures that, if they don't kill me outright, will probably corrupt my soul. All this in a bid to make it home again. But what good is my return if the Ceoghast gets on me?

Isn't it better to just go now and, as Emathi put it, deal with the consequences? Am I better off dead but unblemished?

"I didn't think you'd be dumb enough to really consider it," she says. Without her anger, she looks deflated and tired. "I just need you to pay more attention. Get through today, sleep it off, and figure out what you'd like to do about the bigger picture tomorrow. Can you do that?"

"I can do that."

"Good. Now pay attention and don't move until I tell you."

She returns to the kelpie and releases him from her spell. Blue cloth in hand, she leads it out of the water.

"They're less dangerous away from the water. You still have to be careful, but the ground makes them slow."

She sets the cloth on the ground where the kelpie snuffles at it like a curious puppy.

"Why does he like the cloth?

"This one is fond of pumpkins. Every kelpie has some scent that distracts them for hours."

"Why not bring a pumpkin?" I remember the apple and find the answer to my own question.

"You know why," she says. "Now here's how to cut those bad bits away." Emathi grooms the kelpie for the next hour with a long pair of shears. I even chop a few strands away. Her reminders not to touch the kelpie irk me. I haven't inspired any confidence, but I'm not a complete idiot. The defiance that rises in me is sweeter than a balm and steadier than anger.

By the time we release the kelpie and go inside the house to complete the indoor chores, I'm once again determined to remain unblemished no matter what I face. If my own mother failed to corrupt me, these creatures don't have a chance.

Not if I'm vigilant. Not if I'm good.

We dust and sweep and clean. Inside the house is much nicer than its exterior suggests, though it is small and cluttered. I do most of the work. Emathi's mouth is pinched and her hands flutter. She does not say anything, but she must be in pain.

"You'll have to do all of this once a day on your own," she says. "I'll give you a mark so you can come here and back by the fastest route."

"A mark?"

"A coin. It'll keep your path."

"Magic?"

"More of a compass."

I don't press past the half-truth. We came here by no ordinary route. Maybe all the trails in the Ceoghast are cursed this way. The stories we have about being hunted by the Ceoghast road make more sense to me here. I'm too tired for another argument.

"You won't come with me?" I say.

"No. I don't need to trek here and back again for no good reason."

"So I'll be alone." I haven't been alone since I got stuck here. I haven't had a chance to think or come up with a plan about how I can return.

"You're safe here, if that's your concern."

It is, but right now the thought of my own space, even for a few hours, feels like a miracle. Given a bit of time without interruption, I can figure out how to get out of this. I can figure out how to get back to Midt and have the people accept me.

"I'll be okay," I say. "I can do this."

For the first time since I crossed the border into this horrid land, hope fills me.

Chapter 20

Emathi's face is orange in the sun's last rays, and for a moment I imagine her as one of Knife's Jacks, face full of creases a life in a field brings to its inhabitants. I can't get Jacks out of my head. Particularly mine. We came back from the homestead to find Hum still gone. I worry she won't come back. I worry she will.

I try to focus on Emathi. She is at peace, in control of her transition, until confusion settles over her.

"Who are you?" she says.

Seated in the chair across from her, I go through the rituals that calm her down. I repeat her name each time I speak. When her hands flutter, I give her yarn. If she shudders at the window, I draw her attention back to the room with questions.

"Do you know what you want to knit?" I say.

Her work from the night before is undone. Emathi must unravel it in the morning to give her nighttime self more to do.

"This is too thick for socks, but my feet are cold."

"I can get you another pair of socks, or maybe your shoes?"

"No shoes in the house," she says. She slaps her hands on the arms of her chair and tries to rise.

"Emathi, your yarn."

She pauses.

"What did you say you wanted to make, Emathi?"

Her elbows dip and she lets her weight return to the seat. "A blanket for the winter."

"That sounds nice, Emathi."

"I like winter. It's always..."

Bam!

I leap from my chair as though stung. My head whips toward the other rooms. Did something fall, or...? I strain to catch other noises.

Emathi's knitting needles fall to the floor. "My needles."

Did she not hear that bang? I crouch and give the needles back to her. "I think..."

Three hard knocks ring through the cottage.

"What is it?" Emathi says. "Who's there? Is there someone at the door?"

Her simple question sends chills through my body. Someone? Or something?

Quieter, but still loud enough to reach us in the sitting room, someone drums their fingers against the door.

"Tell them to go away," Emathi says. She's so scared she loses her grip on her needles again. They roll to my feet. "We can't have visitors. They'll touch my things. Send them away." Her voice is shrill. I want to keep her calm.

"It's okay, Emathi."

The fingers begin to scratch. It sounds hard enough to scar the door. I hand Emathi her needles and make my way to the foyer.

I'd rather walk the other way, or dart up to the loft and hide in my bed until whatever is outside leaves.

When I enter the foyer, I grab a broom from the corner so I'm not empty-handed. It's not much, but as Ealey told me, it's better to have a makeshift weapon in hand when you face the unknown.

Another thunderous knock unnerves my confidence. My knees quiver.

"Who's there?" I say.

Excited taps race along the door's edges from top to bottom. The unusual response calms me. Hum?

I drift close enough to look through the peephole.

Hum's carved grin leers at me through the glass. She's so close, she must be pressed against the door. Irritation strengthens my limbs where fear had left them weak. What on earth is she thinking? She abandons me all day, then comes back to scare us in the middle of the night? A lecture boils on my tongue. I yank the door open.

"Hum," I say.

The rest of the words collapse inside me, dead as pumpkins left to rot on a vine. The broom clatters to the floor as I step back.

"What have you done?"

Her stalks are no longer loose undulations. She's grown them, twisted them, made them thick and strong.

Hum has a body. She's fashioned one in a mostly human shape.

Coordination is not yet hers. She shoves her head inside and struggles to get the rest of her new body in. She needs to bend in half like Emathi to get through the door — her enthusiastic growth has left her gangly — and uses three of the four arms to right herself once she's inside.

She leers at me and wiggles her squash head on its thick vine neck.

"Who is it?" Emathi says.

Hum's attention flips from me, and she charges through the house toward Emathi.

"Hum—" I grab for her, but she's too fast, even if she doesn't have good control of her body.

"Darkness save us," Emathi says. "Knife's sent her Jack. She'll kill us all!"

I dash into the sitting room to find Emathi in tears. She hides her face in her yarn like a child too afraid to face the night.

Hum prances about the room in an odd, high-step dance that shows the length and spring of her new legs to great effect. She's every inch a showy fool.

I step in front of Emathi and hold my arms out to keep Hum away.

"It's the forerunner. There will be more. They're coming for us. She'll cut us. She'll take my face."

"Emathi, we're okay. No one is coming," I say. I wave my hands to catch Hum's gaze, and when she glances at me, I point to the door.

Full of play, Hum high-steps to the door and somersaults through. Emathi shrieks as Hum sends the baskets and jars stacked against wall flying.

I storm after Hum. It'll take me all night to soothe Emathi now. What I'd hoped to be a stern walk ends up being more of a chase when Hum tries to circle the cottage to reenter the door from the other side.

"Hum, stop."

Hum pauses in a doorway and tilts her head. The notes she sings seem to ask how serious I am.

"I mean it," I say. I shift my weight back and point at the floor in front of me. "Come here."

Prior to our trip to Jack's Patch, Hum might have slumped and come forward. This Hum is all cheek. She wiggles her head at me, leans forward, and exhales purple smoke. In the cloud she makes, all I see of her is an outline. The defiant pose reminds me of Katta. The similarity feels like a punch, and tears prick my eyes. Defeat settles on me, heavy as dirt on a grave. Will I even see her again?

Oblivious to my sorrow, Hum shoos the large cloud away and proceeds to puff out smoke in fantastical shapes while she flexes her limbs.

Emathi moans in the other room.

"Those are fine new tricks you have," I say.

Hum preens and pats her torso.

"You've frightened Emathi with that big show and caused a great deal of trouble. Is this what you've been doing all day?"

She shimmies. She's too pleased with herself to hear my frustration.

"Go to the loft," I say. "Stay there until I come up. You can show me all the tricks you want then, okay?"

It's not the lecture I want to give her, but if I get angry, I suspect she'll try to make a game of it. She's already caused enough grief.

"Upstairs," I say.

Hum considers my request long enough to make me doubt she'll do as I ask, but then she heaves herself into the rafters and disappears into our sleeping spot.

I want to collapse right here and sleep for the night without another encounter with Hum or Emathi. But Hum would rouse me to show off her new skills no matter where I try to rest, and I'd never sleep through Emathi's wails.

I make my way back to Emathi. She sobs into her yarn and muffles her cries with her fingers. My entrance startles her.

"She's going to get me," she says.

"No one's going to get you, Emathi. You're safe."

"She said she'd cut me. I trapped her, but not enough. Not the right way." I lift the yarn she's made wet with her tears.

"Do you know what you're going to make, Emathi?"

"Make?" Her brows furrow, and for once I welcome the confusion. "Who are you?"

"I'm a friend, Emathi. I'm Cassia Mooseroot. Do you remember me? I've been staying with you for a while."

"Do I know you?"

"You know me, Emathi." The yarn she'd used as tissue is wrapped around her hands and arms. I unravel it as I speak. "You said you want to knit. You want to be warm for winter, Emathi. Maybe you can make a blanket."

"It's already winter," she says. "I'm late. It's already so cold."

"You have time, Emathi. It's not winter yet," I say, though she's right about the cold. Now that Hum's chase is over, I feel a chill in the air, a bite full of autumn and ice.

Like the outside has come in.

The door.

I didn't close it.

Emathi cries out as I squeeze her hands too tight. I let her go and leave the rest of the yarn in a tangle.

"I'm sorry," I say. "Start on your blanket, Emathi. I'll be right back."

"Don't leave me." Panic dilates her pupils, and I know she's about to have another meltdown, but I left the front door wide open.

I leave the room. Emathi begins to cry.

If the knock scared me before, the thought that I've left the cottage open to any creature that wants in terrifies me to the quick. Emathi told me not to open the door. I wrote the rule down myself. How could I be so stupid?

I round the corner and find the door an open mouth. Night presses against it like all the dark will flood the cottage. I start to heave it shut, but then the shadows on the floor and ceiling skitter deeper into the room.

My skin goes cold.

Twig-like creatures scurry in and join the mass. There must be more than a hundred of them.

"Hum?" I say. "Please come here. I need your help."

Emathi calls out and asks who's there. I hope she's too scared to venture this way by herself.

Hum bounds into the room with haste and cocks her head at me. Her sweet note of greeting makes me feel a little off-balance, like my request for her company is normal. Like this is the relationship we have.

"Get them out," I say and gesture at the twig creatures. "All of them. Out."

Hum's arms creak. She untwists a few of the thinner stalks, and with a trill of pure joy, she begins to bat the creatures outside.

Her aim is terrible. She hits the wall and me more often than she gets them out. I open the door wider and hide behind it.

Hum's familiar whip-like thwacks fill the room. Emathi yells. The creatures crack and skitter. This is a nightmare and I'm too spent to be afraid. I'm distant from the horror of it all, as though I'm watching a play and am not an active participant.

Perhaps it's Hum's uncoordinated volleys, or the unusual epithets Emathi shouts at the creatures. Or maybe it's the creatures themselves, broken in ways that don't make sense and trying to reassemble themselves as they flee with no care for order.

Laughter burbles from my belly, then bursts from me in snorts. My hands slip on the knob as I laugh harder and sink to the ground. This isn't the right response, but I can't stop. I slump to the floor in giggles. The door closes halfway, and Hum scours the room.

She appears to have gotten every last one.

Emathi storms into the room, waist and ankles caught with yarn. If her face wasn't pinched with fear, I'd let the giggles have me. Her distress rebalances me, and the momentary levity leaves me empty and exhausted.

I stand and shut the door.

"Was someone here?" she says.

Hum, soft with fatigue from her exertions, tiptoes from the room. Emathi's gaze is fixed on the entryway. She doesn't see Hum slink back to the loft.

"No, Emathi," I say.

"I heard the door. Is someone there?"

I sigh and wish Hum could help me with this, too.

"Come on." I take Emathi's hand to lead her from the foyer. "I'll put on tea for us, Emathi."

Chapter 21

The next morning, Hum is keen to go with me when I embark for the swamp homestead. I'm thankful I won't face the kelpie alone. That said, the mood Hum's been in since she gave herself a body makes me wonder if she'll aggravate the other creature. She's that kind of cheerful. Still, I encourage her to come and let her carry the basket with the blue cloths.

In daylight I have a proper chance to examine her. She towers over me. The way she wiggles her head on its stalk has a serpentine quality. Her body, while modeled after a human's, has a few irregularities that seem more enthusiastic disregard to details than intention. While she has two opposable thumbs, one hand has only three fingers while the other has seven. The other two arms end in thin points with no discernible hands. Both her legs have extra knees, and her torso is short and plump. Without a doubt, she's extraordinary to behold, but also very silly.

We visit the chickens first. Hum is enamored with them and follows them around the yard as I rake the coop. The hens scatter, of course. Hum's nearly twice my height and swings her limbs about in wide arcs like she can't keep her balance.

When she realizes her attempts at friendship are failing, she begins to mimic the birds. Whether its mockery or a sincere attempt to connect, I can't tell. She walks about with their quick steps, headshakes, and wing flutters until I scatter the feed. I half expect her to peck at the meal alongside them but, too thrilled with her new movements, she continues to imitate the chickens around the small yard. It's not unlike a dance, though it's the most ridiculous one I've seen. I bite my lips to keep my smile in check.

Finished with the first task, I pick up the basket and call for Hum to follow me to the swamp. My stomach twists in knots. Without Emathi, I'm unprotected. Hum is as likely to assist as she is to cause a real problem. I'm tempted to leave the kelpie until last, but I want as much time as I can get alone, which means the tough chores come first.

The still swamp comes into sight and Hum bounds past me. She's in the water before I get a word out.

"Hum, get out of there."

She doesn't even turn her head she's so engrossed with her new game. She splashes in the water, then watches the surface like she expects a response. Like she knows the kelpie's there.

"If he drowns you, that's your own fault," I say to scare her away. The kelpie could hurt her.

We see the ripples at the same time. Hum throws water about for a bit longer, then steps back. She moves just as Emathi taught me.

Hum knows how to lure a kelpie. Except she doesn't have the blue cloth. I do. Frantic, I tear through the basket to find the cloth, but I'm too late.

The kelpie rises from the water. Taller than I remember, he must look up to meet Hum's gaze. Hum swings her head closer to his face. The kelpie's inhalation is a roar of wind, like he means to suck Hum closer. He softens on the exhale and steps onto the marshy land.

I let out my held breath. The blue cloth doesn't matter. It's pumpkin that calms him, and a Jack, even a funny one like Hum, must be better than scented fabric.

Hum bops the kelpie's nose with her long vine finger, and the kelpie nips back with a playfulness I wouldn't expect the angry creature I met yesterday to possess.

Caution still guides my work, but Hum's presence is a strong distraction. The kelpie is agreeable to my ministrations. I cut the oily scabs from his mane, then work my way down his body. Fully absorbed as he is, I'm able to notice the shift of muscle beneath his seagrass coat, the way his back dips slightly as though to shape a rider's seat, the webbing at his hocks. He's strange and dangerous, but by the time I'm done and Hum leads him back to the water, I appreciate his beauty. He returns to the swamp with many backward glances at her.

That we met with no misfortune cheers me, and we've kept good time. I have hours to go before darkfall and only the house chores remain. My feet want to skip up the path. When the rickety house comes into view I feel a gush of affection for it.

Hum groans at the sight, like a petulant child.

"You don't have to come in," I say. "I'll just clean it and be done in a couple of hours. Why don't you go to the clearing? There might be other creatures there."

Green smoke huffs from her mouth and she gambols away, delighted with her assignment.

I'm just as delighted. I'm alone.

I scurry into the house and lock the door behind me. For a minute I press my back to it, certain my solitude will not last. The silence assures me no one means to bother me, even as my skin prickles with the possibilities of unexpected dangers lurking inside.

Even though I explored the house yesterday, I do so again today, going slowly and methodically through every nook and cupboard until I'm certain nothing waits to ambush me.

I walk into the small parlor and collapse into a chair. This feels like the first time I've relaxed — maybe in my whole life. The ease is so unfamiliar my muscles spasm. My mind screams that I ought use my time with care, that I need to get up and do something.

If I were home, I'd need to make myself busy with all the little observances and niceties that show my community I care. At Emathi's house, I have to do what I can to stay on the witch's good side and keep Hum out of trouble.

But here?

Here, in the house of a swamp witch, I have no one to impress, no one to appease, no one to guard against. I can act as I want. Do what I would like. So what is it that I need? A way back home. A plan.

Would the swamp witch have means to pass the cobweb woman?

This room is sparse: two green upholstered chairs with a small wood table between them and pinkish-red walls covered in framed sketches of insects. Like the other rooms in the house, a window in the ceiling provides enough light to see by, though it's obstructed in parts from fallen foliage and other detritus. I've explored most of it, but with the thought of finding secrets, I lift the chair cushions and peek behind the picture frames and run my fingers under the small table.

I find nothing, but this purpose fills me with an energy that's impossible to deny. This is the first time I've been able to help myself since I ended up in the Ceoghast.

I return to the foyer and scour what's there. Spiders scuttle out of the umbrella stand I upturn. Dust puffs out of the jacket I pat down, and the single red shoe turns out small pebbles.

Exploration of the study will be more worthwhile than the kitchen. I don't like the kitchen here; it's where the abandonment of this home is deepest. There's no life in a house where people can't take nourishment. Even in Midt, my landlord left me a loaf of hard bread and tea leaves when I first moved in.

I skip the kitchen and enter the study. The walls here are dark green, not that much of them is visible with all the bookcases. Emathi cleaned this room yesterday and assigned the rest to me. I've not had a chance to examine it closely.

From the spine of each book hangs a narrow strip of paper on which the titles of each appear in a neat, cramped hand. I take a book from the shelf, curious about whether the interior is also handwritten.

The book beside it catches my eye. I know that cover.

I move with awe as I pull *The Lightbearer Stories* from the shelf. It's as heavy as I recall, which surprises me as I haven't held it since I was a child. Unlike the one from my youth, this copy is in pristine condition. The version I saw belonged to a Traditionkeeper who went from town to town to read to the youth.

We knew all the stories already, of course, but this book, with its embossed cover and gilded pages, was full of color illustrations that made them more real for us.

I settle on the floor and place the book in my lap. I flip through its pages with reverence and find the glory of the Lightbearers lives up to my memories.

Here is Kerrin who burned back the Ceoghast when it encroached on a mill town, and here is Casper who brought back the light when the Ceoghast blotted out the whole sky.

The lesser tales are here, too: Adriel who killed an ice demon, and Digade who dragged an evil creature from the Ceoghast to face justice.

I read them all and scoot across the floor to catch the sun as it shifts above.

In the margins of the book someone's written notes in that same crowded hand. At first, I ignore them for vandalism and distraction, but then I catch words that repeat often enough to grab my attention: evil, redemption, source. The writer of the notes illuminates the parallels between these stories and identifies a structure that each story follows. The writer calls it the conquest of uncomplicated evil.

Once the format is in my head, it's apparent in every tale: a good person faces evil from the Ceoghast and either destroys the threat —this, it seems, is a privilege reserved for Lightbearers — or confines the threat and brings it back to the community for justice.

The sunlight has brought me to the other side of the room. With reluctance, I return the book to its shelf. I grab a feather duster and walk through the rest of the house to do a quick tidy.

Stories make the Ceoghast seem like the ultimate horror, and yet it's never real. Not like it is for me. In the story, a Lightbearer — or soon-to-be Lightbearer — steps in and the evil crumbles before them. We accept the threat but know it can't touch us because we have such good on our side. Where are the real life Lightbearers for my mess? It's not like I can become one.

Duster poised to tickle a vase, I freeze.

What if I acted like one?

Going back to Midt after I've been here for four days is a death sentence. The only people who make it out of this place without corruption are Lightbearers.

But not everyone in the stories is a Lightbearer. Ordinary people make it out — they become Lightbearers in the process, but they escape and prove their worth to the community. The ones doubted the least and revered above all are those who bring back a creature. Proof of their commitment to the tenets.

What if I bring a Ceoghast creature back for the community to judge? I can do that, can't I? I can make this like a story.

Hum isn't an option. My stomach roils at the thought. Evil or not, after all she's done for me, I won't betray her like that. Besides, she's not evil enough — not in the big, impressive way I need.

Lightbearers capture significant creatures. The kelpie's notable, and if I keep a pumpkin with me, I may be able to lure it the whole way to Midt — but how far can he wander from his water? I wonder if he's even enough. Maybe if Midt experienced a series of drownings, but without that situation, even the water horse isn't likely to save my life.

I need to bring a creature big enough to convince everyone else that I don't have the Ceoghast on me. If I'm here for two weeks like the cobweb woman says, I'll have to find a real monster. One that the Ceoghast will miss.

I jump at the knock on the door.

"Are you in there?" Emathi says.

"Coming," I say. I drop the duster in the corner and run to the door.

Emathi shoves her way in when I unbolt the lock. "Why'd you lock it?" she says. "There's nothing left that wants this place."

"I didn't know that," I say. Not long ago, Ealey asked me the same question. "It's a habit."

"I was worried you'd gone with the kelpie," she says. "When you didn't come back in good time, I thought maybe you hadn't listened."

The sudden end of my solitude makes me unhappy. The time I spent alone seems insufficient. "I wanted to keep Hum out. She'd probably make a mess in here," I say.

Emathi nods. She wipes her finger along the door frame and harrumphs at the dust. Her disapproval sparks my anger, and like a flower in rapid bloom, my answer comes to me.

What town would not delight to have a Ceoghast witch?

"Are you done, then?" she asks.

Hope bubbles in my throat and the urge to grin is overwhelming. I clamp my teeth together to keep my glee inside and nod.

"Good. Let's get back before dark," she says.

That's how I'll do it. I'll take nighttime Emathi. All I have to do is gain her trust.

Chapter 22

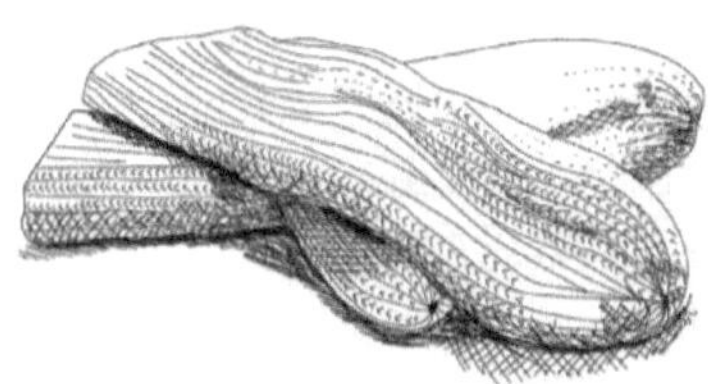

True to our agreement, Emathi takes me to the tree-lined road that evening to see if the cobweb woman still blocks my way.

She does.

Disappointment and frustration are not as keen as they felt yesterday. I have a plan and need a bit of time for it to come together.

"No fight to stay today?" Emathi says.

"It won't do me any good."

"That makes my life easier. I appreciate that." She turns back the way we came. "I'll make us a stew for dinner if you help me cut the vegetables."

We return to the cottage in Speckled Hound Hollow and make the stew. It's one of the heartiest meals I've had since I left Horth, and when darkfall comes, I am half asleep in one of the sitting room chairs.

"Do I know you?" Emathi says.

Sleep startles from me like a flock of spooked birds. I lean forward. "Hello, Emathi. I'm your friend, Cassia Mooseroot."

She cringes, and I wonder if I'm too exuberant. This level of cheer might exhaust her. I force myself to relax and smile.

"I'm here to knit with you," I say.

"Oh." She straightens in her chair. "Do you like to knit?"

"I haven't done much," I say. "I started a pair of mittens once."

"I like mittens." Her brow furrows like she's about to lose our conversation. I place the yarn and needles in her hands.

"Will you teach me how to make a pair? I don't remember much about knitting." In truth, the thought of knitting again fills me with dread.

I'd told Emathi the truth about the mittens — a woman I'd considered a grandmother worked on them with me. But then she'd come to our house with the Ceoghast on her. I'd thought it was a regular visit and crawled into her lap with my knitting. I think she tried to dissuade me, but like Katta is now, I was a child not about to dismiss my own desires. My father found us and chased her out. When he came back inside, he told me why he had to drive her away. That was the first time the Ceoghast became real for me, years before my mother tried to end my life. I never touched the half-done mittens again.

"Beginners don't start with mittens. You can start with a hat," Emathi says. Her pronouncement has authority in it. She looks certain and strong. "You'll need a pair of needles."

"Why don't I watch you for now?" I say. If I leave to find needles for myself, Emathi's focus won't linger and any good I do will be lost.

"Learning is best done oneself." She takes up the needles and yarn. "You can watch for now, but only for a bit. Then you have to try."

"Okay."

"Do you know how to cast on?"

"I don't remember." Even the simplest part is fuzzy in my memory. "There's a loop or a knot, isn't there?"

"Here. Watch me." Though her fingers are twisted and stiff, she manages a neat set of loops. "What was that?"

The sharpness in her voice makes me jump. I turn in my seat to look at the dark room next to ours. Nothing but shadows.

Until Hum scurries by on all six limbs.

I could yell I'm so mad. I told her not to make any noise and to wait for me in the loft.

146

"That's my Jack, Hum." I touch Emathi's knee to keep her attention. "She won't hurt you."

"Not the Jack. I know what a Jack is. The rodent. That rat she's chasing." A moan wheezes through her lips. "I can't stand rodents. Not in my house. Get it out. Catch it and throw it out."

"I'll take care of it." This isn't how I'd planned to win her trust, but it's a good opportunity to impress her — if she remembers I've done it. Rodents don't scare me, and if Hum's already in pursuit, my job should be easy. "I'll be right back, Emathi. You can knit while I'm gone."

If there's no rodent and Hum's playing the fool, I'll give Hum such a lecture she won't so much as peek over the loft's edge. I'll have to start over with Emathi when I return, remind her about the hat we're to knit.

I take a candle and go after Hum. I find her in the small study. She's shoved the upper half of her gangly body under a desk. Her back legs tap out an impatient dance.

"You better have it, Hum," I say.

She scrambles deeper under the desk, not that much more of her will fit. She's so determined to get under it, she pushes it off the wall.

"Get out of the way," I say. "Help me move the desk."

Hum backs out and grins up at me. Her eyes puff smoke red as hot coals. She is fire, and a part of me shudders in fear even as I shove her aside to get to the desk. She watches me struggle to move it for a moment before she steps in and drags it away from the wall with ease. The wood whines as she scrapes the floor, then she leaps over the desk and swoops down on the rodent I still haven't seen.

"We're taking it outside," I say. "Don't play with it."

She crackles and clicks. Not her usual song. Her delight isn't as thorough as I expect. Wariness steals over me like clouds across the moon.

"Hum? Show me what you have."

She spins to face me and shoves her hands in my face. Trapped within her grasp are brown bone creatures with long bodies and mouths that gape with pinchers.

Last night I thought they resembled twigs, but this evening, shadows do not hide their truth. They are half-rotted horrors, with bodies thin as twigs. Dirty, flimsy skin and exposed muscle hold the thin bones together. They have no heads, just wide, sharp mouths.

In the other room, Emathi shrieks.

I grab Hum's arm. "Get them out," I say and run to help Emathi.

The creatures cover the walls of the parlor where I'd been only moments before.

"Nyxies," Emathi says. "Get rid of them. Get them out. They'll set a rot to the wood and steal all my things. They'll ruin us."

"Hum?" I say. Now that I've seen the decay on the creatures, I don't want to touch them myself. Hum will have to corral them out for us.

"My things," Emathi says. Her tea set leaves the room on a wave of nyxie bodies.

The shock roots me in place. I'd thought Emathi's claim they'd steal her things to be a product of her confusion. But these creatures move with purpose. The few pictures Emathi had on the wall in the parlor are gone.

Hum barges into the parlor, her carved mouth full of nyxies who struggle to free themselves. She sings a note that dominates the room and makes my ears ring.

"Get them out," Emathi says.

I run to the front door. "Send them this way, Hum. Herd them."

I open the door. It swings inside with such force I fall to the floor. More nyxies pour into the cottage.

"What are you doing? You're letting them in," Emathi says.

I can't shut the door. "I didn't know there were more outside."

"You should have looked." She wrings her hands. "Get them out. Say the words."

"What words?" If nyxies leave when told, I'm not sure why Emathi wouldn't have done that in the first place. They swarm over my feet and I kick them off. Each place they touch my stockings becomes wet and brown. Not like mud, but like dried blood.

"The words that make them leave."

"I don't know what words you mean." I throw myself against the door but still the force of the incoming nyxies holds it open. They are too many to deal with the way I'd planned. Hum has no chance of herding — or eating — them all.

"This is my home. My place of sanctuary. You are not welcome. Leave now and never come back," Emathi says.

"Those are the words?"

"Yes. Oh, my tablecloth!"

I attempt to step on the corner of the tablecloth as it whips by, but I miss. It goes out into the night.

"Well, the words don't work," I say. "We'll have to chase them out."

"I have no magic. It won't work for me."

"It'll do no good for me either." A spell. She tried to get me to cast a spell. That's what those words are.

I kick at the nyxies on the floor in a rage, but most evade my feet. A few jump to cling to my stockings, and I flail to get rid of them. Memories of the plant hands and candy corn teeth have me flailing wildly. I remember them all too well.

I grab a broom and swat at the creatures. Most flow out of my way, but a few fly back outside. It's enough to encourage me.

"Grab something to hit them."

More of Emathi's belongings scamper out the door. She's no help. She mourns each item that goes past her and makes no effort to reach for them or stop the nyxies. I need real help.

"Hum," I say.

She lopes into the room and grabs nyxies to throw in her mouth. Real fire leaps from her head, and the tips of her stamens throw sparks. She incinerates the nyxies alive, and when their highpitched cries fill the small foyer, I want to send Hum out again. The nyxies' terror and pain strikes my chest as though it were my own. It's too much.

"Hum, stop. Don't do that. Chase them out."

She whirls her head to me, seems to weigh how serious I am.

I want to say "I mean it" but all I can muster is "Please."

With a great heave, she vomits out the mass she'd crammed into her face. Charred remains and still twitching bone limbs spew onto the floor. The stench catches in my throat and sours my stomach. I cover my nose and turn away.

The other nyxies do not seem to care about the fate of their fellows and hurry to take more of Emathi's things out the door. A few of them snatch up the fine bones of their deceased companions and seem to size them against their own.

I've had enough of them. I take the broom and begin to swat at the flow in earnest. Their bones sound like fire crackling as they break, and my way ends up no kinder than Hum's.

Emathi sinks to the floor in a struggle for her apron. She mumbles her spell but tears jumble her words. I wheel to help her, but then I see Katta's face.

Two nyxies run for the door with Katta's portrait stretched between them. Brown stains spread where their twiggy bones touch the paper. Katta's chin is marred, her forehead spotted.

"No," I say, my voice a bark. They sweep the portrait toward the door.

"This is my home," I say. "This is my sanctuary."

A rumble builds in my chest, and I straighten with it. My breath is deep and strong. Ease fills me. The nyxies pause, the entire mass frozen to listen. Without their chatter and clicks, I am as loud as a thunder crack, and I will have my sister's portrait back.

"You are not welcome. Leave now and never come back."

A bam so cacophonous I think the cottage might collapse rings through the rooms as the nyxies drop the items they meant to steal. They depart like an invisible force sucks them into the night, a dark tide that rolls away from us. The room empties, and shock roots my feet to the floor. But then I see Katta's portrait. I rush to pick it up and dab at the brown spots with my blouse. The stains don't budge. My sister's face is smeared. The drawing on the back is a mess of marks.

My knees hit the floor hard. Hum cozies up beside me and sings what could be a lullaby if not for the discordant notes that make me shiver. Emathi shuffles to the door and throws the bolt.

"Oh, my home," she says. "Such a mess, and those nyxies touched my jars." She sounds far away, but when I glance up, she's right before me.

She beams at me. "You darling witch."

I jerk back. My fist closes on the portrait. I let go, but I've wrecked the paper. "Don't say that," I say. "Don't call me that."

That couldn't have been magic. The nyxies only listened to what I said. That didn't feel like anything more than words.

Except it was more. That lift. The rise in confidence. The way I could breathe. Like everything was easy.

I shake my head to dispel the thoughts that begin to bubble in my mind, but then tremors take me, and I can't stop. I don't know what to do.

"We should have tea," Emathi says. "All the cold air's inside now. You're shivering."

When she reaches for me, I let her take my hand. I can't think of a reason to stop her. Where once the thought of her touch had made me worry about contamination, I now find only comfort.

If that was a spell — if I just cast magic — Emathi's not the one who's going to get the Ceoghast on me.

I am.

Chapter 23

I wake with a start in the morning, my whole body tense. My fingers claw for Katta's portrait, and only when they find the well-worn paper do I let out a shaky breath. Twisted with memory, my dreams these days feel too real, and I lie motionless on the cot in case more danger is near.

"Gods' cursed rot!" Emathi says from downstairs. The anger is unmistakable, and I don't want to face it.

On the floor beside me, Hum sleeps curled about her head. She retains her flexibility despite the human-shaped body she's given herself.

"Hum," I say. I prod at her. She slaps me away with one of her stalks. "Come on. Don't make me go downstairs by myself."

She rolls away from me and begins to snore. Given that she's never snored before, I think she fakes her slumber, but I get the message. I'll have to face Emathi alone.

The frustrated outbursts continue below. With haste, I wash and change into my clothes, once again folded and cleaned by whatever magic permeates this place. I may not want to encounter Emathi given her mood, but I won't delay the inevitable conflict. I broke our agreement. Maybe not with any intention, but I disobeyed the rules she set out for me. I don't think she's likely to take my lack of intent into account, or the fact that I did get rid of the nyxies in the end.

My thoughts drift to last night's spell. With the force of a guillotine, I cut them off. I can't consider that now. First I have to appease the angry witch downstairs.

The ladder creaks beneath my feet like it's old and unreliable, and by the time I reach the bottom, Emathi's come into the room.

"Good morning," I say.

"Is it? Is it indeed? This is what you call a good morning?"

I want to fly back up the ladder. I don't know what to say that will ease and not incite her.

"Is there something you'd like to tell me?" she says.

Like a child caught for bad behavior, I flush and lower my eyes. "I let the nyxies into the cottage two days ago."

I pause to let her yell, but she remains quiet. She crosses her arms like she expects there's more to my tale.

"Hum was at the door after dark, so I let her in," I say. "But she scared me so much with her new body, I left the door open."

"You stupid woman. You should have told me then."

"I thought we got them all. Hum helped me."

"The squash has pickles for brains, and you're no better."

"Hum did her best." Indignation on Hum's behalf rises where it will not for me.

"And you didn't?"

I know my actions were dumb, but her tone prickles me. "We both tried to get rid of the nyxies. I'm sorry we didn't. I thought we had."

"Is that your apology?"

I stop and replay our conversation. No matter how I feel about her, an apology should have been first off my lips. I may be stuck in a wild and unruly world, but I am not from one. I know better.

"No, that's not my apology," I say. "I know I owe you one."

Her smirk threatens to cut through my good sense. A deep breath steadies me.

"Emathi, I'm sorry I let nyxies get into your home and failed to tell you. I'm sorry my decision led to this." I gesture at the room where broken crockery lies on the floor beside curtain rods, torn paper, and food from Emathi's meager pantry. "I'm sorry for all this loss and for the damage to your home."

"You're lucky I had enough wits about me to cast the banishment."

For a moment I don't want to correct her. If that were the truth, I wouldn't have to consider what really happened last night. What I did.

Instead, I could be angry with her for using magic in my presence.

But that's not what happened.

"You didn't," I say. I keep my eyes on the ground. How can I look anyone — even a witch — in the eye with a confession of corruption? "You knew the words but they didn't do anything for you."

Shame scalds me. Even my tears feel hot. I swipe at them.

I never should have been in this situation at all. I'm not meant to be in the Ceoghast. Whatever I did last night, it wasn't magic.

"I said the words. They worked for me," I say. Aloud, my frustration sounds like defiance, like I mean to rub my success in Emathi's face, when all I really want is strength enough to confess.

"The nyxies left." My voice is smaller now. I glance at Emathi.

Her lips press into a hard white line, and her swollen hands clamp into fists. "You cast the spell?" she says.

I can't speak. It's too horrid an accusation, even if it might be true. I nod.

"Who are you really? Why are you here?"

Her barbed questions unbalance me. This is no conversation with nighttime Emathi. She is not confused about who I am or why I'm here. She thinks I've lied to her.

"I'm no one. I'm just... I'm not a witch."

I need her to believe me. I need her to tell me I'm not evil inside. There has to be a logical, reasonable explanation about why the spell worked last night.

"Then how did you cast the banishment?" she says.

"I said the words. That's all. It's just a mistake. I don't know why it worked."

"It's heart magic," she says. Her outrage seems undecided, like she may believe me, or she may accuse me of lying about my identity this whole time.

"I didn't mean to," I say.

But I did.

When the nyxies stole Katta's portrait, I meant every word. I just didn't want the words to be magic.

"Were you angry? Scared? What was in your heart?"

Since landing in the Ceoghast, fear and anger have been my constant companions. "I was mad," I say. But is that true?

It started that way. I felt so much rage when the nyxies tried to take the portrait I could have killed them all. But then I felt strong, like I was more solid than I've ever been in my life.

"That's often an inciting emotion," she says. She watches my face like she expects to catch me in a lie. "But, like I said, it's heart magic. It's familial."

"I'm not a witch."

I'm not... but my mom was. What if her corruption did get to me? Have I been evil all along?

"A spell like banishment takes emotion, intent, and focus. Who trained you?"

"Trained me? No one." What does witch training even look like? I imagine an apprenticeship full of dark deeds. My mother didn't teach me any of her evil magic. Or did she? What if she had taught me, but I didn't know because it didn't look like instruction?

"You're sweating," Emathi says. "What aren't you telling me?"

"I am not a witch," I say, as much for her benefit as my own. "I don't know how that spell worked, but it's not because I have magic."

"Heart magic," she says. "It's very specific. Only a woman can become a Heart Witch, but it's a patrilineal inheritance."

Her gaze bores into me. She looks for tells I don't have.

"That means your father's a witch."

The thought makes laughter roll in my chest. If she knew anything of my father, she'd know how ridiculous and impossible an accusation she's made.

Memories of my mother silence my mirth.

I may not be a Heart Witch, but what other kinds of evil are there?

"You're too mousey, anyway. Heart Witches have an unmistakable strength."

"Then I didn't cast the spell?" I knew there had to be another explanation.

"You had something to do with it," she says.

The confirmation turns my stomach to ice. My mind screams incoherent protest. Whatever expression finds its way to my face causes Emathi to cringe.

"But maybe there's something else going on here," she says. "Another explanation."

I want to believe she means that, but one look at her face, and I know she placates me. She doesn't want to deal with a tantrum.

"My heart was probably enough, but I needed someone else to say the words," she says.

Oh, how I wish that were true, but every part of me says she lies. I can't trust her.

"Why don't you help me put the cottage to rights? You can try a few spells and see if they come to anything," she says.

"No." The suggestion makes me sick. The solution here isn't more magic and more spells.

"It's your choice, but it'll help you figure out what sort of witch you might be. If you're a witch at all." She adds the last sentence in a rush, and again I sense she's trying to soothe me.

"I have work to do at the homestead," I say, "and I don't want to do magic. I'm not a witch."

Emathi's face darkens. "You'll come back here and at least do the sweeping. This is your mess, after all."

"I can do that." I'd agree to almost anything if it means she'll stop trying to turn me into a witch. I turn to go up the ladder and fetch Hum.

"I'll have Knave take you to the path today. I'll be far too busy here to make so pointless a trip."

"Okay," I say. A flutter of panic zings through my chest. I force myself up the ladder.

Knave makes me nervous. The way they look at me makes me feel like they can figure out all my secrets in a glance.

And I have a secret now they can't find out.

Chapter 24

Chores at the homestead don't take long. Even the kelpie is easy with Hum's help. I don't want Knave to catch me bent over a book in the swamp witch's library, so I take myself to the kitchen. The room feels more abandoned than the others, and I don't like being in here, but at least I can find work for myself. I empty the cupboards to scrub them down. The work absorbs me. Part of it reminds me of my laundry job in Midt — the repetitive motions, the ache in my arms. It comforts me, even as the homesickness calls sadness into my heart.

I've spent six nights, five days, in the Ceoghast. I can't begin to imagine what will happen when I return home. Will they believe I captured the Heart Witch without the Ceoghast getting on me?

Lightbearer stories parade through my head and show me ways to get home safely, but my courage skitters out of reach.

Outside Hum screeches a greeting that manages to be both enthusiastic and threatening. Knave must be here — who else would Hum hail like that? I remember the growls she first offered Knave; it makes me wonder if they knew each other beforehand.

The front door opens.

"I'm in here," I say. I lift jars of dried spices and herbs back into the scrubbed cupboard. I recognize most of them, even without labels. They're common and ordinary, but fallowfoot is not among the jars. Given its effect, a witch wouldn't be likely to have it, but I still feel disappointed. If I had some, I'd get nighttime Emathi to eat it before I take her to Midt. It's a safeguard I'll have to forego.

"What an industrious worker you are, Miss Mooseroot," Knave says. They saunter through the doorway like an actor takes the stage. Their presence overwhelms me, and my tongue can't figure out what reply might suit.

"I have a surprise for you," they say.

Curiosity snaps my head up to study their face, but distrust narrows my eyes. Then hope floods me. "Is she gone? The... the woman on the road? Did she leave?"

"That wouldn't be a surprise," they say. "That would just be me keeping my half of our bargain. What I have for you is a surprise."

"Surprise?"

"Oh yes. An unexpected delight. Such a decadent little treat."

"It's food?" I don't want to eat whatever they might offer. Their excitement is too sharp; it makes me think the surprise must be meant to shock me.

"No, nothing like that. I'm not here to feed your body. But as to your mind..." They shrug with feline poise.

My cheeks flush. They laugh.

"What is it, then?" I say.

"A surprise." The word is a purr in their mouth. "Follow me. Your Jack awaits us."

"Did you do something to her?"

"Only invited her to join us. She's quite excited."

Hum's company makes me feel better about going with Knave. They pause at the front door. "You're dressed a little brightly for our venture." They grab a brown moth-eaten cloak from the coat stand. "You'll have to borrow this."

They swing the cloak onto my shoulders. It swirls about me
like autumn leaves. Unlike me, Knave is dressed for the occasion in
dark, fitted clothes.

"Much better," they say. "You'll be warm but won't spoil
the fun."

We exit the house, and Hum leaps into the air to bounce
about me. Her delight is infectious and quiets my worry.

"Where is it?" I say. Nothing about the area looks different.

"Oh, it's not here. We're off on an excursion."

"Into the Ceoghast?" I cringe at the words, so stupid and
fearful. Like I'm not already in the Ceoghast. "We have to go
somewhere else, I mean?"

Beside me, Hum continues to bound about. Knave ignores
my question.

"It was lucky timing, really, that Emathi needed me to
check up on you today. What I'm going to show you only happens
once every two months or so, and not at a specific time."

"Is it dangerous?"

Hum wouldn't be so keen if she knew the surprise could
hurt me, but how much did Knave share with her?

"Not in any immediate way. You'll need to stay quiet, but
that shouldn't tax you." Their mouth quirks in a way that suggests
they mock me.

"What happens if we make noise?"

"You ruin the surprise, of course." Knave places a gloved
hand on my shoulder. "You're my way out of here, Miss
Mooseroot. I wouldn't risk losing you but come only if you want.
This is no forced march."

They speak truth but that doesn't mean I'll like the surprise.
Still, when Knave leaves the homestead, I'm right beside them.

Knave doesn't navigate the path like Emathi. They direct
me to stop between a series of stones and step forward with a
particular twist of my left foot. I do what they say and the path
before me shifts, changes to a different place. It's like the bridge
Hum took me under my first night.

"Is that a...?" What had Knave called the strange route that
evening? "One of the pathways? Like the bridge where you found
us?"

"It's one of the Eldritch Ways, yes. Clever of you to remember."

That doesn't feel particularly clever. Nor does the question I refuse to speak aloud: am I using magic when I walk through them?

"You were in a terrible state that night. You're doing so much better now," they say.

Then they study my face and frown. The displeasure makes them look like a sulky god.

"You're not thinking of staying, are you?"

"No." Stay here? Never. Not even if going home means I might die. At least I'd be loyal to my community.

"Good." The way they speak makes the world feel heavy and dark, and I wonder what they would've done had I said yes.

Our surroundings shift more and more with every Eldritch Way we take. If Knave left us here, I'm certain I'd never find my way back to Emathi's house. The somewhat ordinary forest morphs into a different land. We pass through a desert. The air is hot and dry. Sand sucks at my boots and makes it difficult to walk, but it's worse for Hum. She growls and covers her stamens with her hands. In the distance, a curled figure straightens to predatory alertness. Their tattered clothes snap in the wind.

"Step lively now," Knave says, a note of nervousness in their voice. "Through the ruins there on your tippy toes."

I grab Hum's elbow and do as Knave instructs. Behind us, the figure lets out a moan as dry as the desert itself. I plunge through the ruins on my toes and step into a forest so dense that near-perfect dark envelopes me. My eyes are slow to adjust. Humidity covers me like a wet blanket. I want to shed the cloak Knave made me wear, but they grab my hand as I begin to untie the clasp.

"Not here. We're close now, and you'll ruin the surprise if you don't blend in."

"Where are we?"

"The Crepuscular Jungle."

"Jungle?" I've read of jungles in the Lightbearer stories. They're dark places full of creatures made of poison. This forest is so different from the woods I'm used to that I disorient myself

trying to understand it. The trees loom overhead, draped in vines
not entirely unlike Hum's own. The way the greenery hangs over
us reminds me of the plant hands.

"Stay close," I say to Hum. She spirals a stalk about my
lower arm. With her at my side, I duck after Knave who picks a
cautious path ahead.

The air is so moist my clothes stick to my skin. Sweat beads
on my lip and slips down my face. Knave steps with exaggerated
care, then turns to us with a finger pressed to their painted lips.
Hum mimics their movement and brings one of her unusual
fingers to her carved grin. I creep up to Knave.

"We crawl from here, and no more words. Not a peep,"
they say. "We're going to a lookout. Your surprise is over the
edge."

I don't want to crawl but swallow my protest. Knave drops
down and moves with fluidity away from us. Hum trails after, her
rear high in the air.

When I follow, my knees and hands, still sore from my
early misfortunes, seem to find every sharp rock and twig. The
ground is sticky and springy. I move without balance or comfort
and drag my knees through the soil to keep steady. Ahead, Hum
gives up her crawl to slither on the ground. She shimmies to the
edge.

Halfway there, I stop. What am I doing? Since when do I
think sneaking up on anything in the Ceoghast is a good idea? Both
Hum and Knave watch whatever's over the ledge with rapt
attention. They don't notice I've stopped. What could be so
interesting?

Unbidden, my mind answers with horrors grotesque and
half-formed, but the way those two look at whatever's down there
grips my curiosity. It's not like Hum would let anything hurt me. I
forget my fear and squeeze between them.

Below us, a man bathes in a spring. He's half out of the
water and scrubs himself with a bristle brush.

This is the surprise? I flush with embarrassment and fury.
This is what Knave thought I'd want to see? A perverted violation
of another person's privacy? I want to hit them. I push away from
the edge, then stop.

Person. This is a person. They seem ordinary, normal like me. Another person is in the Ceoghast. Except… my gaze alights on their clothes folded near the pool.

No. Not a person. A tremor runs over my sticky skin. Those clothes… this man is a Lightbearer.

I have no idea what to do. I could call for help, but what danger would the Lightbearer see? Tucked next to Knave and Hum, I look like any other ceogot. If I go down and explain my situation, he'd be right to kill me on the spot, whether he believed my story or not. And what of my story can I share that doesn't cast me in a bad light? I saved a Ceoghast creature, boarded with a witch, and have cast a spell.

I bet he'd see corruption all over me at a glance. Next to his glory, I'm worse than mud. He's not my hope. He's not the answer I need to get out of the Ceoghast. I watch him instead and try to absorb his good and light. His radiance is so great the water's become iridescent. We always touch Lightbearers in hopes that part of their grace passes to us, but the light never comes off. We never gain their glow. Why did he give this Ceoghast spring what we — his own people — have always wanted?

By the time he finishes his ministrations, my shame about watching him is gone. If I can't ask him for help in a direct way, I'll take from him what I can: his mannerisms, the way he walks, whatever gestures or expressions might help me pose as a Lightbearer better. It's not much, but it's more than I had before.

Once the man pulls on his clothes, I'm irritated with his normalcy. I want epic poses and private prayers, contemplative looks and a recitation of the tenets. All I get is a lot of neck rotations and hearty scratches at areas I don't want to mention. He moves more like a beast of burden than one infused with Light's highest grace. He's ready to leave, except he looks about the ground like he's lost an item.

That's when I notice Hum's no longer beside me.

My heart races so fast it's hard to draw a breath. I clutch Knave's arm. Their skin is soft and cool beneath my sweat-slick palm. I gesture at the empty space beside me. They nod with a calm that makes me want to shake them. Then they point to the trees behind the Lightbearer. There, with jungle flowers jammed in her carved face, hangs Hum. Her vines blend into the tree she's wrapped around, but even with her attempted disguise, her great orange head is easy to see.

Panic seizes my chest. She's going to get caught. The Lightbearer will see her. He'll kill her and...

"I'll need that back," the Lightbearer says. After the quiet we kept, his voice is too loud for comfort and sends alarm screeching through my limbs.

Hum is at his back. He hasn't seen her yet. He speaks to the whole area, to anyone who might listen.

"I mean you no harm. Only fetch it back to me, and I'll be on my way."

I am still as ice. Surely Hum knows better than to believe him? My gaze stays on her, as though I might pin her where she hangs and keep her safe.

"It can't be worth anything to you," he says. "It's just a knife."

A knife? My fears about Hum shift. Where before I worried about exposure for her sake, now I worry for his. Does she mean to use it on him?

I want to close my eyes. The Lightbearer waits in silence for what feels like an eternity. I'm certain he's about to discover all of us.

"Well, if that's how you're going to be, consider it a gift, then." He readjusts the bag on his shoulder. "I'll be off. Leave it here for me to find again should you tire of it."

His manner is polite, even conversational, which confuses me. I expect a Lightbearer to make demands of evil, to see that good is done. Why would he speak with such respect to anything in the Ceoghast?

After he leaves, the three of us remain where we are for a long time. Stretched out on the ground, my body is sore, but I don't dare stir. What if the Lightbearer means to trick us and catch us out?

Hum is the first to move. She uncoils herself from the tree and drops to the ground with a flourish that looks like a grand bow. She jiggles the flowers loose and begins one of her high-step struts about the pool, a thin silver blade in her hand.

Knave stands and helps me up. I'm covered in dirt, but Knave is as pristine as they were before the belly-crawl to the ledge. "I take it you didn't send your Jack?" they say.

"Of course not. Why would I risk being seen? And what would I want with a knife?"

"Did you know him?"

"Know him? No. Is that why you brought me here? You thought he might be a friend?"

They shake their head. "No. I did think him from your world, though. Was I wrong?"

"Oh. No, you were right. He's from one of our communities."

They nod. "Do you know why they're so obsessed with our springs?" They wave away my confused expression and point to the water. "Don't get me wrong, I love a good shine on my skin, too, but these people keep doing it. Like they don't want to stop shining."

I stare at the iridescent pool where Hum continues her victory dance. "The water makes them glow?" That can't be right. The Lightbearers must leave their radiance in the spring.

Knave has this the wrong way around.

"Just like that." They point at Hum who now splashes in the water. Wherever she gets wet, she glows.

I don't know what to think, never mind what to say. The shock slackens my face, and Knave laughs at me. Their tone is one of true delight. For once, I don't care.

What does it mean that a Lightbearer bathed here? Is that why they glow? Is it not a sign of their good? Surely the Lightbearers would not lie to us. Not about a truth so big.

I shake my head. The man we saw must be a fake. He only poses as a Lightbearer but has none of their gifts, none of their true power. That's why he was so polite to the Ceoghast, too. He's corrupt.

My next breath is deep and long and steady. I feel better. "I'd like to go to the path now, please," I say.

"Was it a good surprise?"

"It was interesting."

Knave motions at Hum. "Your Jack certainly had fun."

Hum's given up her dance and watches us. I motion for her to return to me.

"Can we go?" I say.

"This way, Miss Mooseroot."

I look back at the spring one last time as Knave forges a path out. That's when it occurs to me. How much more convincing will I be as a Lightbearer if I have their radiance, or something that looks like it?

I can bathe here, too.

Chapter 25

I'm so distracted by thoughts of the Lightbearer, I don't linger at the path home or speak to the cobweb woman once I see she still blocks the way. Knave takes me back to Speckled Hound Hollow by Eldritch Ways, and I almost get lost due to my inattention. After one wrong toe twist lands me back in the desert, I try to pay full attention. If Knave hadn't followed me, I wouldn't have known how to find my way back.

When Speckled Hound Hollow comes into view, I thank Knave and shut myself in the cottage. The abruptness with which I leave them borders on rude, but I need to be alone. I need to think. All these tiny parts of my plan come together, but I don't have a sense of how to execute it. I don't have the details set, and I need to get it right. If I don't, I'll lose my life.

Emathi finds me on my way up to the loft and sends me to the kitchen to cut vegetables for the evening meal. Tonight we'll have salads with cuts of meat that are an orange shade I need to believe is the result of a marinade. The alternatives are too gross to consider.

My mind wanders as I work. The big plan to take Emathi to Midt needs its smaller steps now. I still don't know how to get Emathi past the spells that keep her here, and I don't know how to get to the iridescent pool without Knave. Could I ask to see it again?

"Those are small enough," Emathi says. She sweeps the carrots I've minced off the board. "You've all but pureed them."

She scatters the bits onto the lettuce I shredded to herb-sized portions. I drag the meat plate toward the cutting board, but she grabs my wrist.

"Don't you mince this meat. I expect healthy mouthfuls, so pay attention."

I may deserve this reprimand, but from her it makes me prickle. I cut the meat smaller than she suggests, but not so much so that she'd take me to task for it.

Dinner is quiet. We have nothing to say to each other. No common ground or bond. I wait for nighttime Emathi. To me, the two sides of this woman may as well be separate people, so when confusion folds Emathi's brow, delight crows within me. Her rheumy gaze settles on my face.

"Hello, Emathi. I'm..."

"I know who you are," she says with a wave of her hand.

"You do?"

"I never forget a witch." Pride sharpens her features. "You got rid of those nyxies. You're Cassia Mouseroot."

"Mooseroot," I say. I squirm in my seat. This isn't how I want to gain her trust — to be known as a witch — but surely this is a good development?

She sits back with a snort. "Mooseroot. I was close."

"You were," I say with enthusiasm. If she remembers our interactions now, I'll keep them agreeable and positive.

"And what brings you back to my home this evening?" she says.

The lie about the knit hat sits on my tongue, but she's so aware this evening. She's sharper than I've seen her. A question burns within me. I decide to take a chance. "The spell to banish the nyxies," I say. "Can anyone cast it?"

"Oh, don't be daft. That's got nothing to do with your visit. I don't mind if you came to check on me." She taps the table. "I know others might be touchy about that sort of thing, but it's not easy to be alone."

"That's not... I mean, I'd like to hear how you're doing, but I need to know about that spell."

"You cast it. You know all there is."

"But I don't," I say.

This conversation should make my skin crawl, but her obstinacy makes shame difficult to hold. I found the courage to ask the question. And now I want the answer.

"You're a witch," she says. "Of course you do."

"I'm not a witch."

"If you weren't a witch, that spell wouldn't have worked." She wrinkles her nose at me in a so-there gesture better suited to a child, like Katta.

"Is that how it works? You have to be a witch for it to work? No exceptions?" That can't be true.

Emathi huffs a sigh. "Why are you asking me this? You cast it. You know how it works. It's no different from any other spell."

"I've never cast a spell." I'm loud because I want her to hear me, to understand.

Confusion twists her face.

"Emathi?" I say. I need her to stay with me. No one else will have these answers.

"But you're a witch," she says. Her voice is weak, like she's about to lose the thread of our conversation.

"I don't know what that means."

A struggle between sense and confusion bends her expression into a grimace. She wants to connect with what I say. I touch her hand. Her skin is soft and papery beneath my fingers.

"I don't understand spells or witches or any of this," I say.

"No one taught you?"

Again, the thought of an apprenticeship for witches, or formal lessons, shakes me to my core. Laughter bounces within me. It's too ridiculous. A mockery of the ordinary. To think evil is a matter of learning. I swallow the hysteria.

"No one taught me," I say.

"But you're a Heart Witch. You cast a Heart Witch's spell."

"I'm not. I don't even know what being a Heart Witch means."

She stirs from her seat but settles back down before I can help her to stand. "You have a family," she says. "They should have taught you."

Family. Did my mother do this to me? Am I full of the same evil? "I'm not a Heart Witch," I say. I need that statement to be true, but I worry it's not. I worry so much my hands quiver.

"Then what kind of witch are you?"

Daytime Emathi had made a similar inquiry. I have no idea how to answer. I want to tell her I'm not a witch, but even I wonder if I could be wrong.

I clench my jaw and chase every one of those thoughts away. I'm here to gain Emathi's trust, to keep her interest. "I don't know about witches or what kinds might exist. Can you tell me about them?"

Emathi straightens, her mouth a cat-like grin. I feel every bit the bird as she leans over the table toward me. "You really don't know? Not a thing?"

"Not a thing," I say. I really don't, but more than that, I don't want to. Emathi's glee alarms me. This isn't a conversation a good person would have.

"What do you want to know?" she says. "You said you don't know what kinds of witches exist, but that's no easy matter."

"It's not?"

"Oh no. A witch shirks definition for the most part. We can talk about Heart Witches and Swamp Witches, Sea Witches, and Demon Witches all day, but you'll only have general ideas."

Four types of witches roll off her tongue like we discuss ordinary matters. Each one feels like a real presence, like the witches she describes are about to spring from the cupboards and break through the windows and grab my feet beneath the table.

Emathi smacks her lips together, and I leap up to fetch a glass of water for her. I can't help but glance beneath the table to make sure no witches hide there. The childish need feels stupid — especially when a real witch sits in the chair — but I can't quiet the fear that bites me.

I hand Emathi the water. She drinks with greed. "Thank you," she says.

I refill the glass and sit down again but tuck my feet beneath me. "What are the general ideas, then?" I say.

"A Heart Witch's domain is what you would expect: the heart. Emotion. She may know, influence, and change any matter of the heart."

"But how?" I say. That's the part I really don't get. Not that I should want to know any of this. It's just that if I have to gain Emathi's trust this seems as good a way as any, and I can't help but be curious.

She rests her fingers on her chest. "We use our own heart. We feel what others desire, sense their intentions, and with the right force exert our will."

I think of the nyxies and the possessive rage I felt the moment they tried to steal Katta's portrait. That was nothing like what Emathi describes. The spell told the nyxies they were unwelcome, and even if I wanted the words to be true, I didn't touch or twist any hearts. Saying what you want to be true and those things becoming real are not the same thing.

"But that's just the general idea," Emathi says. "How each of us comes to our power changes from individual to individual. It's like... well, anything really. It's like if you and I made cakes. Our ingredients could be different, the flavors dissimilar, but in the end we have a cake. Being a Heart Witch is like that. Each one of us is a cake."

If that was meant to clarify anything for me, it failed. I have no idea what she means. I smooth the frown from my face and nod like what she said made sense, though.

"What about the other types?" I say.

"Different desserts," she says. She looks pleased with herself for a moment, then shakes her head. "No, that's not right. They're not like desserts."

Confusion drops over her. I don't want to lose her. "Emathi, what is swamp witch magic like?"

The question cuts through her mental fog. Her gaze finds mine again. "All creatures and life that touch the swamp are her domain. Her influence is bound by her environment."

"How does that happen?" I imagine the swamp a
malevolent spirit that penetrates unwary travelers and turns them
into witches.

"In each case it's a matter of listening. Every type of witch
depends on listening," she says. "We hear part of the world speak
to us. I hear hearts — all the needs and desires a person can hold."

"So it's like hearing words?" Relief sweeps through me. I've
not heard anything — not a whisper, not a peep. I'm not corrupt.
I'm not a witch.

"You take this too literally," she says. "If you hear voices
you're either a Ghost Witch or mad. No. This is more a sense, like
a feeling."

My mind refuses to consider ghosts. That's too much. But
have I felt emotions I shouldn't know?

She raps her knuckles on the table to reclaim my attention.
"That's how I know you're not telling me the truth. I may not have
my magic, but I can hear a heart's secret."

I feel like she's grabbed my heart in her hand and squeezed.
She knows I mean to take her to Midt. My mind races too fast for
me to catch my own thoughts.

"Who's the witch?" she says.

I'm baffled. Her question doesn't make sense.

"I know your family has one, and you know it, too. So who
is it? Your father, surely?"

"My father's not a witch," I say, more reflex than thought.
She doesn't know about my plan, then. She wants another secret,
one I can offer. "It was my mother," I say. "My mother was a
witch."

The confession winds me, but Emathi claps in delight.
"Yes, yes, yes," she says.

Back in Midt, such a confession would ruin my chance at
acceptance. To share this here is safe, in a way nowhere outside the
Ceoghast could ever be. Emathi applauds this development. My
community would stone me.

"What did she teach you?" she says.

Given who she was, I shouldn't have good memories of
her. But before she tried to kill me, she was my mother. I thought
she loved me.

I remember she taught me how to pour syrup into the snow to make winter sweets. She brought me pen and ink and taught me my letters. We left the garden together with the scent of rosemary stuck to our skin.

"She died," I say. I shove the memories away and bury them alongside her in my mind. "That's why I never learned. She never taught me anything."

Emathi heaves a sigh heavy with empathy. I dig my nails into my palm to keep the tears from my eyes. I shouldn't have such tears. My mother was evil and we killed her. This is a happy end.

"That's a hard lot," Emathi says. "But you're here now, and we can get you sorted."

The thought exhausts me. I don't want Emathi to sort me. I want this conversation to end. I get up from the table and fetch the yarn. When I place it in her hands, she looks bewildered.

"How do we start to knit the hat?" I say and force her awareness to fade.

Chapter 26

My sixth day in the Ceoghast passes in a blur. The kelpie slaps me with his seaweed coat when I rush his grooming. The lash burns, and a trickle of blood runs from the wound. I look to Hum for help, but she shrugs as if to say I deserve no better if I go about my chores so muddled.

My mind is everywhere but the swamp witch's homestead. Even my escape plan can't hold my focus. My thoughts circle the idea of witches like water around a drain. Not just one type of witch, either. My mind invents every kind of witch it can: witches who hold domain over the grass and air, the sea and sky, the ground and trees. Before long I'm half-convinced witches hold sway over the entire world. Is Knave a witch? Or Hum? Tension crawls between my shoulder blades, and I want to shudder or scream to free myself from it.

By the time Emathi comes to fetch me, I've spent hours on chores that should have been done before noon. "You're in a state," she says.

That I'm so easy to read irks me. "Hello to you as well." I'm worn out. All day my imagination shows me horrors so unthinkable that when I face true evil, I think nothing of back talking to it.

"No call to be rude," she says. "Mind you step smart now."

She marches off at a brisk pace that Hum mimics behind her back. I wave Hum off and follow with leaden feet. Hum springs and spins about me. Her joy is infectious, and though I'm tired, her antics make me feel less sharp.

When the tree-lined path comes into view, I'm relieved to spot the cobweb woman. No change means no complications. Her presence reassures me. I turn to start back up the path to the cottage.

"Ain't you even going to say hello?" the cobweb woman asks.

I wheel around. "What? Me?"

"Well, who else?"

Who else indeed. Emathi looks as startled as I feel, and Knave starts down the hill toward us, not about to miss the day I owe them a favor.

"Hello," I say.

"That's better manners."

I wait for her to say more, but she only sits on her black horse and watches me. Like she expects more from me.

"May I go by?" I say. I'm not sure how I want her to answer. A yes would wreck my plan but grant me the freedom to leave the Ceoghast. Maybe I could work out a different way to keep from dying in Midt.

"At any point you please. That's always been the case. But you won't want me to be here when you do," she says.

Disappointment and relief dance in my stomach.

"All that said, I have to commend you on all the hard work you've put in recently," she says. Her praise feels dangerous.

"What do you mean?" I say. I've been at the swamp witch's homestead for days. Why would she care about my chores now?

"Seems like I'll be here for only a few days more. If you keep up the hard work."

"What?" Knave and I speak in unison.

"You're going to leave early?" I say.

"Seems likely."

"What happened to the two weeks?" Surely she won't let me go early on account of my chores. Why would she care? My heart plummets. What if she means the work I've put into my escape plan? I want to retract my question.

"Well, to be fair, two weeks was more of an arbitrary guideline than factual truth," she says.

I step forward. "You lied to me?"

"Ain't a lie if it could be true. Seemed as likely a timeline as any."

"Why would you do that?" The betrayal I feel seems disproportionate — I shouldn't have trusted a Ceoghast creature in the first place. I know better.

The woman leans over her horse's withers and lowers her voice to a hiss. "What do you suppose you would've done if I'd gone and told you that you had no chance of returning? Ain't no hope in that, and a person like you without hope? May as well kept myself tucked away and let you march straight home."

I've not been so long in the Ceoghast that I've forgotten those first nightmarish experiences. However much being here scares me today, the terror of my first night eclipses it in full. If she'd told me then that my stay was indefinite, that I had no hope of getting back to Midt... In those first moments, I was desperate to save whatever good I had in me. I know exactly what I would've done. Her lie saved my life.

"But why?" I say. What motive could she have? Not kindness, surely.

She straightens in the saddle and shrugs. "Ain't mine to say, sugar. Just felt like a thing I could be doing, and that ain't common in this."

"What's changed?" Emathi's words are a whip. She's coiled like she means to pounce, every muscle tense.

The cobweb woman shrugs and faces forward. She assumes the statuesque indifference I've come to know well these past few days. Our audience with her is at its end.

"We should leave," I say.

I'm afraid Emathi will insist the cobweb woman answer her, and if it's because I have a plan now... that has to remain secret. And if it's something else, I don't want to think of the possibilities, but one comes to mind. What if it's because I'll have the Ceoghast on me by then? What if she's blocking my way to ensure I go back corrupted to harm my community?

"I don't like this," Emathi says. "She's got no heart to hear, but I've a bad feeling."

My heart pounds. Good or bad, I can go home. Surely I can keep myself safe enough for just a few more days. "It sounds like I'll be gone soon," I say. "That's got to be good. You can have your home back."

"Seems you've got yourself a lucky break, Miss Mooseroot," Knave says, mockery in their tone.

"There's nothing of luck about this," Emathi says. "Something's changed, and it may not be all good for you. Or us."

"I just want to go home," I say. What I really want is for her to drop the matter. I'll figure this out, figure out how to be safe.

"Yes, we're all aware of that," she says. "A bit more critical thought on your part wouldn't be amiss."

She glares at the cobweb woman, then starts back up the path. I stifle my sigh of relief and let my body relax. Knave snickers. I tense up again.

"I'll be seeing you, Miss Mooseroot."

My nod is stiff. I hurry away but their quiet laughter chases after me.

They know. I'm certain of it.

Chapter 27

The next day I keep my mind on a short leash and direct it to the homestead chores. Without distraction, I finish in record time. Hum runs off to play in the forest, and I sequester myself in the swamp witch's library.

Any one of these books could hold answers to the problems I face, but all I want to do is bury myself in the Lightbearer stories. Still, I consider the other books. But most of the titles disquiet me: *Household Guests from This Realm and Beyond, A History of the Thirteen, Sentient Spellwork, Dawn's Guide to Raising Spirits.*

The one ordinary book in the lot, *How to Keep Chickens,* seems a mistake, and none of the tomes address my particular needs. For that I'd need books with titles like *How to Use the Eldritch Ways Without Losing Your Soul* and *Live Like a Lightbearer: An Abecedarian of Practical Steps.*

I snort at the thought and pull the Lightbearer stories from the shelf. It may not have new information, but it'll be good to reinforce what I've learned from them. My favorite chair in the room is the soft green one. I cozy into it and open the book.

"What are you up to, Miss Mooseroot?"

I nearly jump out of my skin as I leap from the chair. "Knave," I say. My breathless shock changes their name into an accusation. Anxiety roars in my ears.

"Did I startle you?" They lean against the doorway. How did I not hear them come inside? "I've come to see what you're up to. What plan you're hatching. What plot's twisting your heart."

They step into the room, but not far enough to unblock the door. I lower the book to my side. "I don't know what you're talking about." My heart is a mallet in my chest.

They lean forward and walk toward me with their head cocked to the side. "Oh? Whatever else might have changed, then? You don't suddenly get a free pass past death for no reason."

"I don't know," I say. I glance about for a place to go, or a reasonable distraction, but I'm pinned in the corner with nothing to help me. I could call for Hum, but that would only convince Knave that I lie. I need them convinced of my innocence.

Knave snatches the book from my hand.

"Give it back."

They dance out of reach. "What's this? Children's stories?"

"It's nothing." I try to take the book. Knave turns their back on me and flips through the pages. "Please give it back."

If they find out what I'm up to, or if they already know and came here to confront me, I'll lose my chance at a safe return home. Knave spins back to me, finger on one of the bold illustrations. "This is what he was, that person from yesterday."

I want to deny the resemblance, but it's too obvious. The Lightbearer in the book has the same clothes, same knife, same iridescent glow. I need to be smarter than my panic. "Yes," I say. "I was reading about them."

"But you already know about them. They're from your world." They thumb through the book with narrow eyes.

My hands tremble, and I force them to stillness. I won't let fear of my discovery out me with an obvious quiver.

"You know where to find them now that I've shown you the pond. You mean to get one of them to help you."

"They'd kill me." I regret my words the moment they're in the air. That was my out. I could have said yes and let that be the plan they suspect I have. It would've been understandable and forgivable.

They raise their eyebrows. "Kill you? Are you not one of their own?"

Righteous pride swells within me. We kill our own when they're corrupt. We keep the rest of the community safe. But I can't tell Knave that, and now that I'd be the target of such an execution, my satisfaction fades.

"I've been away for too long," I say. "They wouldn't trust me."

"It's only been a couple of days."

"It's been a week, and this isn't a good place."

"Ah, yes. You've mentioned that before. We positively burgeon with evil." The eye roll that accompanies this statement makes me feel childish and stupid. "Tell me, Miss Mooseroot, what is this world of yours like that you want so desperately to go back to it?"

"You don't know? But you said you want to go there."

"I want to leave here," they say, "but maybe your little pocket of desolation and shining boys isn't the world for me. You better tell me straight what it's like so I can make a proper choice."

Their tone taunts me, and maybe this is a trick, but if I have a chance to talk them out of our deal, I'll take it. I don't need them around when I get Emathi over the border.

"It's very strict," I say. I reframe all I know and love about my community in negative terms. "No one is allowed to be different from what the tenets tell us we need to be. If anyone fails to uphold our laws, we banish or execute them. Most of the time, we opt for execution to make sure the evil the person tried to bring into our town ends with them."

"How efficient," Knave says. They look unimpressed. My heart delights to see it.

"Magic is outlawed. The Lightbearers pull all of it from the ground to make sure our land stays pure. The best communities are bone white. Midt's like that. Evil can't get a foothold there." I miss the solidity of magic-drained earth. The Ceoghast is soft and squishy, unstable and immoral. "They don't like outsiders. If you want to settle in a new town, you have to prove you're good."

"Aren't you new?" they say.

"I am." But when I go back, my plan will keep me above suspicion.

"Miss Mooseroot, you've just described a terrible and restrictive place. Why in all the glorious dark would you go back to it? You can be free here. Make your own life."

"I have a sister."

"I do, too. You don't see me rushing to be around her."

"It's not like that." If I had Knife for a sister instead of Katta, I'd not be keen to maintain a relationship either. "She's not like that. I need to go home."

This doesn't hold Knave's interest. With nowhere else to go, I sink back into the chair and wonder how to end this audience.

"Such a strict world. And these stories... Such single-note heroics." They close the book. "I've always thought those who see the world in black-and-white are the easiest to fool. They lack critical thought. They root out variance because they see it as a threat. They're delightfully homogenous sheep." The smile they share is a twin of Knife's creepy grin. "It's easy to pull the wool over their eyes. Wouldn't you agree?"

My reply catches in my throat like a fly in a spiderweb. Knave's too close to my intention. Not that I mean to fool my community. I just need a way to show them I'm good. I need to survive my return long enough to prove my worth. "No," I say. "They're vigilant about tricks. They know what evil is and what it means to be good."

"Such a simple dichotomy. That's why you're going to pose as a Lightbearer."

I feel like I've been punched. Air rushes out of me.

"You walk in all shiny and special and voila: no murderous mob for you."

My chest constricts. I forget how to breathe.

They know.

I fight for control of my mind. For rational thought. They know I mean to pose as a Lightbearer. That's all. Nothing about that should alarm them. Except, perhaps, my disproportionate response.

"I was thinking about it," I say. Maybe this isn't so bad. They could lead me back to the pool when I need to bathe. I still have to work out how to get Emathi, but this could solve that one obstacle. It could work.

"I haven't read all these stories, Miss Mooseroot, but it seems to me there's more to this whole Lightbearer business than a glow." They tap the book. "Being better acquainted with these tales, I imagine you know you need proof beyond that shine. You need evidence of your trials. You need something like a monster's head."

This conversation needs to end, but I can't think of how to get out of it. I could shout, throw books, storm past them... but none of that gets them off my trail.

"I'm almost done," they say, as though they sense my discomfort. They smile when I squirm, like a Lightbearer might when interrogating a ceogot.

"You need a little more," they say. "You're too attached to your Jack to let anyone hurt her — to say nothing of what Knife would do to you if she caught wind of any such abuse."

The suggestion sends such a spine of fear through me I draw in on myself.

Knave continues like they missed my response. "And who knows if so small a creature could sway a mob from murder. Not worth the risk. That's why you're going to take Emathi at night. Because a real-life witch... who wouldn't that impress?"

"What? That's not true."

"You are a terrible liar, Miss Mooseroot."

My breath comes short and sharp. I sweat guilt. I don't know how to get out of this. If they tell Emathi... My thoughts run wild with the punishments she could devise. She could twist my heart. Make the whole of me evil. Destroy my soul.

Knave tosses the book on the windowsill and sweeps toward me. They grab my hands and kneel in front of me. "No need to be so scared. You see, I'm going to help you."

"What?" The room spins. I don't understand what they mean. I tear my hands away to clutch at the chair arms and close my eyes. "I think I'm going to be sick."

"Take a deep breath instead. Slowly. In..."

I time my inhalation to their voice. It takes a while, but the nausea passes. I want to keep my eyes closed, for Knave to go away so I can think this through in peace. Instead, I look at them and say, "Why?"

Because that's what I don't understand. That's what doesn't add up. I told Knave about Midt. They know what could happen to Emathi there.

"I need to get out of here, and you're my ticket, Miss Mooseroot. If the way to get you home in one piece involves bringing another witch along, I'm at your service." The purr in their voice makes me blush.

"But you know what could happen," I say. "To Emathi."

"My dear, I'm counting on it. She and I have a span of unfinished business, at least on my end. This will settle things between us."

"This is revenge for you." My stomach flips. It feels wrong to let them help me. It makes kidnapping her personal, and I don't have anything against her.

"Retribution. Reparation. Nothing to be uncomfortable about. It won't change your plan. It just means you'll have help." My plan has so many holes in it, and Knave could fill almost all of them. Every obstacle I foresee goes away if I let them join me. Is refusal even an option? Who knows what Knave might do? They could tell Emathi. They could ruin everything.

"I'll let you think on it." They retrieve the book and place it in my hands. "It's a lot to consider. You can let me know when you come to the path this evening. A simple wave hello will be all the confirmation I need."

They sashay from the room before I can reply.

The book sits heavy in my hands. Knave knows what I'm going to do. They know. And this book told them. I stand and lift the chair's skirt. I dig at the fabric on its underside until it rips. I can't let anyone else find these stories.

I shove the book inside the hole I made and position it so it won't fall out. I don't need to look at it again. I already know what to do.

Chapter 28

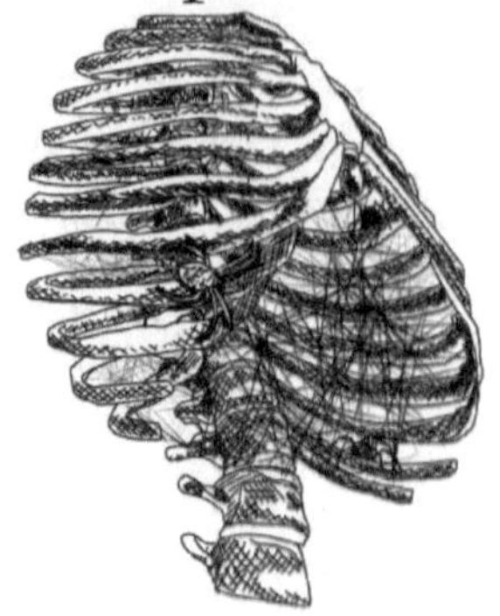

Emathi meets me at the homestead with a scowl threatening to flay me. "Well?" she says.

"I'm finished," I say, even as I realize she probably wants to know what's changed with the cobweb woman. Let her think me meek and simple-minded.

"Is there anything else you want to tell me?"

I shrug. "The kelpie didn't seem as bad today."

She twists her mouth in disapproval before she turns and walks toward the road. Relieved, I follow. Today the silence between us feels like cracked glass. A word from either of us could shatter this combative quiet and turn it into a conflict I suspect I'd lose.

We reach the hillcrest, and Emathi moves like a storm cloud toward the tree-lined path. At first, I don't see the cobweb woman. My stomach flips and twists. She steps onto the path as I come closer.

"Hello," I say.

"Remembered your manners today. Ain't that nice." The spiders in her abdomen are still, and her skeletal arm looks less raw. She's still a horror to behold, but she's healed a little from the first time we met. She leans forward and scratches her horse's neck. "Have you come to say goodbye?" she says.

"Are you leaving now?" I say.

I'm not ready. It's too soon. I still haven't figured everything out. Even with Knave's help I couldn't pull the plan off today, and if she steps away now, I'll never get Emathi to come with me.

"Not at this precise moment, but soon. Ain't likely you're going to see me again."

"Why would you leave?" Emathi says. "Why now? Tell me what's changed." She's snappish and sharp, but a whine underlies her demand. She's afraid.

I'm scared for a different reason. If the cobweb woman tells Emathi any part of my plan, it'll ruin my escape. I whirl on Emathi. "Why does that matter? I'll be gone and out of your hair. This is a good thing."

"You're hiding something," she says. "I know you are."

She reaches for my arm. Hum slaps her hand away with a growl and covers my shoulders with a protective stalk. "Don't touch me," I say. "You have no reason to. The only thing I want is to go home."

"What's the verdict today?" Knave says as they come down the path. Their joviality sounds forced, like they heard the exchange between me and Emathi and intend to blot it out with cheer.

I lift my hand and wave. They brighten. I wish they'd not been so obvious. Emathi will notice the shift.

"It sounds like I'll be home soon," I say. "Maybe as soon as tomorrow. She told us this is probably the last time I'll see her." "It's about time you had a bit of good news," they say. "And as soon as tomorrow? That's a bundle of good fortune right there."

"It's not good fortune," Emathi says. "It's scheming and tricks."

Knave's laughter, sharp as a blade, startles me and Hum. We jump, and Hum's stalk tightens around my shoulders. "Are you serious?" they say. "Sweet darkness, Emathi, is your evening paranoia getting to you when it's still bright out? How long until you lose what remains of you to the soft-witted woman you become every night?"

Emathi pales. The hand that had reached for me with such conviction begins to shake. "That's not what this is," she says. She doesn't sound certain, and her sudden insecurity floods me with shame.

"Are you sure?" Knave says. "Because it sounds no different to me."

Emathi tightens her jaw to stop the quiver in her chin. I look away. I can't stand her vulnerability. It makes my stomach tense. She looks too much like an old woman who needs help and not a witch. I have to remember what she is. Hum croons, a single note of sympathy like she understands my struggle.

Emathi straightens to glare at Hum. "We're leaving," she says. "Get out of my way."

Knave steps aside with the grace of a dancer. With Emathi's back to us, I catch their gaze and nod. We're in this together now.

Chapter 29

Emathi shuffles about the cottage in a daze. "Where are my jars?"

She doesn't speak to me. I've hidden myself by the front door, ready to go outside the moment I'm certain she's forgotten I'm here. I don't want her to follow me into the yard.

"I need my jars." She hasn't called me for a while. I should be safe. I ease the door open and slip outside.

Hum whistles a greeting when I step onto the porch.

"Hush," I say. She shrinks from me, and I shut the door. Without a glance at her, I tiptoe into the grass.

Overhead the sky is black and cold. Speckled hound pumpkins stretch out in every direction and make the task ahead of me seem impossible. Beyond them, the suspended lights of the barrier twinkle.

I pause in the grass, afraid of what else might be out there. If Knave and nyxies can pass through the barrier, other creatures may find their way through. On top of that, I'm not sure where to start, or what I need to look for. Somewhere in this hollow is a way to take down the barrier that confines Emathi at night. She spends so much time outside it has to be out here. Why else would she send me into the cottage just before darkfall? It can't be solely for fear of nyxies. Besides, it's not like she'd trust nighttime Emathi to leave the key to the barrier alone if it were inside.

A breeze cool with the threat of winter sweeps by me. I should've borrowed a blanket to sling about me. Arms crossed for warmth, I explore the yard, focus torn between finding what I need and identifying any threats before they grab me. I refrain from touching the barrier but examine the lights closely in case they may hint at its removal. The barrier almost looks like netting made of light. It takes me ten minutes to realize what a fool's errand this is. When I lap the cottage for the seventh time, I stop.

This isn't going to work. I can't wander about and hope to happen upon the key to a magic spell I don't understand. Do I honestly expect to stumble on a solution to this problem by luck?

I pull the blue cloth I took from the kitchen out of my pocket. I'm fairly certain Emathi only rubbed the pumpkins with this cloth so she'd have a way to deal with the kelpie, but I can't dismiss the chance that this is part of the barrier. I scrub at one pumpkin, then another, and try to listen for an answer. I work my way about the field until my hand cramps and my arm is sore. The barrier's steadfast film stands unchanged around the hollow. I throw the cloth at an oblong pumpkin in frustration.

"What are you doing?"

My irritation overrides my startle reflex. Hands on my hips, I wheel toward Knave. They saunter across the barrier and lift the hem of their lace skirt to sweep through the pumpkins. Next to them, the tingle of sweat and dirt from chores on my skin feels heavier.

"I'm trying to figure out how to take down the barrier that keeps Emathi here," I say. My hands want to fidget with my hair and adjust my blouse. I force them to stay on my hips. "Why are you here?"

"I knew you'd be at your preparations. I've come to help you." The bow they execute makes my heart skip beats. Their elegance is more love story than real life.

"There won't be a plan if I don't work out how to get the barrier down. I thought the pumpkins might have a connection to it, but I can't work it out. Any ideas? Why can you and I pass through and she can't?"

Knave looks about like the pumpkins are below their notice. They wrinkle their nose. "I don't dabble in spellwork. Ask your Jack. Why's she lurking over there, anyway?"

Hum hasn't left the porch. She hunches over near the corner, her stamens flat. Guilt steals over me. I've been short with her as of late. "Hum doesn't know witch magic," I say.

"If the magic involves the pumpkins, she may have insight."

They have a point, and I don't have a better idea. "Hum?" I say. "I need you. Will you come here?"

My words are like water to a starved plant. She perks up and bounds over. She stops in front of me, aquiver with pleasure and anticipation.

"I need to take down the barrier." I gesture at the boundary. "I think we have to do something with the pumpkins, but I'm not sure what. Can you find out?"

Hum trills her affirmation and wanders away. She begins to sing to the speckled hounds, and though I worry Emathi may hear her from within the cottage, I don't shush her.

"Let's hope she can figure it out, otherwise we're in for a long night," Knave says. "So, what's your plan, Miss Mooseroot? We take down the barrier and force Emathi to the borderlands?"

"No. Not like that." My hope is that she'll come on her own if I tell her the right story, but that seems naïve now that I need to share the thought with Knave. "I need you to take me to that pool after darkfall tomorrow. I can sneak out like I did tonight."

"With Emathi?"

"No, just me. We'll come back for her after. She'll follow me out, and then we can go to the path."

"Late night," they say. "It's not a fast trip to the pool."

"I can't go before dark. Emathi's already suspicious enough. I don't know what she'd do if I show up glowing before her confusion sets in." I might not know what she'd do, but I can imagine all sorts of reactions, and none of them are pleasant.

"So long as you're prepared, I'm here to help. But what makes you think Emathi's just going to follow you out? She's terrified of the night."

Hum trumpets triumph and bounces across the yard to us, a pumpkin in her hands. I'm happy to avoid Knave's question and give Hum my full attention as she pushes the pumpkin toward me. Nothing extraordinary marks it as any different from the other ones in the field. I wouldn't have known to pick it out.

"This will remove the barrier?" I say.

Hum whistles affirmation. The barrier still stands all about us. To take the pumpkin is not enough.

"What do I do?"

Hum straightens with importance and wiggles her head. She mimes holding the pumpkin and smashes her pretend gourd on the ground. I want to be certain I understand. "If I wreck the pumpkin, what will happen?"

Hum throws herself into a wild, convulsive dance. It's an odd way to communicate, but now I know for sure. If I break the pumpkin on the ground, the barrier will dissipate. I hand it back to Hum with care. "Put it back where you found it," I say.

"What are you doing?" Knave says.

"We know Hum can find the pumpkin. We don't need to bring the barrier down tonight."

"You need to make sure that's how it works. What if that's just the first step of twenty?"

Hum was so assured with her find, but how could she be so confident?

"Wait," I say. I take the pumpkin back. This time I notice its weight, the way it pulls toward the barrier. Knave's right. I have to know for sure.

I lift the pumpkin over my head and smash it with all my strength.

Wind rushes through my body and fills me with a heady exhilaration. I inhale it. Hold it. When I breathe out, the barrier scatters.

Knave grins. "Looks like we have a plan."

My smile is unstoppable. Tomorrow, I go home.

Chapter 30

"Get out of bed."

I jerk upright and blink against the dark. The sun's not fully risen yet, its orange rays just beginning to lighten the farthest patch of sky.

"Now," Emathi says from below the loft.

Hum grumbles and rolls away from me as I fight free of the bed-sheets to stand on legs still half-asleep. I stomp my feet against the floor to wake them up before I climb down the ladder. I'm halfway down before my mind breaks from its soporific state and offers me the reason for Emathi's early morning anger. My hands tighten on the rough wood as I consider scurrying back up the rungs.

Last night, when the final piece of my plan fell into place, my euphoria overrode any thought of repercussions. Now the consequences await me at the bottom of the ladder. I gather my courage like a cloak and descend. I won't give anything away. This might not be about the barrier.

"Is something wrong?" I say.

Emathi's face is splotchy, and I realize too late my naïve act will only incite her fury. "You filthy, lying guttersnipe. Did you think you could come here and wreck my home and that I wouldn't notice? That I wouldn't see your malice for what it is?"

My temper rises to match hers. Guttersnipe? My aim should be to calm her down, but no witch is going to insult my character.

"What's your problem? You wake me up, start screeching at me and insult me for no reason. I'm not the one full of malice, and if anyone here's a guttersnipe, it's you."

"What did you do to my protection spell?"

It takes me a moment to understand she means the barrier. Still, I opt for ignorance. I feel spiteful. "What are you talking about? I haven't touched any of your spells, and I don't want to." I slather each syllable with contempt.

"I know you took down my protection spell. You and your magic. You destroyed it. Did you think I wouldn't know? That I can't hear the jeer of your spellwork?"

"My spellwork?" The anger from before was a spark compared to the inferno that rages in me now. I'm tired of being called a witch. "That took no magic. All I needed to do was smash a pumpkin. You call that spellwork?"

"You admit it," she says. "You had no right. How dare you?"

Hum swings down from the loft, all snarls and smoke, and steps in front of me.

"Get out of my way, you shrunken squash, or I'll scorch your stalks from tip to toe."

"Don't you dare threaten her." I press past Hum to look Emathi in the face. "You will not touch her."

"Get out," she says.

"What?"

"Get out of my home. I want you gone."

All my bravado wilts. "I can't leave," I say. I've handled this all wrong. She can't kick me out.

"This is my home," she says. "I can do what I want. That means you're going to leave. I never want to see you again."

I need to change her mind. I speak with force and confidence. "You need me to stay."

Emathi's expression softens for a moment. Then her glare draws down like a knife. "You manipulative witch. You think you can change my heart? Mine?" Each word is shrill and tight. "Get out of my home before I twist your heart into a hollow and leave you for the monsters to take."

I place a hand over my chest, as though I can keep my heart safe that way. I didn't try to change her heart. I don't have that ability. All the same, the accusation and threat frighten me.

"I can't go out like this," I say. My clothes are upstairs, along with Katta's portrait. All I have on is the borrowed nightgown and boots.

The air beside Emathi cracks open, and suddenly my belongings are on the floor in a neat pile. She reaches down and plucks the pendant that allowed me to travel to the swamp witch's homestead from my things.

"Keep the nightie," she says.

I collect my possessions from the floor. Katta's portrait rests between my blouse and trousers. "Will you let me get changed first?"

"Do it in the yard, if you must. You're no longer welcome here, so leave."

She doesn't need to shove me with her magic. Her anger is enough to move me. I retreat to the front door, Hum at my back, and step onto the porch. Behind us, Emathi slams and locks the door. And just like that, my plan derails.

Panic claws my throat. I heave in the wet morning air and hurry into my clothes. Without the pendant to the homestead, the only way for me to get anywhere in the Ceoghast is to travel by foot. I can't walk away from Speckled Hound Hollow and expect to get anywhere good or safe. I need help.

"Hum, find Knave. Bring them here as fast as you can. I need their help." They're the only one who can help me.

Hum grumbles a little but lopes away when I give her a stern glance.

If I'm going to pull my plan back together, I'll need Knave's help. I have no idea what to do about Emathi, but for now I have a more immediate problem: getting away from the cottage in one piece.

Chapter 31

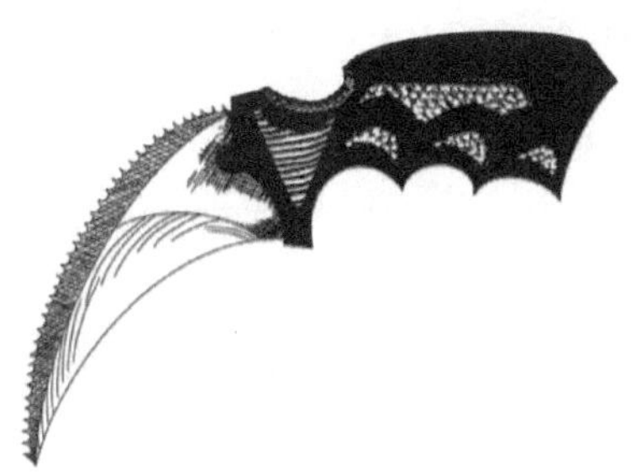

Knave meets me at the edge of Speckled Hound Hollow dressed in clothes so somber I don't recognize them at first. The straight lines and unembellished fabric lack the frivolity and joy their clothes usually have. They seem a different person. Maybe that's the point. Today we both take steps that will change our lives.

"She forced me out," I say. "She knows I broke the barrier."

"Couldn't talk your way out of it?"

"I wouldn't be standing here if that were the case." A chill from the ground seeps into my boots, and I step in place to warm them. "She was furious. She doesn't trust me."

"Nor should she," they say. "But this does throw a bit of a scarecrow in our path, Miss Mooseroot. What's your plan now?"

Even though I have a revised plan — it's all I've thought about out here — Knave's non-involvement irks me. After this morning, I'd hoped for a stronger sense of partnership, but Knave makes it clear they're a tagalong.

"I haven't changed my plan. Not really. We can do a few things earlier, like the pool because it doesn't matter if I glow all day now. Then we'll come back after darkfall."

This is the best revision I have. I don't know what else to do. It's not like I'll hunt down a different Ceoghast monster to present to my community. Everything hinges on Emathi.

"You're just going to wait and see what surprises Emathi might have for you here?"

"I don't have any better ideas. Do you? It's not like I can spy on her."

They shrug. "At least you'll have from the start of darkfall to figure it out. That trip to the pool was going consume a lot of your time."

True, but I don't like the fact I'll probably need more time now to take down whatever new barrier Emathi devises. If I can disperse it at all. "Will you help me for the day?" I say.

"My only other job was to watch your path home. I stopped by on the way over here." They pause, and my breath hitches in anticipation.

"Is she gone?" I say.

"Your way back is clear, Miss Mooseroot."

Most of me wants to run to the path right now and forget the plan. The small, rational part of me squashes that urge. I breathe in patience. I'm almost there. Almost home. I won't wreck my chance.

"Let's go to the pool first," I say. I didn't have a chance to do so much as wash my face this morning.

"And so it starts," they say. "This way, Miss Mooseroot."

With the loss of my lodgings, I'm unmoored. The Ceoghast feels more dangerous, like it would pounce on me if not for Knave's presence. I stick close to them and shoo Hum away when she tries to squeeze between us.

By the time we reach the pool, I'm thankful we've made the trip by day. The foliage here is so dense it makes the path hard to see. I'd injure myself if I traversed this path in the dark. Even the air slows us down. It clings to us and forces us to a slower pace.

Unlike Hum, Knave gives me a modicum of privacy as I undress. The ground around the pool is slick with a spongy moss that squelches between my toes. Even in the nude, the air is so humid I'm as hot as I was in my layers of clothes.

Hum sits by the edge of the pool and drags her long limbs through the water.

"Don't touch me," I say as I slip into the lukewarm pool. The last scare I need is her eel-like stalks grabbing me from under the water, which seems like the exact sort of prank she'd pull. She smokes a green sigh and traces patterns on the water's surface as I sink deeper.

Is this all I have to do? Soak? For all my gaze never left the Lightbearer, I can't remember his exact ministrations. I lift a hand to see if I've gained any iridescence, but the water rolls off without a trace. "This may take a while," I say.

Knave steps into the area and sits on one of the few mossfree rocks. "Those others take their time, and it's not as though we're in a rush." They lean back and pull a small, blue-bound chapbook from their coat pocket.

"Do you think we'll be able to get back to Speckled Hound Hollow?" I say.

They don't look up from the book. "She can't change my Ways there. We'll get back when we need without a problem."

"No, that's not what I mean." I hadn't even thought of that problem. The idea that areas of the Ceoghast could wink out of existence, or somehow hide themselves from me, is a new concept. One I don't like. The thought isn't unreasonable either, not in a world where a road can hunt you down, or a single path can lead to many different places.

"I meant back on the property. Will she change her barrier spell so we can't even get in?"

"Oh, she'll have a new protection spell. Wouldn't you do the same in her place?"

I would, but I'd also not stay where I felt unsafe. "Will she even be there?"

"Emathi's got nowhere else to go. She's burned a lot of bridges, and besides, can you imagine what nighttime Emathi would do in a new place?" They chuckle, low as a dog's growl. "No, she'll be there."

"But we won't know how to bring down the spell that traps her in there," I say. "Not if it's new."

Knave shrugs and flips a page. "You'll figure it out."

"But if we can't get in…"

"Look, there's only so much she can do in the time she has. I don't touch spellwork, but even I know this much: she'll want to make her protection spell strong, and that takes time and energy. That means she has to choose between keeping herself in, or keeping us out. Which would you choose?"

"I'd keep us out," I say.

"And let your half-mad evening self wander into the Ceoghast?"

I'd not considered that part. Hum begins to croon. The jungle consumes her song and makes it flat. Hum knew what to do last night. No matter what, if Emathi uses the pumpkins, Hum can help me again.

"We'll figure it out," I say as Emathi's words come back to me. She said I took the barrier down by magic, but that's not right. Surely I'd know if magic touched me. Even if the last barrier didn't require magic, this new one might. What will I do then?

I lift a pruned hand out of the pool. A dim shimmer clings to my skin and tears sting my eyes. I wish it were real. That I were good enough to create my own light, to be one of Light's true channels. After this venture through the Ceoghast, do I even have a chance? I drop my arm into the pool again. None of this will matter if I don't make it back.

If Emathi's new spell needs magic to break it, I'll do it. I'll do whatever it takes to get home.

Chapter 32

Even with our early start, Knave, Hum, and I don't make it back to the barrier until an hour after darkfall. In the starlit night, my skin is a second moon. It may not be a real Lightbearer glow, but I feel regal. I walk with my head high and shoulders back. If one of the plant hands leaps out at me today, the courage to face it is mine. It's a heady sort of power.

That said, I may have overdone the glow. I couldn't remember if the Lightbearer's hair was meant to shine, too, so I soaked my head and may have overdone the effect. Knave offered me better clothes to go with my transformation. The offer tempted me, but I wouldn't be able to explain the new wardrobe to my community members. Instead, I wear the clothes that I wore into the Ceoghast eight days ago.

Knave hangs back when we come to the edge of Speckled Hound Hollow. "Time to test your protection spell theory."

"You want me to go first?" I shouldn't be surprised, but the ease with which Knave suggests I venture into potential danger first reminds me that our relationship exists to fulfill a bargain.

"You're the best one of us for the job. Unless you want your Jack to tempt the black?"

"Tempt the black?"

They wave a dismissive hand. "Find out what might be lurking. To go into the unknown first."

"No." I hate the suggestion.

Hum stands beside me. She'd go first if I told her to, but the thought makes me sick. She chirps at me and flexes her fingers. The pool's iridescence adheres to the stalks she kept submerged. She didn't keep them in the water evenly, so the glow is spotty.

"Stay here," I say. I cross into the yard. The air shifts around me but allows me to enter Emathi's safe space. I wait a moment to be sure nothing means to spring upon me, then I motion for Hum and Knave to join me.

"Easygoing so far," Knave says.

I touch Hum's hand. "Can you find the pumpkin to take down the barrier?" She whistles and darts off. Her song this evening is low and dark and full of a self-satisfied malice. I watch her until she ducks behind the cottage. "Barrier down. Emathi out. Then it's off to Midt," I say. Only three steps left, really.

"You're getting closer to home," Knave says.

Hum trots out from behind the cottage with three pumpkins cradled in her arms. She sets them by my feet and dances about delighted.

"I don't understand," I say. "Do I just smash all three of them?" That seems too unsophisticated. Emathi wouldn't repeat her previous spellwork and just triple it, would she? She knows I figured that out the first time.

Hum makes a guttural sound of displeasure. At least my instincts are right.

"What do I do, then?" I say.

Her squirmy shoulder shimmy informs me I'm on my own with this one. She doesn't know any more than I do.

"Okay. I can figure this out."

I lift the smallest pumpkin and examine it. Like the one from yesterday, it's indistinguishable from the others in the field. Nothing marks it or the other two as distinct, but they are special. Hum picked up on it. I have to do the same if I'm to work this out. I close my eyes and listen to them the way Emathi described.

At first, Ceoghast noises clog my ears. Hidden in the shadows both within and outside the barrier, nyxies crackle and snap as they move. A breeze flicks leaves to life and chases them over the ground. Hum's stalks creak. Around Knave there's a silence so deep it seems an abyss.

In my hand, the pumpkin tocks like a timepiece. By my feet, the other two answer with their own metronome. I hold my breath to better hear them.

They don't align with each other, nor do they work in complement. Like siblings who refuse to admit a relation, they strike out their own beat. I move them about. Different arrangements and distances do nothing to change their solemn tempos.

"Hum, can you hear them?" I say.

She shrugs, neither a yes nor a no. More of a "not really" gesture.

"I don't suppose you can?" I say.

Knave snorts. "Plants and I haven't had cause to communicate. As I've mentioned, spellcraft isn't an area of interest to me."

Given our need to unravel a spell, their insouciance seems foolish. And this isn't spellcraft — all I do is listen.

I settle on the ground with the pumpkins arranged in front of me. I could break them and see what comes of it, but who knows what traps or tricks I may trigger if that's not the way to bring down the spell. I tap my finger against the nearest pumpkin and consider my options.

It taps back.

I grab it in surprise and find its tempo changed. It carries the beat of my finger. Is this the key? I try a few different patterns on the pumpkin. It adapts to each rhythm I give it. On a hunch, I tap out the beat one of the other pumpkins keeps. They fall in-sync with one another. The barrier fluctuates.

This is it.

I snatch up the third pumpkin to teach it the song of its siblings. In my haste, I mess up the rhythm twice, but then it has it. All three play together.

The barrier falls.

Hum looks about startled. She chatters at me with concern.

"We need it down," I say. "Stay here. Both of you. I'll go get Emathi."

"I'll be here if you need a hand getting her out," Knave says. They sound certain I'll need such assistance. But I'm determined to do this alone.

I slip inside the cottage. "Emathi?" I say. It's oddly quiet. I expected her to be at her usual jar search.

"Who's there?"

I follow the direction of her voice. "It's me, Emathi. Cassia Mooseroot."

"Cassia Mooseroot?" Confusion has her, but when I walk into the kitchen, she smiles. "I know who you are."

"Hello, Emathi."

"You can't be here," she says. "I have to ask you to leave."

"Leave? Why? I came to talk to you." I'd hoped this would be easy. I don't know how Knave and I will drag her away if she doesn't come on her own.

"I remember," she says. "No more outside witches in the house. It's a rule."

Most of me feels relieved daytime Emathi only managed to get one rule through to her nighttime counterpart. But this also complicates my plan.

"I'm not an outside witch, Emathi. We're friends. You know me."

"But you don't live here, so you can't stay."

For that I come up with an easy solution. "You can invite me to live with you." Of course, if she invites me to stay, I'm not sure how I'm then going to turn around and convince her to follow me out. Maybe if I tell her I need her help to move in? That feels flimsy. She's not physically fit to assist with move-in work and we both know it.

She draws herself away from me. "One witch cannot live with another. We have no relationship." She sounds scandalized.

"What kind of relationship do we need to have?"

"Blood or contract, of course," she says.

I think of the agreement I made with daytime Emathi. Had she thought me a witch even then? "We could make a contract, Emathi."

"You want to be my apprentice?" Her eyes are wide. I don't know if it's hope or horror in her gaze.

"Could I stay, Emathi? If I were your apprentice?"

"Of course. You can do and have whatever you want. I'll teach you everything I know." She clutches my hands in hers and shakes with an excitement better suited to youth. "I've waited for an apprentice for so long. I gave up hope years ago and thought the same mistakes would happen all over again. I didn't know what I was doing, and I had to teach myself. Heart Witches are so rare. The lineage..."

Confusion bends her brow. I squeeze her hands to get her back. "I'll be your apprentice," I say. Already a new part of the plan forms in my mind. "But we need to get my family's permission."

"Your family?"

"They don't live far. We can go tonight. Then I can be your apprentice."

"Who is your family?" She sounds like she's about to lose her place in the conversation.

"My mother was a witch, Emathi. Remember?"

"Witches on both sides," she says. "You should be trained already."

I let her assumption be. "But no one taught me. I don't know anything. I need you to teach me. That's why I want to be your apprentice."

"An apprentice." She beams.

"So we'll go tell my family." I tug her hand to lead her from the room.

"Yes, yes," she says. "We'll do everything right."

My heart pounds with triumph. This is even better than I'd hoped. I have a story to last all the way to Midt.

"Wait," she says. "Wait. We can't go like this."

"What do you mean?" Anxiety replaces my joy.

"Well just look at me." She gestures at her soup-stained apron, mismatched woolen stockings, and patchwork shift. "I'm not fit to go anywhere dressed like this."

"You look fine, Emathi." I've never seen her in anything different. If she decides to wait until she whips up a new outfit, I'll have to figure out another story to get her out the door.

"I'd never let any witch apprentice under someone who looked a ragamuffin." She sounds cross. "You stay here. I'll be back in a minute."

"I should help you," I say. I don't want her out of my sight. She could forget.

"With my toilette? I think not. I won't be but a moment." She sets her jaw, and I resign myself to the wait, hoping she doesn't keep me long.

Ten minutes later, Emathi re-enters the room in a delicate lavender gown with lacy sleeves and decorative ribbon. Her thin gray hair sits against the nape of her neck in a tight bun, and she's washed her face.

"How about this for a transformation?" she says. She spins in an awkward circle, and the skirt flutters about her ankles like butterfly wings. She giggles.

"It's a beautiful dress. You look lovely," I say, and I mean it.

"I made this for myself a long time ago for an occasion that never came. The poor thing's languished in the wardrobe ever since." She pats the skirt like it's a pet. "But here we are at last, and a better special occasion I couldn't dream of at my age."

"We should go now," I say. Her joy twists my stomach.

"I'll make a good impression, won't I? On your family?"

I nod. The lump in my throat is too big to speak around.

"Off we go, then," she says.

Knave and Hum are on the porch. Emathi's startled at first but takes it in stride. "Come to escort us?" she says.

"We have," Knave says.

"That's good thinking. Who knows what trouble we'd get up to. Two witches in the dark." She cackles like she's made a grand joke.

Hum mimics the laugh and puffs out smoke. We must seem a jolly group to any observers, but my insides are in knots.

"This way, Emathi," Knave says as they strike out.

Emathi glances at me. "My dear, why are you glowing? Did you fall in a boonabog? We should get you washed."

"No, I'm fine," I say. The last thing I need is for her to remove my glow. "My family likes when I visit them like this. It's important."

"That's an odd custom," she says.

"We should go," I say. "Knave's getting ahead of us."

Emathi takes off with the eagerness of a loyal old dog. I clench my teeth against the guilt that rises in me and follow.

Chapter 33

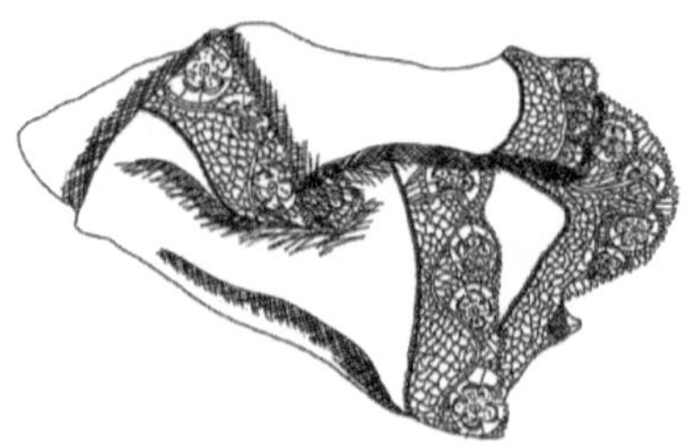

We arrive at the tree-lined path a less jovial group. Emathi sags into herself as we pause to look down the road. She's exhausted from the walk. Sweat stains the armpits and back of her dress.

"Are we here?" she asks.

"No," I say. All the tension in me clings to my terse reply. I glance at our surroundings. No sign of the cobweb woman, but is she really gone? "Wait here a moment.

Emathi needs no further encouragement to rest and trundles over to sit on a rock, while Knave remains standing where they are. Only Hum takes a few concerned steps forward. My own steps are slow and cautious. It's not until I walk beyond the area the cobweb woman once occupied that I feel confident she's gone.

"We can go," I say.

Knave helps Emathi to her feet, and Hum bounds over. "Why is there a crowd on the road?" Emathi says. "Where'd all those people come from?"

"It's just us, Emathi," I say. Her eyes aren't focused on me, and I worry we're about to lose her to confusion. "I'm going to be your apprentice. We just need to tell my family and get their permission.

"But who are all these people? They're all on horses."

Her paranoia makes me glance about, afraid the cobweb woman has appeared. But no one is in sight. "We're the only ones here, Emathi."

I look to Knave for help, but the bemused quirk across their lips tells me they're more likely to tease Emathi than reassure.

I tuck my arm into hers and hustle her down the road. "Are you excited to meet my family, Emathi?"

"I'll make a good impression, won't I?"

Her gentle insecurity tugs on my heart. "The best," I say. Beside me, Hum sings her agreement.

"You have to get rid of her, you know," Knave says. "Your Jack."

It's like they've thrown ice water in my face. All this time I've been preoccupied with Emathi, I gave no thought to Hum. "I know."

"Well, now's the time." They gesture to the road ahead. Beyond it, within an easy walk, is a track of bone white land where magic has no hold. The borderlands. My home.

I unhook my arm from Emathi's, and Knave leads her forward alone. Hum sidles up to me with an inquisitive chirp. She's so tall I have to look up to see her, even though she lowers her head to better meet my gaze. She's changed, entirely different from the little stunted squash I met my first night. I inhale her cinnamon smoke scent, let it curl inside me like a contented cat, then breathe it out. I want to hug her, to part on kind terms, but I need her to understand I'm not coming back and that she can't follow me.

"You can't come with me. You have to stay here."

She crackles at me, thinks I joke. I force my face into a glare.

"I'm leaving, and you're not welcome. Stay here, Hum."

Her expression falls into confusion, and I don't wait to see comprehension or obedience dawn on her face. I start down the path. I can't stand the thought of seeing her hurt, and I have to do this. If she leaves the Ceoghast, my community would kill her. Torture her.

Maybe I shouldn't care, but I do. The thought of someone hurting her strengthens my resolve. Better harsh words from me than death by another person's hand. With a growl of protest, she pursues me. I spin and shove her back. Her stalks bend beneath my hand.

"No, Hum." My throat is tight. I swipe at a tear so hard I scratch my cheek. "Stay. You can't come with me."

She barks a protest, her smoke tinged red with determination. How can I make her understand? All the times she helped me, she never asked for a reward. Being together was enough for her. She's pinned all her hopes for a future on me, and I need to destroy them. I need to keep her here, keep her safe.

I clench my fists. "I don't care what you want. You have to do as I say. You're not coming with me."

She gurgles a cry and reaches for my hand. I slap her away, then shove her for good measure.

"No. I don't want you. I don't like you." My chest fills with a hurt so deep my heart might stop. But mine isn't the heart that matters here. When she tries to come close, I kick her. "Go. Get away from me."

She warbles in confusion, makes herself small and extinguishes her smoke. I want her to understand it's not safe for her outside the borderlands. That this is for her sake as much as mine. But if I show her compassion, I worry she won't get the message.

She cries and scrabbles at my feet. I step away from her. A deep breath steadies me, and I arm myself with the air's chill.

"I never want to see you again," I say, forcing hate into my voice. "If I see you, I'll cut all your stalks until you don't have a body and smash your head like the pumpkin from the other night." Her wail pierces me.

I can't take it. I walk away. Then run. My pulse thumps the apology I can't utter. Bile rises in my throat.

I come abreast Knave who frowns at my tear-streaked face. "You sure you can do this?"

I don't mistake the question for concern for me. "We're leaving the Ceoghast," I say.

I grab Emathi's hand and haul her down the road faster than is easy on her, but I need to get away. I can't stand Hum's mourning cries. My reasons for returning, for abandoning Hum, are flimsy until I think of Katta. If I stay here, she will grow up like I did, under doubt and suspicion — everyone waiting for her to turn, to become a witch. It's no life, and I won't let it happen to her.

Don't look back. Don't look back.

I train my eyes on the magic-drained land ahead and keep them there until Hum's cries die out. Then I can't help myself.

Hum lies in a curled heap in the middle of the road, an inanimate lump. I whip my head forward again and bite my cheeks to stop the tears. Hum's a Ceoghast creature. She doesn't matter. I want that belief to drive out the regret, to blot out the ways I hurt her and silence my own aching chest. I quicken my steps, as though I can outpace the pain that grows in me.

This is what I want. This is what matters. I'm finally going home.

Chapter 34

Emathi's hand is clammy and her breath reedy before I let her slow down. Knave glances over at me like they don't trust me to stay with the group or keep myself together. Like they expect me to go back. The truth is a lot of me wants to go back. I want to collect Hum and tell her I'm sorry and take away all the hurt that made her cry. But I want to go home even more, to make sure my sister is safe from any harm I could cause her if I disappear into the Ceoghast, and that keeps my feet on the right path.

Knave leads us to the edge of the woods. Beyond them, the ground begins to lighten and the plants thin. "Will you be good from here?" Knave says.

"I need to sit down a moment," Emathi says. She eases her clammy hand away from mine and sits on a nearby stump. I hardly notice. My heart is full.

This is it. The edge of the Ceoghast. "I'll be fine," I say. For the first time in eight long days, I believe it.

"What's your plan?"

I lean my head out of the trees. "I'm going to walk toward Midt. A border patrol group should find us before we reach town. I'll tell them what happened. Well, my story anyway."

"Best not get confused on that point."

"After that's done, I'll hand her over." I soften my voice so Emathi doesn't hear. She hasn't been confused since we left the cottage, but she also seems adrift, like she's not aware enough to know she should be jumbled.

"Then I have kept my part of the bargain and done more for you besides."

"You have." I wouldn't have gotten all the pieces in place without them.

"Then you are bound to keep yours."

I'd once thought to cheat Knave after they delivered me from the Ceoghast. Now I know I can't withhold the favor I owe them. Not even if I tried. Their words wrap around me like gentle chains. Soft for now, while I'm in compliance with their request. But spikes lie in wait, ready to spring should I stray, and for the first time, I understand more of them. And with that knowledge, my vision clears. They are deep and dark and sublime — utterly other.

"You're not a person, are you?"

The grin they offer is all teeth. "Not even in the slightest. I'm offended you'd even think it possible."

"And you've been trapped here." Emathi had a role in that.

"But not for much longer."

"No. Not much longer," I say.

Maybe if I was a real Lightbearer, I'd sacrifice myself to keep Knave in the Ceoghast. I'd call the deal off and turn away from all that's bright and good in the world. But I need the good too much to let it go. I extend my hand. "I'll see you in the Light," I say. The traditional parting brings tears to my eyes. I last said those words to Katta when I left Horth for Midt.

"In the Light," they say and fold my hand in theirs. "I'll find you."

It's both promise and threat. "I know."

"Just one more thing, then." They reach up to my hair and yank out a few strands.

"Ouch. What was that for?" I cover my stinging head.

"One part of you here to match one part of you there. This is my bridge." They roll my strands into a ball and tuck them into a chest pocket. "It's how I'll get through."

Unease sloshes my stomach, but all I say is, "Okay."

"Goodbye, Miss Mooseroot. Until we meet again. In the Light, as you say."

"Where are they going?" Emathi says.

I go to her and take her hand again. She's unsteady as she gets to her feet. "Are you ready to go, Emathi?"

"But where did they go? Did they leave?"

I glance back, but Knave is gone. "It's just us, Emathi. We're going to meet my family. Do you remember?"

"You're going to be my apprentice." The pride in her voice is impossible to miss.

"That's right."

"Do you think they'll like me? This is my best dress." Dark stains mar the lavender fabric from hem to knee and wet patches expand from her underarms. Leaves and dirt from the stump cling to her backside.

"You'll get along well," I say. I need to keep her calm and focused. "And it's not far now. Let's go, Emathi."

I tug her forward, and together, we step out of the Ceoghast.

Chapter 35

Away from the trees, Emathi and I are easy to spot. The glow of my skin illuminates our location no matter how black our surroundings. And it is dark. The sliver of moon that earlier lit our way retreats behind heavy clouds. Our feet hit the white ground of Midt's distant border with a shock.

Gone is the spongy give of dirt laced with magic. My heels clomp against unyielding ground. Each step sends a jolt up to my knees. This is what ground should be, but after so long in the Ceoghast, it's strange to me. More lifeless than sacred.

"Is it much farther?" Emathi asks.

"No." I'd expected a border group to spot us the moment we left the trees.

"I'd like to rest."

"Not yet. We're almost..."

"You there. Stop," a voice says from behind us as a sharp whistle pierces the air.

Nerves clutter my stomach, and I spin on my heel. A pair of border guards approach us, weapons not yet out.

"Stay here and don't say a word," I say to Emathi.

"Can I rest?"

"Only for a moment." I step away from Emathi to intercept the duo.

"I need your help," I say.

The guards slow, near identical frowns on their faces. "I don't recognize you, Lightbearer," the shorter woman with freckles says.

I muster bravado and throw back my shoulders. "I don't expect you to. I need your help."

"Forgive us, Lightbearer, but we need your name and business," the second guard says. The hair at her temples is gray with age. "You seem set on our town, and it's our job to monitor all those who want to come and go this time of night."

I breathe in courage. "My name is Cassia Mooseroot. I..."

"Cassia Mooseroot? You're the woman that went charging into the Ceoghast with some monster?" Her hand is poised over the knife at her hip now. She seems uncertain as to how she should receive me. Here I am, worse than a criminal due to my earlier actions, yet now elevated by Light.

"I have been in the Ceoghast for eight days," I say. "The Light found me there and made me a vessel worthy of its radiance." The statement rolls off my tongue with the ease of constant practice. I'm proud I pull it off without a quaver in my tone. If this were real, if Light had truly found me, I'd be humbler. But this is a performance meant to safeguard my life.

"I return to bring Light to Midt, and more besides. I have the Heart Witch of the Ceoghast." I gesture to Emathi who sits on the ground and rubs at her swollen legs. She doesn't cut an impressive figure.

"That's a witch?" the freckled guard says.

"The Heart Witch," I say. Emathi's age alone should be enough of a reason to suspect the Ceoghast is on her. The guard's question has my thoughts scrambling to give Emathi an air of intimidation or danger. "She tried to curse me with a spell, but Light protected me. Her curse struck her instead. It's left her temporarily simple-minded. It won't last, but for now she's relatively docile."

"The spell rebounded?" The disbelief in her voice makes me worry I've overstretched.

"Hail, Lightbearer," a different voice says. Two more border guards cut toward us, one young and one old. They move with an ease the two before me don't display, like they've already decided I'm not a threat.

"In Light we meet," I say. The newcomers extend their hands and repeat the traditional greeting as we clasp arms.

"Who's your companion?" the oldest of the group, a silverhaired woman, asks. No one has gone to Emathi or greeted her. She fidgets with her dress on the ground.

"Lightbearer has a witch," the freckled border guard says.

"A witch? Are you certain?" the oldest says.

"She's a Heart Witch," I say. "She tried to curse me in the Ceoghast, but Light delivered me."

"She says the curse rebounded," the freckled guard says. "This here's Cassia Mooseroot."

At this both of the new guards stiffen. "We heard you made a run for the Ceoghast, consorted with monsters," the oldest says. Her voice is colder.

"I chased a monster into the Ceoghast to kill it," I say. I can't let my story stray too far from the one Ealey will have told them. "My partner at the time mistook my actions and tried to kill me."

"How long ago was that?" the oldest asks.

"I was in the Ceoghast eight days." I have no sense of whether they believe my story or not. My palms are slick with sweat.

"Eight days?" the youngest says. "Light save you."

"It did," I say.

"So it did," the oldest says. She doesn't sound convinced, like my story doesn't add up even in this basic form. I don't want to give her more time to consider it.

"I need your help to take the witch to town," I say. "She's confused, but it won't last."

"Rebounded spell left her simple," the freckled guard says. She's picked up on my story as though she was a witness to it. She lends it weight.

"We can accompany you," the oldest guard says. "How do we contain the witch?"

"She's docile right now, a little disconnected from the world. You should be able to just lead her to a holding cell."

"Lead a witch?" the oldest says.

I don't want them to distress Emathi or hurt her, but my suggestion is too kind to pass muster. "I need you to follow my instructions exactly. She hasn't had fallowfoot to block her magic, so it's important to keep her calm. It's easy right now because she's so confused. She believes…"

"Here." The freckled guard hands me a pinch of fallowfoot. "Can you convince her to eat it?"

I take the herb. Its bitter scent stings my nose, more astringent than I recall. "I can," I say. "Stay here. I'll call you over when it's set."

They speak in hushed tones as I walk away, and I worry they don't believe me. What if they see the holes in my story? The lies are so obvious to me, I don't know how anyone else could believe a word, but I'm in this now and I mean to keep my life.

Emathi glances up when I stand before her. Her rheumy eyes droop with exhaustion. "I can't make it," she says.

"I have help for us," I say. "I have friends who will help you along the way." I shove images of the guard mishandling her out of my mind.

"We just need you to eat this." I hold out of the fallowfoot. "It tastes awful, but it will help your energy."

She takes the herb. "I know this plant."

My heart stutters. If I have to force her to take it, the guards will leap to help. Emathi will be hurt.

"It's my family's custom to eat it," I say. "It's how they welcome visitors."

"I don't remember what it's called."

"That's okay," I say. I won't give her the name in case it jogs her memory. "You just need to eat it so you get your energy back up. Then my friends will take us to town. We're really close."

Emathi places the herb in her mouth. Her face contorts, and I'm afraid she might spit it out. "This is awful," she says.

"If you swallow it, it's better than chewing," I say.

I remember the taste all too well. My father made sure we ate it with every meal. My stomach drops to my feet. Did he know?

Did he think I was a witch and made us eat fallowfoot to block whatever witchcraft might stir in my blood?

I shake my head to lose the thoughts. No. Everyone in Horth kept the custom. He was strict about it because of my mother. We had to keep up every appearance of obedience.

Emathi finishes the herb with a loud noise of distaste. "When will I feel better?" she says.

"Soon. But I'm going to invite my friends over now." I glance at the guards who watch me with expressions I can't read. "They're going to take you to a waiting room. I won't be with you. I have to fetch my family. But I'll be quick and then you can meet them."

"I'm such a mess," Emathi says. "Will I have time to freshen up?"

"You can do whatever you want in the waiting room," I say. The freckled guard begins to walk over with the oldest. I bend close to Emathi. "Don't tell them anything, okay?"

"Who?"

"My friends. They'll be jealous, so don't tell them about the apprenticeship or anything." I want to tell her not to talk to them at all, but the guards reach us.

"Everything all set here?"

I note deference in her voice. For now, they believe me a Lightbearer. The relief I feel is so immense I could cry. "Yes," I say. "She ate the herb."

The oldest guard motions to the other two. "They'll take you to the town council, Lightbearer."

She reaches down and grabs Emathi's bicep. The freckled guard follows suit. "We'll see you in town," the freckled guard says.

Emathi looks over her shoulder at me as the guards drag her away. "Cassia?" she says.

"This way, Lightbearer," the youngest guard says as she comes to stand next to me. She gestures down a different path, one that will take us to Midt's town center.

"Cassia?" Hysteria frays Emathi's voice. I breathe out through my teeth to settle my growing dread and then turn my expression into a smile. It's so forced I must look as manic as I feel, but the guard beside me gives an answering grin.

"Lead the way," I say.

Chapter 36

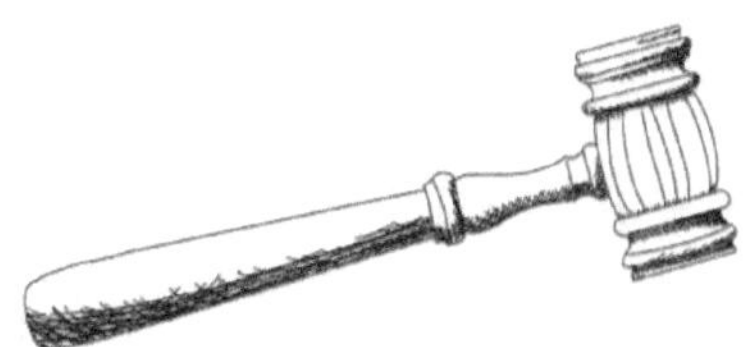

Walking through Midt, homesickness swells in my belly and threatens to overwhelm me. I want to touch every building and kneel to kiss the cobblestones. Yet even as the community's familiarity comforts me, I can't shrug off the dangers present even here. Maybe especially here.

My mouth and throat are dry when I enter town hall and take my seat at the round council table. I'm so scared I don't think my tongue will move enough to answer any of the council's questions. Across from me sit two bearded men who may be brothers. They didn't greet me when I walked in, and they stare at me when they think my attention drifts to other parts of the bland room. I don't have the courage to meet their inquisitive gazes, but I'm aware of every shift they make.

My Lightbearer guise is flimsy, and I wait for the moment they see through me. Two more council members hurry to their seats. Each one tips a nod in my direction, but neither speaks. No one will until the last member arrives. I dig my fingers into my thighs to keep from squirming.

Councils consist of five community members. Only the best and most virtuous people are selected. I sat before such a group after my mother's execution. That council wanted to know if

I was a witch. This one seeks confirmation that I'm actually a Lightbearer.

Another minute drags past. It's hard to hold myself still and upright when every instinct I have screams at me to cower and hide. The door behind me scrapes open. Rushed footsteps jog forward and a woman slides into the last seat. Relief and panic flood me. We are done waiting. Now the interrogation begins.

"Lightbearer, we are sorry for the necessity of this interview," the woman who arrived last says. "It's clear to all of us that Light's blessed you, but we still need to host this meeting. Our apologies."

I freeze in my seat. All desire to fidget gone. Is this a trick? In none of the scenarios I imagined of this moment did I think deference would be the council's tone.

"You have to," I say, awkward as a startled goat. "You, we, have to do what the tenets command."

Except they're not doing that. Not really.

"As you say," the woman says. If she notices my discomfort, she hides it well.

The councilor to her right clears his throat. "I call for the interrogation to begin."

"Seconded," the woman says.

I strangle the moan that fights to rise in me and incline my head in acknowledgement. Better not to speak when I need to pull myself together. If I mess up now, I'm bound for whatever death they deem appropriate. What punishment does one even get for impersonating a Lightbearer?

"Allow me to introduce the councilors, Lightbearer," a man in glasses says. He's so reverent it should be mocking, but he strains his face in his desire to express sincerity. "My name is Willer Carros. I've served on the council for five years after my father retired."

He gestures to the woman who had come in last. "This is Milhewna Laventi. She's served on our council for more than a decade."

Willer continues this way through the remaining three councilors, as though we meet to take tea and not decide my fate. I try to remember all their names: Willer, Milhewna, Russ, Eni, and

Ryder. Their last names and time they've served on the council leave me the second after Willer says them.

He pauses after the last, and I speak into the space. "My name is Cassia Mooseroot."

"Thank you, Lightbearer. We know," Milhewna says.

"We'd like to hear your story," one of the bearded men says. I think his name is Russ, but I'm not confident enough to use it when I reply.

"I can share it," I say.

"Thank you, Lightbearer." He motions to the others around the table. "This is the first time any of us has witnessed a Lightbearer's return after they came to the Light. I'd like you to know what an honor this is."

"Oh," I say. I don't know what to do with the awe he exudes. In no way do I want them to suspect I lie, but I also don't like how docile they are. This should be a proper interrogation per the tenets, and maybe a real Lightbearer would correct them. I won't dare. Despite my unease with their ingratiation, it's to my advantage.

I start exactly as I practiced. "I lived in Midt three weeks before I had my orientation for the border patrol."

"We were given to understand you didn't want the role," Eni says. In another tone, that statement would be the cross-examination I expect of an interrogation, but she speaks with soft encouragement. An invitation to elaborate. Even though it's only been eight days, I don't remember exactly what I said to Niehe, the border patrol leader. I remember how I felt, though.

"I was surprised. I thought it was a simple orientation. I didn't expect Light would grant me so large a role."

Eni nods. Two of the others murmur their understanding. I continue. "My partner and I took one of the quieter routes."

"Ealey," Willer says to the room.

"He's become such a menace," Russ says. "The way he behaved when he came back. It was unbecoming of a good person."

"At least now we know why," Milhewna says. "Please continue, Lightbearer."

Whatever story Ealey shared when he returned changes in their minds as I tell my side of things. I hold no fondness for Ealey, but after this, if the community allows him to stay, his life will be difficult.

"We split up," I say. "I encountered a Ceoghast creature while I was alone."

"Split up?" Ryder, the other bearded man who's been quiet until now, leans into the table and taps it with a forceful hand. "Why was this not reported? No road near the Ceoghast is to be traversed alone. Tenets guard us... The risk to our community... What if this is a common practice we haven't known about?"

"Thank you for bringing this to our attention, Lightbearer," Milhewna says.

"You must know, of course, that we have rules against such risky behavior," Willer says, as though they're the ones under my scrutiny. "We'll launch a full investigation into this. I'll start it myself at daybreak."

I am so uncomfortable with their reactions, I return to my practiced story without any acknowledgement of their concern or promises. My stomach twists as I think of Hum. What must she be doing now? "I began to chase the creature into the Ceoghast — I meant to kill it — when my partner returned and presumed me to be a witch."

"How could he have gotten it so wrong?" Russ says.

"Arrogance." Willer polishes his glasses. "We've seen it before."

"He must have the Ceoghast on him," Eni says.

"I believe he's already on notice," Milhewna says. "But we keep interrupting you, Lightbearer. Please continue."

I want to yell at them. They're supposed to interrupt. They're supposed to ask questions. Their whole purpose is to doubt my story. Instead, they turn on their own community members and let me lie without suspicion. This is better than I'd hoped for, but I hate it. I should have to struggle to convince them of my ridiculous tale. Instead, like overeager puppies at a bowl of warm milk, they lap it up.

"I ran from him, found the creature, and smashed its head in with a rock." This idea I lifted from the story of Lightbearer Lyra who crushed a demon's head between two stones.

"Such a sacrifice. To go into the Ceoghast like that," Eni says.

"I didn't expect to come back." Whatever emotion I put into that line during my practice sessions is gone now. I'm as lively as fallen wood and half-convinced these councilors will believe anything I tell them. "I just thought of Midt, and of the harm that creature would do if I let it get away."

"You were destined for Light," Willer says.

Anger stirs in me, a monster roused from a long, deep sleep. If I were destined for Light, I'd not have to parade through this sham interrogation. I wouldn't have taken up with a witch, saved Hum, or bargained with Knave.

My whole life everyone tried to see the bad in me. Tried to find corruption where none existed. Now, because I glow, all they see is good.

The more they look at me, the cheaper my faith in the tenets becomes. Everything about this feels false, like we're all in on a larger lie together.

"Why didn't you come back right away?" Russ' question cuts through to my sensible side, the part of me that wants to survive this ordeal no matter what.

"I couldn't find my way back."

"It's common," a new voice says as the door opens. "Many a Lightbearer wanders for a long while in the dark places before Light redeems us."

My sharp intake of breath seems a scream in the suddenly silent room. The false Lightbearer, the one I saw bathe in the Ceoghast waters, strides into the room. His poise, confidence, and glow are everything a Lightbearer should possess, but I know his truth.

Which means he can guess mine. He smiles at me like he can read my thoughts.

"Lightbearer Cassia," he says and walks up to my chair to grasp my shoulder. I tense. This is it. He'll expose me, turn me out. I shake beneath his palm. "When I heard I had kin returned from the Ceoghast, I had to come greet you. Your trials were long and hard, but by Light's grace and the tenets' goodness, you're with us again. One of the chosen. I am Lighbearer Erik."

I don't know how to respond. His welcome must be a trick, but I don't see how.

"You honor us with your presence, Lightbearer Erik," Willer says. "My. Two Lightbearers here. This must be good fortune."

"The only fortune one should desire is the fulfillment of the tenets," the Lightbearer says.

Willer flushes at this minor chastisement. "Of course, of course. We have been listening to Lightbearer Cassia's story."

"And what a story," the Lightbearer says. "To lure a witch from the Ceoghast? This is no small task. Even I haven't managed to bring so great a prize. You are to be commended."

I want no praise or acclaim from this fake. He's so lavish in his approval I suspect a trap. Yet he does not expose me as a fraud. Instead, he turns to the councilors. "I inspected the woman Lightbearer Cassia brought from the Ceoghast. She is a witch. All the marks are upon her, so have no doubt."

All the marks. No one ever specifies what those indicators are. What we need to look out for beyond the vague moniker of corruption and decide what those might be in the moment. The only mark I can imagine upon Emathi is age. So few elders remain in our communities — their minds too often slip into the Ceoghast's corruption — but is that even true? What if confusion is just part of being old?

"You've done us a great service," Russ says, ripping me from the broil of doubt that churns my mind.

"Truly, to have two Lightbearers working in tandem to protect the community... It will invigorate our commitment to the tenets." Eni sounds on the edge of unrestrained emotion. "It is, as Russ says, a great service to us."

"What sort of witch is she?" Milhewna says.

"A Heart Witch," I say, though her question may have been for the other false Lightbearer. "She's the Heart Witch of the Ceoghast. She keeps the evil strong. Without her, the Ceoghast will weaken."

My rehearsed lines are vulgar to my ears and the silence
that follows my statement confuses me. Was that what finally read
as a lie to them? The one piece of truth? Are they quiet in disbelief
or understanding? "She lost her mind when she tried to curse me.
Light saved me," I say. I mean to smooth the situation, but I feel
like I'm digging my own grave. And part of me doesn't care.

"By all that's bright," Willer says.

So they believe me. I glance at the Lightbearer. "It will only
last the night," I say. "She won't be in this state after that. She'll be
dangerous. You'll need to confine her."

"We'll deal with her immediately," the Lightbearer says.
"Wake the community, councilors. I'll retrieve the witch myself.
Are you done here?"

The shift happens so fast my mind races to understand
what he's suggested. I'm not ready for them to take action. I need
time to get used to the idea.

"Oh, quite," Willer says. He removes his glasses to rub his
eyes. "It's obvious to all of us this Lightbearer is a child of the
tenets."

"A stoning, then?" Milhewna says.

For a horrible moment, I think she means me. When I
realize she discusses Emathi's execution, my stomach continues to
pitch. No one stones witches. They're meant to be hanged. A
stoning is… I picture the event and start to shake.

"Good enough," Russ says.

"It's always better when the whole community can
participate," Ryder says. "The young ones learn best this way, and
with such a witch, too."

Eni beams at me, all gratitude and pleasure. I wait for
elation to fill me, but my only companion is a cold, growing horror.
I want to warn Emathi. Explain to her what's about to happen. But
this is for the good of Midt, my community. This is what needs to
happen. This is how I stay safe.

"I have clothes you can use, Lightbearer Cassia," Milhewna
says. "You'll be more comfortable in something clean, I'm sure."

I flatten my hands on my thighs to keep them still. "Thank
you," I say.

"We'll convene in thirty minutes," the Lightbearer says. "Get the post ready and I'll bring her up. Unless you want the honor, Lightbearer?"

"No," I say. Too fast, too hard. I scramble to hide my revulsion. "I've had quite enough time with her. I mean, I dragged her here so..."

"I'll take care of it, then."

Maybe I should thank him, but I can't bring myself to do it. Everything feels out of control. I made this plan, and it's gone off without a hitch, but I never really thought it would go this far.

Or maybe I never let myself think this far ahead. If I had, would I have stolen Emathi away from her home? Could I have handed her over to die? I stand and knock into the table in my rush. The councilors look at me with surprise, and I'm afraid of them discovering my lies all over again. Is this what it's going to be like? Me scared one of my community members will learn the truth about me for the rest of my life?

"Oh, Lightbearer Cassia," the Lightbearer says. His casual tone prickles my spine.

"Yes?"

"Your father is here. The town summoned him to answer for your crimes."

The floor tilts beneath me. I grip the table to keep upright, as the roar in my ears blots out all other sounds. "What?"

"We took his statement earlier today," Milhewna says. "I can see now how we prejudiced him against you with how we misunderstood the situation. We'll have to rectify our records once we're done here."

He spoke against me? I wait for shock to accompany the thought but all I feel is a deep knowing, an utter lack of surprise. Of course he did. What wouldn't he do to save himself?

And I already forgive him, because in creating distance from me, in speaking against me while I was gone, he would've protected Katta too.

"My sister?"

"Your father mentioned she'd stayed behind, which is a shame now. How proud she'd be to see you like this," the Lightbearer says. "How proud your father will be."

"We'll have to take another statement," Willer says.

"In the morning, once all this is settled," Milhewna says.

"Yes, we need to act quickly now and put this witch to death," the Lightbearer says. "We don't have much time."

And just like that my sham of an interrogation comes to a close, and we prepare to kill Emathi.

Chapter 37

Milhewna leaves me to dress and make my own way to the town square. "I'd love to escort you, Lightbearer," she says, "but I have to help prepare the stage."

Stage, as though I'm not the only one performing. Milhewna leaves me more clothes to choose from than I've owned in my life. Each piece feels fine and soft. I change into a blouse and skirt, the plainest I can find, and then leave for the square.

The night is cool and carries wood smoke in the air. I correct my posture as I walk. It's hard to hold my shoulders back when I'm used to slinking from one place to another to avoid attention, when I want to avoid my father now more than ever. I worry he'll see through me, that he'll turn others against me.

I sling my shoulders back. I don't have to cower now. For the first time since my mother died, everyone who sees me will know I'm good, that my soul is unblemished. The glow proves it. Even if it's not true Light. My father can't change what's so easily apparent for everyone else to see.

I hesitate as I draw near my destination. My name moves through the crowd like wind through leaves, a rustle in every mouth, and I freeze at the edge of town square. So many people are here they hardly fit. Elbows press into backs and small children sit atop shoulders to avoid being trampled. Even during Horth's Judgement Days we didn't have so big a crowd — and the whole community came to those gatherings. Midt is larger than I thought. So many souls determined to keep our lands safe from the Ceoghast. It's only been an hour since I returned, but everyone is here.

I clutch my skirt to keep my hands still. I should step closer, join my community, but my legs won't move. This feels dangerous. What if I'm not welcome? What if they think I have the Ceoghast on me after all? With so many people, surely one of them will call out my lie.

"She's here!" a voice says, and the people in front become a sea as they bob and sway in an attempt to locate me. My heart sends a sharp jolt to my stomach. I don't want to be found by so many eyes, to have everyone's attention on me. When people look at you, they see all the faults, all the ways you don't measure up to the tenets. A hand on my arm makes me flinch, and it takes all my will not to pull back. I want to jerk away. I want to hide.

"Cassia," the woman says, and my name doesn't sound like my own. Her breathlessness, her awe, it makes my name light and ethereal. It makes me sound holy. "Lightbearer. We've been waiting for you."

All my energy is in coils, twisting and turning my stomach, but her voice soothes me and gives me the courage I need to look at the people who stare at me. My name, whispered in wonder, moves in waves away from me as people catch my gaze. They smile, and for the first time since my mother's execution, I feel safe. Hands reach for me, brush against my clothes, my hair, my arms, my face. This. This is everything I've ever wanted. To belong.

All the years I stood outcast and apart due to the blemishes of others slide off my shoulders like string. Untethered, light — this, I think, is happiness. Safety and belonging. This is what I've worked my entire life to achieve.

My smile is effortless, like my face is unbound by the tension I've always known. I meet every joyful face with my own, and I dip my head to let everyone who reaches out touch and welcome me. The crowd gently pulls me forward, hands soft with reverence, and so I move deeper within the group toward the center of the square.

And that's where I see her.

Emathi still wears the lavender dress she pulled from deep within her closet when I told her I wanted her to meet the rest of my family. She'd wanted to make a good impression. That was so important to her.

The once bright fabric now drips with rotten food and manure. The hand-knit lace and skillfully embroidered skirts are covered with filth — torn and ruined. Emathi's wrinkled face is splotchy and tears run down her swollen and cut cheeks covered in slowing blood. Six ropes bind her arms and legs so tightly she'd not be able to stand if the ropes themselves didn't hold her up. Six of the strongest community members hold the ends and take turns yanking at them to tighten their grips.

Where the ropes touch Emathi's small, withered body, darkness spreads downwards. I remember holding her papery soft hand in my own as I led her here. Her hands are so tiny and frail, her skin so thin. I know the darkness to be blood from the scrapes and cuts. She is small and old and surrounded by people who want her dead. People I brought her to.

I can't do this.

Panic takes hold of me, and I resist the people who urge me forward. This isn't how this is supposed to go. This isn't what an execution should be like. It isn't what I pictured. It's supposed to be neat and painless and not public. I never saw what happened to my mother. Everything was done behind closed doors. Emathi's not supposed to know what's happening.

I want to go back. I want to get away from this and forget I ever saw it, and as I struggle to turn around, Emathi's gaze finds mine.

"Cassia?" she says. Though her sobs hitch on what she says next, I hear clearly every word. "Oh, Cassia. Help me. They're hurting me. Make them stop. Please. I want to go home. Please, Cassia. Take me home. Make them let me go. Please, Cassia. Cassia!"

My ears are too full of the crowd's laughter, high and fast and sharp, for my brain to process what Emathi says. I don't know how to respond to her. I don't know how to fix this. Emathi's lips continue to form pleas as saliva-thinned blood falls to the cobblestones, but the hollers and laughter are all I hear.

"Cassia's not yours!" a voice I know says. I recognize Ealey then. The vine slash Hum gave him the night we met is an angry red scab across his forehead. He's one of the rope bearers and jerks his end to punctuate his speech. "She's one of us!"

"She's a Lightbearer!" another person says from somewhere behind me. "She brought you here to die so evil will be purged from us! You're a blight!"

This statement renews the volleys of filth. Emathi cries out as a hard clump strikes her face. She doesn't lift her head again and instead sobs without control, like a child lost in a grief too great to hold.

The horror that fills me spills onto the square. I crouch and heave and empty my stomach onto the stones. This is what I wanted. Acceptance and protection from the communities that had held me in contempt all my life. I have it now. I'm welcome and wanted and respected. And none of that is due to committing my entire life to the tenets. It's not the result of hard work and obedience. None of that matters.

All these people care about is that I have a glow and brought them a person to hate and kill. That's what they want. The community defines itself by what it is not. It is not evil. It is not the Ceoghast. It is not different. To be good we follow the tenets and keep the community's beliefs. We put in the same hard work, and we watch for evil in the same way. We watch for anything that is not like us, and when we find that outsider, that difference, that variation we perceive to threaten our existence, we kill it.

My arms shake. What am I supposed to do? I don't want Emathi to be in pain. I don't want her to die. Why did I bring her here? How did I not think this through? We could have stayed in the Ceoghast. If I hadn't been so focused on coming back — on this foolish idea of coming back to Midt and being forgiven — I would have seen the home and community that welcomed me in the Ceoghast. I wouldn't have left Hum.

The sudden rustling around me sounds like the hisses of a hundred snakes as the people of Midt pull stones from their pockets. Each person seems to have a preferred style: sharp and jagged, flat and round, big and heavy. How often have they done this that they've worked out such personal taste? Crouched on the ground, surrounded by a community keen on murder, I'm more scared now than I ever was in the Ceoghast.

"Lightbearer Cassia?" a small girl says beside me. Curled as I am, we are about the same height. She is young with wide eyes and a shy smile. "Where are your rocks?"

"I don't have any." My mouth tastes like acid. "I didn't know..."

Didn't know what? That I'd brought Emathi here to die? That I'd kidnapped a kind and generous old woman, one who welcomed me into her home and made a place for me in the Ceoghast, so I could earn a place among people who will turn on me if it suits their needs?

Dread skitters up my throat. That could be me up there. Even now, as a Lightbearer, I am not safe. If I stand out, speak out, walk out, I will no longer belong. I will be out. Even this little girl could judge me unworthy and I'd be gone from the grace I've found.

"You have to bring your own rocks to a stoning," the girl says. "Everyone knows that. Did you already throw them? We're supposed to wait, you know."

"I didn't know," I say. "I thought... Isn't there time still?" My thoughts feel trapped in a too-small room. I have no way to speak on Emathi's behalf. They've hosted no trial. Even if they did, would they listen to me?

Surely I have some power. I'm a Lightbearer now. I can find the right way of explaining this. I can tell them Emathi can be rehabilitated and saved. We could get the Ceoghast off her. She could live here and...

And what? Spend her days under the suspicion and hate of an entire community? Feel friendless and alone? Be removed from a world that not only makes sense to her but also loves her?

No. She can't stay here, so I'll convince them to let her go. I'll have to. I have no idea what I'll say, but I can speak up for her if we have a trial. I'll figure out how to keep us both safe.

I stand, and the girl pushes a hard object into my clenched fist. "You can have one of mine," she says, "But don't throw it early, okay? It's my special rock. It helped kill that last witch, so it'll help kill this one, too."

"But we should have a trial?" I say. "I'm a Lightbearer. I've seen the Ceoghast. They'd want me to testify."

"I told you." The girl pulls another rock from her pocket to replace the one she gave me. "Ceoghast creatures don't get a trial. We just kill them. Why would we listen to anything an evil creature wants to say?"

"I want to say something," I say.

"Oh, you'll speak after. It's the Lightbearer's job to tell us when we've piled on enough stones to break the body after the stoning ends." The girl frowns, and the suspicion that crosses her face ties my stomach into knots. Not this. I don't want to be outcast again.

"Don't you know all this?" she asks.

"Yes, I..." I what? Changed my mind? "I'm just excited and forgot."

The weight of her judgment doesn't shift but the girl says, "I guess that makes sense. Remember don't throw your rock until it's time."

I glance around to see how many people witnessed our exchange, but it's like I don't even exist. Everyone's focus is on Emathi.

The first stone hits her knee, and she yells in pain and surprise. The crowd inhales as one. Their faces twist into wild grins that would be better suited to the turnips and pumpkins in Jack's Patch.

Another rock, small but fast, strikes her throat. I hear a wet gasp and gurgle from Emathi's mouth and shove through the crowd to the square's center before my brain catches up with my body. My hands stretch toward the community members I'd wanted to please more than anything, and I shout, "Stop!"

If joy marked their expressions before, fury clouds them now, and I realize even my title of Lightbearer will not protect me from their rage if I side with Emathi. In a community taught to shun and hate anyone different, any defense or plea I make to save her will turn them against me, too. But as I rush toward Emathi, who gasps quietly like a fish stuck on shore, I know where I stand.

I've focused on being accepted by the wrong people my entire life. I've followed tenets that taught me to hate myself. I spent every day trying to work harder to prove to people who don't care about me that I'm good and that I matter. So wrapped in prejudice for anything that wasn't the perfection of the tenets, I lied to one of the first and only friends I've ever had, and worse, planned her murder.

This stops now. If being an upstanding community member means killing a person who tried to help me, I want no part in this. My mother already paid that price, and she shouldn't have. For the first time in my life, I know where I belong.

"Emathi," I say, "I'm so sorry. I'm going to take you home."

Her eyes, sharp and beady, lock on mine. "You stupid woman."

Shock roots me in place before her. "Emathi?"

The air around us grows heavy, and the ropes that hold her loosen. I glance at the guards whose job it is to keep her bound. Mouths slack, they seem wholly unaware. The crowd around us seems frozen.

Heart magic.

With a cry, Emathi sinks to her knees. "Do you see where your mousing gets you?" she says. "I wanted to stop this cycle." Blood drips from her lips. She shakes out of the ropes that hold her.

I want to ask her how she can work her magic when she ate fallowfoot. I want to cry with relief. The desire to know how long we have to escape rises up in me. Apologies press at my mouth. I shove all these urges aside. "We need to leave," I say. "How long can you..."

"We don't leave from this."

"We can't stay. They'll..."

"Help me up." Her voice is strained, a wetness clings to each word. "I can't hold them back and do everything."

I wrap my arms about her and lift her up. She places a hand on my shoulder to steady herself. "Can you walk?" I say. It's a stupid question. She can barely stand, and who knows how long she can hold the hearts of everyone here. In the corner of my eye, Ealey twitches, his hand tightening on the rope.

"It shouldn't be like this, but here we are. I wanted it to be different," she says. "This is how we all come to it."

"Come to what?"

"Come into our own."

She slaps her gnarled hand against my chest then curls her fingers into my flesh. I scream as the skin over my chest splits like overripe fruit. Hot blood runs down my stomach, into my belly button. I reach for her hand, but muscle and bone within my chest snap open like an elastic band, and the cold wind that rushes inside me blacks my vision. My body freezes, held in a chrysalis of pain. Her fingers wrap around my heart and squeeze. I cry at the pressure and scream again as spikes of pain race up my neck and down my arms.

Emathi pulls her hand back, and I collapse on the ground. Every breath hurts, and I grab at my chest to hold the most inner parts of myself in. But my scrabbling fingers find no bloody hole, no gaping wound. Only the blouse torn open over smooth skin. Like blind ants my fingertips search for the opening. Under the luminance of my glow, my chest is a tapestry of dark, angry bruises.

Emathi's words hiss by my ringing ears.

"What?" My voice croaks. Tears slip down my nose.

"You'll need a jar," she says.

The world jolts into movement. The moment her heart magic fails, the crowd takes a sharp inhalation, and panic seizes me. We were supposed to get out. We weren't supposed to be here.

Emathi sinks next to me. The little time she bought for us is gone. Murmurs rise as people regain awareness and control of themselves. The confusion will not keep. I have to move now. I have to stop this.

I stand and hold out my hand, bright with the Lightbearer's luminance. I raise my voice so everyone in the square will hear. "You will not kill her. You will not..."

My tongue falls leaden in my mouth. In the crowd, my father's black eyes glare at me. He's seen what I've done.

"Father...."

He hefts a rock black as night, and I reach for him, though I don't know if I mean to block the rock or ask him for help. From the corner of my eye, a terrible darkness rushes at me, but not until the rock hits me in the face do I realize I'm too late.

My chance to save Emathi is over.

And I've lost.

Chapter 38

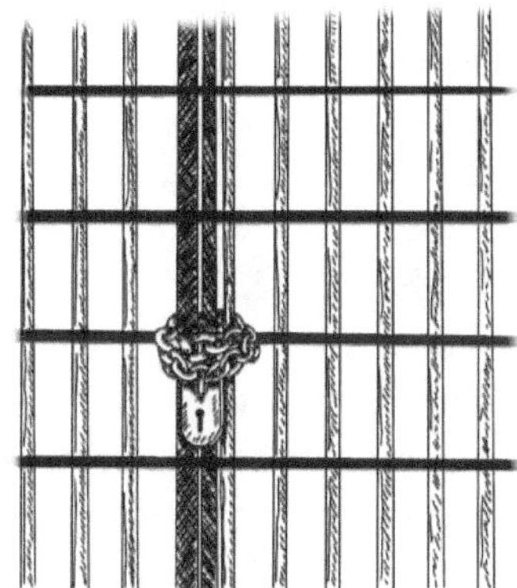

The floor is cold and wet beneath me, and for a moment I wonder if I lie on the rock that hit me. The thought is hard to hold. It slips away. The world sloshes. Darkness crowds in.

I wake many times but never stay in the room long. And it is a room. That much I work out and start to remember. Daylight doesn't reach this place, but noise from the morning makes its way down to me. My glow gives off all the light I need to see my surroundings. Stone floor, iron bars, and four walls I can touch at the same time. It has to be a cell.

When thoughts of Emathi come to me, I cry, which sends bolts of pain down my neck and makes me feel worse. I try not to think of her. I try not to think at all. My chest throbs. The skin where Emathi tried to tear my heart out has become a squishy welt. I close my eyes and wait for unconscious to take me again.

"Get up," a man says. I've heard him before, but I can't place the voice. I open my eyes and ease into a seated position. The room slides into place. My head feels fragile, like even my heartbeat might shatter it.

Three people stand on the other side of the iron door: the Lightbearer, the councilor with glasses, and the border guard leader

I met the night I went out for border patrol. None of their names come to me, but I'm certain I knew them once.

"Where's Emathi?" I say.

"The witch is dead," Lightbearer Erik replies.

My heart twists. Dead. Emathi is dead. I killed her. A low moan wheezes through my lips, and nausea bucks in my stomach. I start to curl onto my side but the throb of my head holds me still.

"We are here to try you for witchcraft and the impersonation of a Lightbearer," the man says.

The accusation seems too small to matter in light of the greater evil I've committed. They've missed the point. They don't see my true crime. "Witchcraft," I say.

"You enchanted us to make us believe you good," he says.

How quickly they can convince themselves of whatever fits their worldview with the most ease. Relief diminishes my anxiety. I'm evil in their eyes and in my own. I don't have to pretend anymore. I don't have to be what they think is nice and good.

"You did that on your own." My tongue feels fuzzy, so I scrape at it with my fingernails. "All it took was the glow."

The Lightbearer stiffens at this. Maybe he knows his secret isn't safe with me anymore.

"How did you trick us?" the border guard says.

I want to answer her, but my tongue is disgusting. My fingernails come away green. "Oh," I say. I should have recognized its bitter flavor. "Fallowfoot. That's smart."

"How did you trick us?" she says, louder this time.

I wipe my fingernails on the skirt Milhewna lent me and raise my eyebrows at the Lightbearer. "Magic," I say.

"You confess," the man in glasses says.

I sigh, tired to my bones and rest my head against the wall. This is the worst place I've ever been — a place I worried my whole life I'd end up. I'm in front of people who want me dead.

And yet I'm not interested in their opinions about me. I don't want to impress them. I have no interest in trying to please this community.

I feel free.

"You don't need to try me," I say. "I confess to it all. I'm not a Lightbearer. I've cast spells more than once. And if I belong anywhere, it's in the Ceoghast."

I wish I'd realized that sooner. I could have avoided all of this. And Emathi... I swallow hard as the fallowfoot's bitter sting rises in my throat. I can't think of her just now. Not yet. It's too much.

"We should go," Lightbearer Erik says. "We have a confession. Her father already spoke against her. No sense in listening to whatever evil this thing wants to speak."

His disdain revives my habitual fear, my need to fit in. My mind scrambles for ways to show them I'm good, but I dismiss them all. The time for that is past. I'm done with it.

"She needs to understand the severity of her crimes," the man in the glasses says.

"I understand what I've done. I've spent my whole life under the tenets." I take a breath to steady the throb in my head. "I endangered the community. I consorted with evil creatures. I even made friends with one and named her. I cast magic more than once. I brought a witch into town and tried to save her. I'm sorry I didn't succeed." Despair chokes my words and I have to force my way through. "I don't want to be like you. I don't want to belong here. Everything you consider good hurts any person who's different. You think it's okay to kill people because they don't live up to your impossible standards. Even my father thinks it's okay to kill me."

"That's quite enough," the border guard says. Niehe. Her name is Niehe. She grabs the man in glasses by the arm and turns to leave.

"It's not even close to enough." I struggle to my feet but only get partway up. I lean against the wall. "You killed a helpless old woman who was kind to me, and that's my fault. If you execute me for anything, it's going to be for that. She deserved so much better."

"You will die for being the festering evil you are," Niehe says.

"Go." Lightbearer Erik steps in front of them and blocks my view. "I will finish here."

"You should be ashamed of yourself," the bespeckled man says.

"I am ashamed. I'm ashamed of what I did to Emathi!" Pain pierces my chest so sharp I look down to see if one of them shot me, but all I see is the swelling wound beneath my torn blouse. Tears run down my face. "And Hum. I hurt her, too."

"Let's go," Lightbearer Erik says. "We've seen enough."

Niehe, the man, and Lightbearer Erik head for the door. I sink to the floor and cover my face to cry.

"You're going to pay," Niehe says. She stands by the door. "You think you can march into my town and make fools of us? Cast doubt on our security?"

Anger flickers in my chest. She wants to cow me with her threats. But I'm beyond them now. I know who I am, and even if I never make it back, I know where I belong.

"It was easy," I say. "And you can threaten me all you want. I'm not afraid of you."

"You will be when I pour the spiders down your throat," she says. "I'll see you in the square."

Spiders? I open my mouth to ask what she means, but the door slams shut. Is this how they kill people like me? Spiders? I try to picture it for a moment, being held while spiders crawl down my throat, but then I realize I've seen this before. The cobweb woman. She did say she was a warning. Am I to become like her? Spiders roiling in my belly long after death? Or did she die that way? Perhaps these people killed her too.

Exhausted, I ease onto my side and curl into a protective ball. My eyes are an endless hot well. This is the worst that can happen, and now that my end is here, it's almost liberating to be at the bottom. To be resigned to what's coming.

I won't see Katta again, but I think my bold, smart sister would approve of my courage, if nothing else. She was never one to back down from a fight, even when it was in her interest.

I try to picture her face, but my focus frays. I left her portrait in Milhewna's room. I thought I could go back for it. I thought so many things. So many stupid things. I shouldn't have come back from the Ceoghast.

Chapter 39

I cry until I have no more tears, until lightning bolts of pain threaten to split my skull in two. The tears are not for me. They're for Emathi. For failing to help Emathi. Regret whips at me with a steady, focused hand. To make amends, the tenets counsel surrender, to attempt to salvage what I can of my soul. If I want to live by them even now, the only role left to me in this community is to accept my death at their hands.

But I have no intention of dying here.

I pinch my swollen eyes closed and listen as I did when I held the speckled hound pumpkins. What answer I expect, I can't say, but when a sound stirs from inside my body, I nearly pull back.

There, deep within my stomach, the fallowfoot I'd been fed while unconscious giggles like a child spent after a good game. At first I want to scream at this invasion, but then...

I prod at it, and it swats away my intrusion. Settled within me, it means to have its fun. It doesn't feel so different from the pumpkins, though it marks no beat I might change. I feel its heart and know how to stop its interference with my magic.

My magic...

For all I've shunned this community of Light, it's a far reach to embrace this dark. Even if it doesn't feel evil. I managed to convince myself of innocence before. Tell myself it wasn't real magic, just luck or coincidence, and something I ought not examine too closely.

This is different.

Hush, little herb. It's time to rest.

Stubborn as a toddler, the fallowfoot rails against me, but loses to the weight of sleep when I adjust its heart. Just... so.

With it dormant, my power expands, full as a long deep breath after short, shallow sips of air. I sit in the roiling waves, match my breath to its lunge and heave. Am I really this? Is this what I want?

I want to live.

I pull until the magic drifts out and down. So little lives here. The bone white ground starved any plant that might grow here long ago. Yet deep within the earth, roots the Lightbearers couldn't drain reach toward me as my mind drifts past. They are too small and too stunted to help me. They need my help instead.

The tentative brushes remind me of Hum. I lose the connection at the thought and tumble back into sorrow. Back into the cell and its too close walls.

Above me, feet walk across the floor. I shove my emotions aside and listen to the plants again. I skip past the roots and go farther and deeper until a shadow tugs my mind into the Ceoghast. My magic thrums along the endless dark, unable to find any walls or wells. It is endless. Abundant.

Darkness coils about me and sighs like a cat contented with its prey. So much life burgeons within it. How did I ever set foot there without being overwhelmed by the magnitude? By the endless voices?

The Ceoghast's pull is like a warm blanket on a cold day. It makes promises of comfort and security, if you don't mind the wickedness and dangers.

I pull back, and it scrambles after me.

Yes. This.

Come find me, I say. With the invitation, I stir the plants along the Ceoghast paths to wake and stretch. To move.

Then I return to the cell.

A mob gathers outside, loud enough to echo in my cell. I seek them as I sought the Ceoghast, and their hearts pound into sharp relief.

They are more complicated than the plants. Not one person possesses clarity or focus. Their emotions are so layered it's impossible to separate one feeling from the next. And it is all feeling, no thoughts, and stirred to extremes. Each person clutches at what is easy — hate, fear, malice — and ignores the nuances of their emotions.

I can yank the layers up. I can change their hearts...

But I never wanted anyone to touch mine.

I let them go and return to my cell. Just because I have that power to manipulate them doesn't mean I have the right. I may have strayed from the tenets and abandoned my community, but I will not abuse people.

A bolt-lock slams. The stairs beyond my cell take on an iridescent glow.

"Hello, Lightbearer," I say.

He enters the hall before my cell without the pomp he displayed earlier. Hesitancy guards his approach, and he watches me as one watches a snake ready to strike. Our places could be reversed. He is no more a Lightbearer than I.

"They'll come for you soon," he says. "You don't have long."

"I don't intend to be here." Already, the Ceoghast feels closer. "But I'd like to leave without hurting anyone."

"I'm afraid that won't happen."

I'm not daunted. "It will if you help me."

"As I said, that's not going to happen."

Nausea crests and falls as I gather my thoughts. "I know your secret," I say. "I saw you bathe in the pool."

"You took my knife," he says, nonplussed.

His indifference riles me. "Actually, my Jack took your knife. She's fond of playing tricks." The hard edge of my words keeps my tears away. When he lifts his eyebrows in surprise, I feel a small, petty triumph.

"I'll expose you," I say. "You're no more of a Lightbearer than I am."

"I am, actually," he says. "And I'd intended to take you back with me to make you a real one, too."

Uncomplicated truth rests in his heart. I choke out a laugh. "You're not. I know where you get your glow. You're not a Lightbearer."

He glances behind him when my voice pitches up. He is afraid. "Look, I am a Lightbearer, but none of us glow. That's a myth we've been forced to take on, and the pool serves that purpose."

If not for my touch on his heart, I'd call him a liar, but what he says is again true. Or at least true to him. "I'll tell them. I'm proof enough such a pool exists."

He shakes his head. "That won't help you escape. No one here will let you go, and no one's going to listen to you either."

"Which is why I need your help." I point in the direction of the Ceoghast. "It's coming for me. The Ceoghast. I've called the road here."

Alarm crosses his features. He opens his mouth to speak, but I cut him off. "I don't know what creatures are on it, or what else might follow the path it makes."

"Are you mad? You're bringing the Ceoghast here?"

"I told you. I won't stay here."

"Do you have any idea how many people could die?"

"That's why I need your help. I need you to be a real Lightbearer and keep your people safe. Keep them away from me and the road."

His face is unreadable, but his heart flutters like a trapped bird. "You're lying. Why would you want to save them? They're going to kill you."

My frustration builds until I want to scream in his face. "Why would I want them to die? I grew up in a community. I lived in this one. I may not want to be a part of it anymore, but that doesn't mean I want to kill them."

He doesn't move. Above us, the muted crowd noise shifts. Cries punctuate the rising murmurs.

"Here comes the Ceoghast," I say. "Right to your front door. Right down here if you don't let me out."

"You can't leave it here. The Ceoghast. If I let you out, you have to take it away." Sweat beads his forehead. He believes me now. I grapple for satisfaction, but all I feel is spent. "The moment you leave, it goes too."

I'm not sure if I can convince all the plants along the Ceoghast road to retreat, but I nod my head. The headache crashes against the back of my eyes, and I wince.

The Lightbearer approaches the cell door. "You can't hurt any of us."

How odd to be a threat, especially when I feel this awful. His fear seems comical. "You have to keep them away. Do that, and no one will get hurt," I say.

The lock clicks open. The Lightbearer flees.

I rest a moment. The road's not here yet and movement hurts. In this state, I'll not move quickly along the road. I need the Lightbearer to keep his promise. If he doesn't... I brush the hearts above me. I'll change them if it means my life.

I leave the cell in an undignified crouch. An upright posture invites too much nausea. Each stair is a silent torment, and by the time I reach the top, the road is close. I put my ear to the door, as much to rest as to listen, and push it open. The jail office is empty. I shuffle to the exterior door.

Outside Lightbearer Erik shouts instructions to a frazzled crowd and ushers them away from the jail. People shout about the darkening dirt, but none of them mention me. They think me contained, and a larger threat approaches. The door resists until I put my whole weight into it, then it swings open on well-oiled hinges. I step outside and the ground darkens beneath my feet.

The Ceoghast is almost here.

Which means this is it. I'm bound for evil and gone from what I thought was bright and good. I may have judged every person in the crowd ignorant for the hidden layers in their hearts, but I hardly know my own. Doubt hounds me. Can I really do this?

That's when my gaze stumbles on Emathi's crumpled corpse.

A wail splits the air, and I'm slow to recognize it as my own.

Too slow.

"The witch!" The mob shifts. Lightbearer Erik tries to call them back, but they see me. Even with the approach of the Ceoghast road, I'm the more immediate threat.

But then it's here. Right at my feet. A black ribbon of Ceoghast dirt suffuse with plants on either side. "Aren't you clever," I say, and I mean it. It found me. It shakes through me like a dog pleased with itself.

I glance at Lightbearer Erik who's forced his way through the mob and stands before them. "Form a line," he says. "Don't touch the plants. We can't let her through." As though I'd want to go that way.

The mob rushes to follow his instructions. A few people carry household implements — knives, pitchforks, scythes, and heavy pans — and stab them in my direction. A weak keep-back sort of warning.

I step onto the road. Magic wells within me, so playful and uplifting I think I may fly. Joy sparks in my heart as it reduces my pain, and all around me those stunted roots I'd felt earlier burst from the ground.

"Stay back!" Lightbearer Erik says. "Those plants are poisonous." The crowd doesn't need the warning. Terror holds them. Even the bravado of borderland dwellers has its limits.

Even I recoil. Not for what they are — for I know them now better than I did the first time I saw them. These beautiful, complicated, scaly plants with bulbous heart-shaped flowers. I stand in a patch of Evil's Triumph. The same plant my mother summoned to kill me. But now I know them, and that knowledge is painful and freeing.

These plants are better-called Heart's Joy, and my mother was not the one who called them up so many years ago.

I was.

She died to keep me safe, and my father watched me eat fallowfoot every day afterwards to sever my connection to the Ceoghast. So I would never know.

He knew and never told me.

She's dead because of me, and because I didn't know — because I was so afraid of my own truth — I killed Emathi too.

It's too much.

I want to fall to my knees and scream or turn on the mob and rip out each of their throats. But neither of those acts renders me safe.

I reach out and pick one of the Heart's Joy flowers. These flowers feel as much a part of me as my breath and body. Each one's roots go down so deep, like the veins of a body, connected to the Ceoghast but also to me. A living part of my soul. I tuck the bloom in my blouse. I then walk along the dark dirt road to Emathi's body. I use the remains of her once beautiful dress to wipe her face, then bundle her in the fabric.

I lift Emathi's corpse over my shoulder and begin the long walk home.

Chapter 40

The Ceoghast road takes me the most direct route back to its border, but with what remains of Emathi over my shoulder, the walk is long and hard. When I reach the foot of the tree-lined path where the cobweb woman used to stand watch, my legs give out. I fall forward, and Emathi's corpse tumbles onto the ground. I heave deep breaths that would be sobs if I had the energy.

"What are you doing here?"

I lift my head. Knave storms toward me, not quite as they were when I left. Their beauty is undiminished, but their humanity has ebbed. They tower on spindly legs no longer human in shape or height and move with an arachnid's rush. Their hands curl into clawed fists, and when they speak, the sibilant words squeeze through a mouthful of needle-like teeth. I recoil from them, try to pull Emathi's body out of their way.

"Why are you back?" they say.

"I couldn't stay." I'm too tired to respond to their anger, and I left fear in the cell when I decided to escape, but their transformation sends shudders through my limbs. They are wholly themselves, a creature of nightmare, and more beautiful than ever before.

"You need to go back. We have a bargain," they say.

Not even for the promise of Katta's company would I return tonight. I value my life too much, but more than that, I want nothing to do with the communities I left behind. I don't want to see them, or hear their tenets, or feel their drained earth beneath my feet. "No."

"You don't have a choice. We made a deal, Miss Mooseroot. You must honor it." Their words stir the Ceoghast, and it begins to push me out in the same way it had once pulled. "You're the anchor. Go do your job."

A tiny flutter tickles my neck, and I remove the Heart's Joy flower from my blouse. It's flattened, but still alive, still connected to the larger plant I left behind.

I offer it to Knave. "I won't go back, but this is my flower. Take it instead."

Knave slaps the flower from my hand. "You think a flower replaces the life I need to leave this place?"

"That flower is as much a part of me as my hair. I called it from the ground in Midt and gave it life. It's my Heart's Joy. Let it be the anchor you need. The rest of it still grows in Midt."

The flower has to work. Knave can't make me go back, not even if the bargain continues to reshape the Ceoghast to push me out. I'll fight Knave if that's what it takes to stay, though I don't expect to come out well from the conflict.

"You are the anchor, Miss Mooseroot." Their needle teeth flash in the moonlight.

"And enough of my heart is in the plants I left behind to guide you there." They're full of my joy — surely that is enough to free Knave. "But you have to go now. The townspeople will burn the flowers after they drain the ground again."

"Now? I was to have time."

"You wanted time, but this is it. This is how you leave. Time wasn't part of the bargain."

Knave snarls but snatches up the flower. Their face softens for a moment, as though they, too, listen for its heart. "This is enough for a bridge," they say. "I will go, but you will still owe me a favor, Miss Mooseroot."

"No. This is it. After you leave, we're done." I won't let them take advantage of me. Our bargain was a safe way out of the

Ceoghast for me, and a favor in return for them. "The bridge is your favor. Take it and go."

Knave tilts their head, their eyes hold none of the monster apparent in the rest of their body. "You've changed, Miss Mooseroot. I think I preferred your mousey ways."

My laugh is more a cough, strangled in my too hoarse throat. "I didn't."

Knave examines the flower before they tuck it into their dark hair. Even transformed as they are, sharp and spindly and edged in razored angles, their beauty leaves me breathless. They walk past me with a smirk, as though they know my thoughts, and slip into an Eldritch Way.

The Ceoghast relaxes, no longer the enforcer of a bargain not kept, and I vow I'm done with unstated favors, no matter how desperate I get. And it's likely desperation is about to be a regular companion of mine.

I fold my legs beneath me and settle on the road to gather my strength. I cast my gaze up the hill ahead. "Hum?"

Tucked behind a tree off the path, Hum crouches low. I'm so relieved to see her, I hop to my feet. "Hum."

She gives a short growl. I'm neither welcome nor wanted. New tears spring to my eyes. She's here, though. That has to mean I might have a chance to heal the rift between us. Or maybe she has nowhere else to go.

Nowhere but Jack's Patch.

I'm about to call for her to come, then reconsider. The work is mine to do. My knees and back protest as I climb the hill, and my head begins to ache again. I shuffle my way up. Hum's growls turn into snarls as I draw near, and I stop before I reach her to give her space between us. I am so happy to see her. I want to make things right again.

She's made herself so small it's hard to make out her face. I'm tempted to crouch but don't want her to feel crowded.

"Hum, I'm so sorry." My apology is weak in the face of all the pain I caused, but it's a start. "Everything I did was stupid and selfish. I shouldn't have… I should never have left you."

Her growl is both warning and threat and chills my marrow. With the bond between us fractured, she's free to hurt me if she wants. For a moment I don't see my friend. She's a Ceoghast creature as wild and unpredictable as any other monster I could encounter here.

Except, I know her. I love her. And I owe her an apology. "If you let me, I want to earn your trust and friendship again. I want…"

Hum crawls out from behind the tree. I gasp. Her face is cut and battered like she beat herself with her own limbs. Her body is torn. Stalks hang half-shredded from what remains of her arms and legs.

I did this to her. This is my fault. "You deserved so much better. I'm so sorry I wasn't the person you needed me to be. I can…"

She lashes out at me. Her broken stalks whip against my skin. I fall, and she races forward. Angry shrieks fill the air as she rails against me. I don't try to stop her. I don't know how to fix this. I don't know how to heal her broken heart.

But where the first lash cut, those that follow are the angry hammerings of a child. Each one hurts, but they're not meant to maim me.

After a while, she rolls away with a moan and wraps her stalks about herself. I uncurl from my fetal position. When she doesn't react to my movement, I sit next to her.

The sadness between us threatens to drown us both. Hum always brightened my mood when we were together, but now that role falls to me. I don't know any songs that aren't based on the tenets, so I sing nonsense words to a tune similar to one Hum once sang to me.

I run through it three times before Hum shifts. She chirps a correction at me. I repeat the part with the proper note. She corrects me again a few lines later. I make that change, too.

She lifts her head, dissatisfied with my performance, and hums the line herself. I do my best to mimic her, but even to my untrained ears, my attempt is flat. She snorts disapproval but doesn't disappear into her coils.

"I have to bury Emathi," I say after a while. "I thought I'd live in the cottage until I figure out where I can live here and how to get by." The next part is hard to share. I'm so scared. If she

rejects me, I don't know that I'll ever recover from the loss or find
a way to forgive myself. "I want to make this whole thing up to
you. Will you come with me? I'll take care of you the best I can,
and I won't hurt you again. Not ever."

Hum's whistle isn't enthusiastic, but it's a start. I stand and
offer a hand to help her up. She takes it and stretches onto her
tattered legs. I glance back down the road. "I have to take Emathi's
body with us. It needs to go back to Speckled Hound Hollow. I let
people kill her. I thought..." I shake my head. "I thought too many
dumb things."

Hum follows me down the hill. Both of us are stiff. I bend
to lift Emathi, but Hum stops me with a touch. She wraps her
stalks about Emathi, then stands with the corpse cradled to her
chest.

I reach out to the plants along the Ceoghast road and ask
them to take us to the cottage. I walk in front, all too aware that
while the earth-bound plants deign to work with me, not all
Ceoghast creatures will look on me with courtesy. This may be the
home I've chosen, but that doesn't make it safe or kind.

The road ends at a hollow, but not one I recognize. This is
a crater dark with a rot so thick it's sludge. I don't understand
where we are until a pair of nyxies skitters by us.

A square of collapsed stone marks the place where
Emathi's cottage once stood. On the far edge of the clearing, three
pumpkins crumple in on themselves, a brown sludge leaking from
their concavities. Next to them lies Emathi's apron, covered in dirt
and rot.

This is Speckled Hound Hollow, or what remains of it. The
magnitude of the damage I've done hits me on a wave of fatigue.
Hum chirps, a question to which I don't have an answer. I'd
thought to bury Emathi in the hollow, but now...

The words come to me now, and this time, I don't hesitate
to speak them. "This is my home. My place of sanctuary. You are
not welcome. Leave now and never come back."

The nyxies shriek and scatter. I watch them go and wonder
if it will be enough to keep this place safe. "We'll bury her here." I
gesture to the lip where Emathi's boundary had once stood. Close
enough to mark the hollow, but not covered in the nyxies' rot.

Hum sets Emathi's body down nearby, and with my hands, I begin to dig.

Chapter 41

I try not to use magic, but as I dig in the ground near so many plants, it becomes as hard as not breathing. I warn roots to move out of the way and accept help from curious grasses and hardy tubers. Still, hours pass before I have a hole that will hold Emathi's remains.

When Hum brings me a handful of candy corn, I shovel the whole of it into my mouth without checking for teeth. My stomach groans in appreciation and complaint. It's not the most satisfying meal, but I don't know where or how to find food here yet. When I back away from the hole, Hum lowers Emathi's body inside. Together, we fill the grave with dirt.

I have no words for a service. I left those ceremonies behind in Midt. I don't know what Emathi, day or night, would have wanted said or shared. The realization makes me sad. I never really knew her. To speak of her myself, to remember her the way the dead deserve to be honored, is too hypocritical for me to consider.

She deserved so much better than this. Her death hangs about me like a tangible weight. What is left when all you can say or do fails to make any of this okay or right?

I bury my hand in the grave dirt and ask the speckled hound pumpkins to grow here. Not a single spark of life stirs. The pumpkins won't come. I stretch my senses into the ground and ask what will.

Tiny green shoots push from the ground and blossom with heavy-headed blue flowers that drip down like tears. The plant whispers its name: Heart's Sorrow. These flowers will guard the grave from nyxies, keep it safe and whole, a memorial Emathi shouldn't have needed. Exhausted, I remove my hand and sit back. Hum settles across from me. Silence, comfortable and companionable, stretches between us.

I have no home. No food. No friends. No real knowledge of the Ceoghast. But I have a chance to heal my relationship with Hum, and right now, that's as much of a foundation as I need.

"I'm sorry, Hum. For everything." I wave my hand through the air to capture all my misdoings past and present.

Hum sighs a single note. It's less chilly than her chirps have been. Hope nestles in my chest, quiet and sweet.

"I don't know what to do, and I don't have a plan. You should probably know that. This was as far as I had thought ahead. Get to the cottage."

Some plan. I didn't know what nyxies could do, and even if I had, they'd not crossed my mind at all. Hum picks at the grave dirt. Her hunch suggests she's as tired as I am. We need a place to stay.

"We could go to the swamp witch's homestead," I say. It's the only other place I know, and without Emathi, no one else is around to take care of it.

Hum's shrug is noncommittal. I don't blame her. There's not much to the idea. "The homestead needs a caretaker. Emathi promised to look after it, so it's my responsibility now."

Hum shifts with discomfort, then stands. The sight of her wounded legs sends a stab of pain through me. I've given her nothing to trust. Not yet.

"I'll look after you like I always should have." I stand to face her. "I'll treat you like family, because that's what we should be, Hum, family. I'm going to need a lot of your patience, and probably your help. I have no idea what I'm doing or how to live here, but I'll work hard to figure it out as fast as I can."

Hum gargles appreciation for the idea, and a small purple light sparks off her stamens.

"Will you come with me, Hum?" That's all I can say. The lump in my throat is too big to speak around. I clench my teeth to keep my chin from quivering.

When Hum whistles agreement, relief winds around my heart.

I reach out to her, but pain spears through my chest and forces me onto all fours. I lift my hand to the wound to assuage the hurt. A bulbous, wet lump meets my palm. I stop breathing, hoping somehow my stillness will make this better.

I try to push the protuberance back into my chest, but the squish shrieks through my whole body and nausea burns my throat. The bulb slips, oozes as my chest gapes open. I cradle it in my shaking hand as though I hold an injured bird. The pain stops.

My heart is the ugliest, slimiest hunk of blue-red meat I've ever held. It beats my panic against my palm. I jab at my chest with my free hand, try to find the hole it came from, but my flesh is smooth and unbroken. My vision sparks black at the edges, and I try to take deep breaths.

Hum chatters a question, but I can't move. Horror holds me too tight. She slips her vines around my heart and lifts it from my hand.

"No," I say, but it's too late. She carries it to her chest and places it with care inside. Her vines knot closed around it.

"I don't understand," I say. "What did she do to me?" Will I die like this? Is this Emathi's revenge? Her last words don't make sense. That we come into our own. That I would need a jar.

I remember her obsession with the jars. Had this happened to her? Was that where she kept her heart?

Her death threatens to bury me. There's so much I don't know, and I have no one to ask. All my own fault. Heartless, I stand on shaky legs and brush the blood from my hands on the skirt. The pain ebbs as I glance at Hum. She doesn't seem at all perturbed by the fact she now houses my heart. Maybe in time I'll learn what Emathi's done to me.

I hold out my hand for hers. She entwines her seven fingers in my hand.

"Ready?" I say.

The Ceoghast road thrums beneath my feet, and Hum chirps assent.

Epilogue

Four years pass before I'm strong enough to visit my family's home in Horth. Not strength in magic — the Ceoghast road is happy to deliver me to almost any destination at any time — but confidence and stability of self. At first, I was afraid to leave my heart at home — it lives in a jar next to what I recovered of Emathi's, and both seem to be doing well there — but mostly I've been afraid of seeing my family again. I understand and trust myself enough now to confront my father and face my sister. It's a meeting I've pictured a hundred thousand times.

But I could never go home as Cassia, the woman who knew every tenet by heart, who bowed and scraped in hopes of a scrap of approval. I return to them the Heart Witch.

Still, I pause on the steps at the front door. Hum groans behind me, all too aware of my wavering resolve. She reaches through my arm and opens the door.

And thus, I'm delivered home.

The scent of warm yeast and wood polish drags me back to the years I lived here, so desperate for anyone to acknowledge me as good. I shrug past's shadows from my shoulders and make my way to the kitchen. A night like this deserves tea, and it seems too abrupt to march into my family's private bedchambers.

Coals flicker in the stove and are happy to wake for me. Hum sets the kettle to storm and begins to rummage through the cupboards, a habit I've never convinced her to shake. I recline in the chair closest to the kitchen door and wait. My father doesn't keep me long.

Hair matted against the side of his head, dried drool in his beard, he rounds the door with a walking stick clutched in both hands.

"There's no need for that, Father," I say.

"Cassia?"

I can't tell if he recognizes me or not, though I'm not much changed in looks since I left. The fire leaps to provide more light, and the candles on the table smoke then burn. His face is ruddy in the sudden glow. Horror and anger fight for dominance in his expression.

"Yes. It's me," I say.

"What are you doing here? You have to leave. Get out of here. Now!"

I knew better than to expect a warm welcome — he was a willing participant in my stoning after all — but his reaction still hurts.

"No one saw me come here. We have some time," I say.

"Get out of my house."

Hum snarls, loud and cat-like, and my father takes in my monstrous Jack. Her face is more animated than mine these days, and the scope of her expressions seems limitless. Fire black as night leaps from her carved mouth. My father retreats, feet tripping over themselves, until his hip hits the table hard.

"Hum, that's a bit much."

She snorts to extinguish the flames and twists her face into a devil's countenance. My gaze traces over her self-inflicted scars, now thin silver slivers where she'd hurt herself after I abandoned her. We've healed, but those marks remind me daily to make better choices. With playful daintiness at odds with her hellish expression, she brings me a cup of herbal tea.

"What do you want?" my father says. "Why have you brought this demon here?"

I stamp out the sorrow that springs in me at his piteous tone. I don't believe he's scared. He's got too much anger in him for that. He was ready to exorcise me from the house without another word a moment ago. The only reason he doesn't continue in that vein is Hum.

"I came to talk," I say. "It's long overdue, I think. You have answers I want."

He stays pressed against the table and tightens his grip on the walking stick. "What do you want to know?"

I want to know everything, but first, the most important question. "Why did you let Mother die? You knew she wasn't a witch."

"You come all the way here to ask that? You know why. She confessed."

"To save me." The wound is as raw and immediate as the first day I realized her sacrifice. I take the hurt and use it to stoke my rage. "I'm a Heart Witch, Father, and that's an inheritance I could only get from you. It's patrilineal. You knew I was the witch, but you let her die and never told me a thing."

"What do you expect me to have told you? I tried to raise you right. I taught you to live in the Light."

"You taught me to hate myself. I lived a lie."

"We don't live a lie. You were just never good enough, Cassia. I don't know why I bothered."

I am so far from my childhood, yet he calls up all the old shame within me with ease. "Why did you bother?" I say. "You fed me fallowfoot, taught me the tenets, gave me all your hate for the Ceoghast."

Behind me, Hum drops a glass canister on the floor. I glance over and find her scooping sugar and glass into her mouth. Her mischief grounds me and helps me find my center again.

"I wish I hadn't," he says, "if this is all you've become. Another meddlesome Heart Witch. I gave you the best chance I could."

"The chance you wanted," I say.

"The chance I took. The one you nearly spoiled."

His heart is too loud for me to ignore, though I've never been good at human hearts. Most of it's a mess of rage and hurt, but part of it is clear. "You came from the Ceoghast," I say.

"I belong in the Light."

The constant vitriol he has for the Ceoghast makes more sense now. I always thought my mother was the cause of his hate, but this is deeper. It's personal.

"Why did you leave?" I say. I can list a million reasons why a person would want to leave the Ceoghast, but I want his.

His nostrils flare, and he glares at me with such black-eyed hate I worry Hum may step between us. "Why would I stay in a place where magic is might and those without it are no better than drowned ponies at a horserace?"

"You have no magic?"

"You were my magic. I was gifted the lineage of the Heart Witch, which left nothing to me and everything to some nonexistent child." He's dagger-sharp and loud. I'm surprised no one else has come downstairs. Surely his wife or Katta should have heard him.

A feeling of dread crawls into my belly. I ignore it. "You left because you didn't want to have the next Heart Witch?"

"I left so I could achieve something in my life. The only chance at greatness I had there was you." His scorn stings, and Hum, with a mouthful of sugar, growls a warning.

Understanding slips into my body. Just as not everyone who lives there is strange or made of nightmares or has power beyond mortal reach, not everyone who looks mortal and lacks power is without their own monstrosity. Hate drove my father every day of his life, and when it was not at the helm of his choices, fear took over.

I gesture at the room. "But what greatness did you ever achieve here? Your life is small and petty and mean."

"You made it that way," he says.

"I was a child."

"You were a witch."

"Is Katta?"

My change of subject catches him off-guard. "What?"

"Is Katta a witch?" I say.

"No." His face is a storm cloud.

Relief and disappointment wash through my empty chest. "Where is she?" Hum's made so much noise even the dog next door barked in answer to her clatter. "If you've done anything to..."

"She's gone," he says.

I feel like the floor's opened beneath my feet. "What do you mean?"

"She ran away," he says. "A year back or so."

Not dead, but not here. "She hasn't come back? Where did she go?" She's my main reason for coming here.

"I don't know," he says. I touch his heart and find truth.

"You didn't look for her?"

"She made a choice. We gave her everything."

"She's a child," I say. I've held her as my center for so long I feel unhinged. "You should have gone after her. Looked for her."

"Child or no, she's no better than a ceogot. She was mouthy when you were here, but after we kicked you out, she was a menace. She thought herself above the tenets, started to talk back."

Hum throws a serving dish at the doorway by my father's head. Her aim is impeccable. He ducks and comes up, face pinched white. But Hum's right. I have as much as I'll get from him. If Katta's not here, I have no reason to linger. "We're done," I say.

He shies from me as I stand, his stick before him like a barrier. "You're leaving?"

"Yes."

"And you're taking that thing with you?"

"If you're rude she might decide to stay until you warm up to her," I say. Hum leers and wiggles her head at him. He retreats from the doorway as we approach.

"Where's your wife?" I say. If she were here, she would have come down.

"She left. After Katta."

I don't blame her. All my life the voice inside my mind that judged my every action was his. If I'd had the smallest ounce of self-respect earlier, I would have left him, too.

Hum opens the front door and steps outside where she stretches into her full height.

"Don't come back here," he says to my back.

For all I know he's not worth the pain, his words cut. "I'll take that under consideration," I say.

Hum shuts the door behind us. We stand on the step and listen as he drags something heavy across the floor to bar the door. As if that would keep us out if we wanted in. Hum scratches at the door, and for a moment I consider stopping her, knowing she's carving a mark the people of Horth will consider a sign of evil. I let it happen. My father has done enough harm, and this slight revenge feels the least we could do, especially as he abandoned Katta.

Katta. Hum chatters to me in melancholy tones. She echoes my every ache, as the shock of not seeing my sister sets in. I finally found my courage to face her, and she left long ago.

"I don't know, Hum." I lace my arm through hers as we descend the stairs. "I'll look for her, but maybe she's found her place. I found mine."

I half-believe it, too. She wouldn't leave home without a plan, and if she was smart enough to leave our poisonous father, she's smart enough to stay out of trouble. My sister — strong, stubborn, relentless Katta — must have found her way. And one day, that way will lead her back to me. I'll make sure of it.

The End

Glossary of Characters

Cassia Mooseroot (she/her): protagonist of the novel, a young woman of Horth who moves to Midt

Corna (she/her): a woman of Midt who works in the laundry with Cassia

Ealey (he/him): a member of Midt's border patrol and Cassia's border patrol partner

Emathi (she/her): the Heart Witch of Speckled Hound Hollow

Eni (she/her): a member of Midt's town council

Father (he/him): Cassia and Katta's biological father

Hum (she/her): stunted squash of Jack's Patch

Katta Mooseroot (she/her): Cassia's younger sister

Knave (they/them): a mysterious stranger

Knife (she/her): Keeper and Carver of Jack's Patch, sibling of Knave

Lightbearer Erik (he/him): a Lightbearer

Milhewna Laventi (she/her): a member of Midt's town council

Niehe Almadon (she/her): leader of Midt's border patrol

Owers (he/him): a member of Midt's border patrol

Pansy (she/her): a member of Midt's border patrol

Rasmo (she/her): Cassia's childhood friend

Russ (he/him): a member of Midt's town council

Ryder (he/him): a member of Midt's town council

Willer Carros (he/him): a member of Midt's town council

Glossary of Creatures and Other Living Things

Boonabog: a light-producing pond found deep within the Crepuscular Jungle

Candy corn: a tri-colored, triangle-shaped creature known for its razor-sharp teeth and swarming habits

Ceogot: a person or being suspected of having evil within them, to be a ceogot is to have the Ceoghast itself within them

Elementrill: a small, invasive pest known for causing havoc in the form of natural disasters of varied scale, may involve fire, electricity, water, or earth

Evil's Triumph: a plant native to the Ceoghast identified by its complicated, scaly body with bulbous heart-shaped flowers; this flower is called by witches from the ground where many seeds lay dormant; the bloom is said to be an outward expression of a witch's evil triumph

Fallowfoot: a common herb known to suppress a witch's natural talents

Faery: miniature, winged, humanoid creatures with warlike tendencies

Feryot: a skeletal bird-like creature known to cross great distances; seeing one is considered an ominous omen

Glows: disembodied faery parts that coalesce in colorful floating orbs, most frequently found in and around trees

Groll: an undead troll-like creature known to bite the skin of whatever creature it can reach; repelled by feathers, fur, and other skin-coverings

Heart's Joy (flower): a plant native to the Ceoghast identified by its complicated, scaly body with bulbous heart-shaped flowers; this flower is called by witches from the ground where many seeds lay dormant; the bloom is said to be an outward expression of a witch's joy

Heart's Sorrow (flower): a flower native to the Ceoghast identified by its heavy-headed blue flowers that drip like tears from its green stalk; this flower is called by witches from the ground where many seeds lay dormant; the bloom is said to be an outward expression of a witch's sadness or regret

Jack: a sentient pumpkin-headed creature with a body made of vines originally created to protect the Ceoghast

Kelpie: an equine-like water creature that enjoys drowning nonaquatic beings

Lightbearer: a person blessed by the Light to preserve and protect the traditions and boundaries of the Tenet Lands

Nyxies: headless, twig-like creatures with wide mouths full of sharp teeth whose bodies are in a constant state of rot

Screambane: a small shrieking sprite known to attach itself to whoever or whatever disturbs it; commonly found under low-lying plants

Sight-hound: a type of dog bred for its ability to hunt by sight and speed

Stunted squash: a squash that comes to life having consumed magic intended for the Jacks, considered an invasive pest

Traditionkeeper: a person within the Tenet Lands designated as a recorder and monitor of a community's rituals and habits

270

Glossary of Places

Borderlands: the neutral land between the Ceoghast and the Tenet Lands

Ceoghast (pronounced kyoh-gahst): a place and entity that encompasses all lands beyond the Tenet Lands, known by outsiders to be a place where evil thrives

Claug: a border town that abuts the Ceoghast

Crawling Zone: a group of trails that connect Midt to the borderlands abutting the Ceoghast

Crepuscular Jungle: a dense jungle in southern reaches of the Ceoghast

Horth: a middle-sized town in the center of the Tenet Lands

Midt: a border town that abuts the Ceoghast where Cassia currently lives, east of Horth

Morrow Road: a group of trails that connect Midt to the borderlands abutting the Ceoghast

Rider's Pass: a group of trails that connect Midt to the borderlands abutting the Ceoghast

Shivireen: a border town that abuts the Ceoghast

Speckled Hound Hollow: a deep, round hollow where speckled pumpkins grow, home to the Heart Witch's house

Jack's Patch: magical grounds where Jacks come to life, cared for and guarded by Keeper and Carver Knife

Witch's Watch: a group of trails that connect Midt to the borderlands abutting the Ceoghast; the Ceoghast frequently encroaches upon this set of trails

Glossary of Terms

Ceoguts: a derogatory term

Darkfall: the moment the last of the day's light leaves and anytime thereafter until the sun returns

Eldritch Ways: ancient paths created by witches to expedite travel from one area of the Ceoghast to another; to use the paths, one must know the exact movements required to access them

Judgement Days: a multi-day event in Horth during which time all grievances and accusations are brought to the town council for resolution

Light, the: a sacred deity and / or ideal worshipped in the Tenet Lands; the source of all good

Light's Day: a celebratory day in the Tenet Lands that marks the sun's return and the withdraw of the days of long darkness

Acknowledgements

Much of writing involves staring into space as characters
and places dance through my mind, swapping pen refills as I
handwrite my way through scene after scene, and filling those 80-
page spiral-bound books I buy in armfuls from Staples when they
go on sale. The part I love and fear in equal measure involves
taking those pages and placing them in the hands of so many other
people. This intimate act requires an immense amount of trust and
respect, and I am so very lucky to have the most amazing group of
Hell Yes People in my life. The cheerleaders who encourage me to
continue while also pushing me to do the very best I can as I wend
my way through Story.

Moki, you've been with me (willing or no) since the
beginning days of play time and horse stories, then JTT, Sailor
Moon, and N'Sync fan fiction. You were the first person I made
cry with my stories, and the power I felt was absolutely
intoxicating. Thank you for breaking your heart on my words. You
read everything I ask you to look over and are never shy with your
feedback. I love you. Thank you.

Gabe, my love, my heart, you have been the one with an
intimate behind-the-scenes look at my writing life. Without you, I
wouldn't be able to build these wild worlds...or produce an
audiobook of any quality. You put in hours editing my spoken
words; your journalist eye forces me to be a better writer; your
technological know-how elevates my books; and your love allows
me to be a better person. I am endlessly thankful to have you in my
life. I love you. Thank you.

Dawn Ius, you created a safe space for me and my stories.
You held me through my burnout and made sure I saw the good in

my work. This novel would not be here without your constant support. Thank you. Dear readers, go read Dawn's books — my personal favourite is *Lizzie*.

Erik Grove, your insight, encouragement, and novels push me to be a better writer. I am so glad to have a writer as tortured by an abundance of novels as I am, and the pace you set inspires me to keep my own. Thank you. Dear readers, find Erik's stories — they will haunt you in the best way.

Janice Leadingham, thank you for bringing me into your mischief. You have been my constant cheerleader, and I am in awe of your stories. Thank you. Dear readers, seek out her words — they're magical.

Marie Bouvier, your heart and encouragement never fail to uplift me. Thank you. I am smitten with your stories and so excited for the rest of the world to read them. Dear readers, you will love the wonder Marie spins in her stories.

Brian Brett, you mentored me, made me a better writer, and ushered me through my MFA. During our first conversation, you slammed your fist on the table and upset the water glasses as you expounded on the necessity of people to write in every genre. Your uproarious passion and dedication to Story terrified and delighted me, and I knew I'd found my Thesis Advisor. Thank you. I wish I could have gotten this story into your hands so you could see where my words have gone since you last saw them. Dear readers, you'll be delighted with all of Brian's work, but I most enthusiastically recommend *Trauma Farm*.

Tiffany Dae, your artful worlds are pure magic, and having you create my cover art has been such a thrilling journey. You pour the whole of yourself into all you do, and I am so thankful for your experience, whimsy, and generous spirit. Thank you. Dear readers, you can find Tiffany's art at TiffanyDae.com and even commission her for stunning paintings as I have, or have her paint live at your wedding!

Monte Lin, your copy edits have made my work so much stronger. I am grateful for your careful eye, attention to detail, and ability to question what I made unclear. Any remaining errors are entirely my fault. Thank you for your kindness and committed eye.

Kristina Osborn, your cover design absolutely floored me, and working with you to ensure the cover did everything we needed it to was a joy. Thank you so much for your creativity and care. Dear readers, you should check out her press at https://trubornpress.com.

My little dead poet loves, you'll never be able to read this, but I love each of you so much and am so grateful for all the time you spend with me — often abducting my writing arm for your pillow and reminding me that I'm meant to be paying attention to you, not bringing stories into this world. Every moment with you is such a joy. I love you. Thank you.

Finally, I would like to thank you, dear reader. You've not just bought this book — you've supported an indie author, her pack of misfit monsters, and creatures like Hum, who have yet to make their way into this world. We hope you'll join us on our next adventure. Thank you from the bottom of all our dark hearts for joining us for this one.

Reading List

I can't ignore an opportunity to tell another about books. These stories are not like Heart Witch — you won't find similar reads here. What you will find is a short list of stories I love and recommend wholeheartedly:

The Last Unicorn by Peter S. Beagle: This is the book I read almost every year, and each time I go through its pages, I am swept into a story as intimate as my own life yet new and fresh. The story grows as I have grown, and each time I read it, the more magic I find within.

The *Lockwood & Co.* series by Jonathan Shroud: If comfort food is a thing, comfort reads also exist, and this series is one of mine. The audiobook is great, but the narrator changes partway through the series — prepare yourself for the jolt (thankfully, both narrators are wonderful).

Every story written by Janice Leadingham: Janice is the witch you want in your life. Her words are spellbinding. You can find a list of her published work at https://www.hagsoup.com/words

The September House by Carissa Orlando: I highly recommend this one in audiobook form because the narrator brings this character to life. Such good spooky fun.

The Indian Lake Trilogy by Stephen Graham Jones: I don't know if a more perfect novella series exists for horror loves.

Four Thousand Weeks: Time Management for Mortals by Oliver Burkeman: Burkeman's book departs from the usual time management / self-help model that tells us we can do it all if only we master our minutes. Instead, tearing down the idea of optimization in favour of mortality-based alternatives, suggestions, and encouragement. I'm better at organizing my life thanks to this book.

Schubert's Winter Journey: Anatomy of an Obsession by Ian Bostridge: This is a book you don't realize you need until you're already deep in its pages, wondering how you've been without it for so long. A story of single-minded passion, Bostridge shows how psychologically, emotionally, and physically singular Schubert's composition is.

Stereoblind by Emma Healey: I kept Healey's poetry in my bag for years. A quiet sort of friend you can pull out when you want out feel more human.

The Murderbot Diaries by Martha Wells: This series is one of my all-time fav re-reads. If you want to laugh, grab the first book in the series *All Systems Red*.

Land Acknowledgement

This book was written and recorded on the traditional unceded homelands of the Ojibwe, Odawa, and Potawatomi Nations, also known as the Council of the Three Fires. Many other tribes, including the Myyamia, Peoria, Ho-Chunk, and others called this area home, and it remains home to a diverse Indigenous population today.

About the Author

Justus Joseph is what happens if you mix Sailor Moon, Glenda the Good Witch, and Snow White together — if they all had a love affair with dark fantasy and horror and had terrible chronic illnesses. Originally from British Columbia, Canada where she grew up surrounded by forests, animals both wild and domestic, and a library of books, Justus has called Canada, Japan, and the United States home.

She currently lives in Chicago with her husband, her six dogs, two cats, and a rotating crew of foster animals. When she's not writing stories, she's sculpting clay, drawing portraits of pets and people, training dogs, or wondering why she's so tired.

You can find her upcoming stories and artwork at justusjoseph.com or at instagram.com/justusijoseph, but for the best updates, you'll want to join her newsletter *Lessons in Monsters and Magic* at https://justusjoseph.substack.com/

Extras
An excerpt from the next book
in the Ceoghast Collection

Black Kate
Chapter 1

The dark side of a schooner loomed over Black Kate like a tidal wave, and she yanked the oars to avoid running into the ship's broad side. Curses flew from her mouth in whispered hisses. Ordinarily, she wasn't a bad navigator, but that wasn't the first ship she nearly hit that evening. In the fog, the moon's cold light was hardly enough to illuminate any of the vessels moored in Destruction Bay. Everything was dark and gray, color leeched from it like life sucked dry. Her need to get back to her ship, the Rue, before the captain caught her missing drove her to take stupid risks, and that damned night wasn't making the journey easy.

She regarded the unlit lantern at her feet, and again considered whether to kindle a small flame to help guide her. She shuddered at the fool's idea and kicked the lantern under the far seat, along with the temptation. She was no night fisher out to lure baitfish with a bright show, and even if she were, she'd know better than to cast any nets on a night like this.

She squinted into the black. She couldn't be far from the Rue but damned if she could see so much as a shadow. Still, she didn't need a light. She just had to keep rowing and keep quiet.

The oars glided through the water as silent as she could make them, each stroke sustaining a steady pace. Her shoulder ached with the tension of such control, with the reflexive flinch she suffocated with every drip and splash. The whole world sounded muffled — not even the pitiless seabirds dared make a sound — which meant sirens lurked below her rowboat.

When the sea was so calm at night, even the landfolk knew to stay well away from the water, which made Kate's presence all the more unforgivable. She knew better. The siren silence wasn't the stuff of tales. Memories of sirens dragging people into the sea's dark green depths rose in her mind like a flock of birds taking flight. All those folks drowned, the only warning they ever had was the uncanny soundless night.

The sea wasn't always that way. Even when Kate came to the Outer Ports only five years earlier, sirensong was not so fatal. The sirens would lure sailors off their ships, drown a few of them for sport and fun, and none of the seafaring folk minded much. They knew the risks. But then the sirens changed.

The seafarers noticed the silence first. A preternatural calm that pillowed even wind and wave. The waters grew murky with grease, and then white flakes — like fish skin left to rot in sunlight — would float to the surface.

At first no one knew enough to be afraid, especially among Kate's kind. Fear never came easy to pirates, so even if their instincts screamed at them to run, those first pirates leaned over the deck rails and dropped their dinghies into the water to have a better look.

Kate wasn't at sea when the sirens committed their first massacre, but the few who survived made sure seafarer and landfolk alike all heard the tale.

The sirens were sick. Their voices had changed. Nothing of play was left in them. They sought only to kill those unlike them, on nights just like this.

Kate scanned the surface for white flakes as she rowed. She shouldn't have left the Rue at all, but the money was too good to pass up, and the job was supposed to be quick. She could never say no to money like that, so she snuck off the ship and found her way to shore.

"Sitting ducks," Kate's evening employer had said about the grab he wanted her and a handful of others to complete. He wasn't wrong, either, but those others he'd hired were idiots.

Kate wouldn't have been late if Kay Creevin had kept his wits about him and not stabbed himself in his own thigh. A bad wound, too. Not a mistaken glance but a deep cut that gushed. Kate's wasn't clear on how he did it. It would've been better if his blade had gone deeper. Instead of dying, he slowed the group down, which was far from preferable. On top of that, he couldn't haul his share of the load they'd pilfered. Useless.

Perhaps if they'd been an established crew and not newly acquainted hired hands, one of the others would've done Kay Creevin in and sped things up for the rest of them. But if you didn't know who you were dealing with, no sense in getting involved in a potential blood feud for killing a fool. When you didn't know who you were working with, best behavior tended to keep the greater bloodshed at bay.

"Hello?"

The soft voice startled Kate into jumping. Her oars launched out of the water and unbalanced the dinghy. A siren! She dropped the oars to grab the fixed blade at her hip. The paddles dropped with a deafening splash, not that quiet mattered now that a siren had found her, and with no flakes in the water to warn her beforehand.

"I'm sorry. I didn't mean to scare you."

Not a siren. Just another dumb mortal looking for death on the water. Irritation warred with her relief. "Keep your damn voice down," Kate snapped.

"I'm sorry."

Kate slammed her knife into its sheath and turned towards the voice. "And I'm not scared."

When her gaze found a woman in a rowboat, she didn't understand how she didn't catch sight of her earlier. The woman was close enough Kate should have seen her, and with hair that gleamed like pure silver in the moonlight even the shadows couldn't have hidden her away.

"I need help," the woman said.

Kate snarled. At this point, it felt likely they'd both need help. The woman did nothing to moderate her voice, so she either didn't know about the sirens at all — an unforgivable offense — or she didn't understand how they hunted.

Not that the siren threat was the only reason this woman should be more cautious — she was out in pirate waters asking for help. Like any of them would act outside their own interests. Her ignorance and neediness stirred Kate's anger.

"Help yourself, then," Kate said. Her voice hissed across the water, reminded her of the greater threat beneath the waves.

Not only would this woman rouse the sirens with her chatter, she'd call Kate's captain down on both their heads. Kate grabbed her oars again.

"No, you don't understand." The woman still hadn't softened her tone. "I need transport back to my island."

She was in a bloody boat. She didn't need help. "Then start rowing. I'm not interested," Kate said, each syllable a punch.

"I can pay."

Even with her pocket heavy with coin earned from the evening's ill-done venture, the offer tempted her. Money always did. Like an itch beneath her skin, the promise of safety she'd never known. Maybe some people were called to the pirate life for what it offered, but for Kate it was a paycheck, and her current work aboard the Rue didn't line her pockets fast enough. Not if she was going to make good on the boat she'd arranged to buy. With only twenty-eight days left before the annual seafaring auction, she had to have enough together for the sloop she'd wheedled down to a nearly accessible sum. But even with the promised lower cost, she was short nine gold cronies. At this point, she couldn't afford to be picky about offers of pay that came her way.

That said, this woman would have to offer enough to cover Kate's pay for the next months plus cushion because if Kate didn't get back on the Rue now, she wouldn't have a job. Half-drowned and clearly friendless, if this woman had real coin, she'd have found transport already through more legitimate means, even on a night like this. She wouldn't be out here shouting at the first rowboat that happened by.

"You have nothing I want." Kate began to row.

"Please," the woman says. Her voice skipped across the water like a large stone. Not a chance Kate's crewmates and captain didn't hear her. If they caught Kate out here in the dinghy...

Kate's cutlass didn't help the noise, and it caught the moonlight as much as the woman's hair, but she wanted to be as clear as possible. Anger helped dismiss the risks.

"The only reason I'd row over there would be to cut your head off," Kate said. Even in the state of pique, her wrath wasn't all for this woman — but she was an easy target. "Leave off."

"I'm sorry." The woman recoiled then pawed at the water on either side of her boat. Was she trying to call up the damn sirens? Vitriol piled on Kate's tongue, but then she saw what the woman was doing. That's how the woman paddled out here. By hand. She didn't have oars.

Pity stretched in Kate's chest like a too-old cat unhappy to be disturbed. She'd been in situations similar, with no one and nothing, but she got out on her own, and so would this woman. Relying on other people never did anyone any good. Kate turned away from the pathetic figure and paddled the last few meters for the Rue.

The dinghy ties still hung where she left them, and no one had poked their head over the side yet. It was hard to believe she was the only one who heard the woman's commotion, but she'd take the luck if it stayed true. She glanced out at the water, but the woman was gone from view, which was just as well.

Kate scaled the knotted rope she left hanging to board the ship. It, like stealing the dinghy, violated many of the Rue's rules. Not that she didn't understand why those sorts of laws existed — she even agreed with the sense most of them offered — but Kate never allowed a rule, good or bad, stop her from doing what she wanted. They weren't made with her in mind, so she didn't mind them when they obstructed, rather than served, her purpose.

She reached deck level and peered through the salt-scarred wood railing onto the ship before hauling herself over.

"I expect better of my crew, Black Kate," the captain said in a low whisper.

Damn.

Kate froze halfway to her feet, like a child caught at mischief. Her stomach squirmed with that juvenile feeling and made her uncomfortable enough to free her from the fear. She was no child.

With a haughty glare, she straightened her shoulders and spun to face Captain Mullen, whose stony expression told her none of her bravado was impressive. Captain Mullen's weather-rough face said she'd seen it all before. Broad as an ox, Mullen towered above the whole crew, and across from her, Kate's below-average height seemed downright spritely.

"You left the Rue, stole a boat, abandoned your watch, exposed the Rue to infiltration — and all during a siren silence. Did I miss anything?"

"Back now," Kate said. "No harm done."

"Plenty of harm," Captain Mullen said. Her black eyes sparked with the rage she'd suppressed to have the conversation. Any other member of the crew might have tread lightly, but Kate couldn't make herself back down, not when it was for her own good. And especially not when others would think think it for her own good. She wasn't there to please anyone.

"Not that I see," Kate said.

"You're not carrying your weight, Kate. A ship runs when the crew takes their even load of the work. You're a problem."

Kate leaned against the deck rail, determined to be at ease if she had to sit through a lecture again. This one had become one of Captain Mullen's favorites.

"I do my work," Kate said, almost by rote.

"Not on the Rue you don't."

"Name a single time I've failed to keep my fair share." She was a good worker, a hard worker. She didn't go around asking and owing favors.

"This time. Right here. You're more than an hour late for watch. Riesl's up there covering for you, which means you've cut into her rest. And for what? Some side job to put a few extra silvers in your stack?"

Kate wished the job had paid so well, but all she got was a handful of tridevil glass and half-pieces. The jobs she lined up for tomorrow promised to make up for it.

Captain Mullen rubbed her face. "It's enough for me to fire you. I'm tired of this, Kate. I'm not your nursemaid or caretaker, and you're not stupid. You know the rules we keep here. You agreed to them when you signed on. You're either on the Rue to be on the Rue, or you're off. We don't keep in-between spaces here. So, it's no side-jobs, or only side-jobs. Your choice."

That was not how the lecture usually went. Kate covered her shock with a snort.

"I'm too valuable to let go." The bravado came out flat, but her mind was busy with new calculations. Neither neither salary on the Rue, nor the income she got from outside employment, would produce enough money for a ship on their own. She needed both if her plan was to succeed. But if she had to give up on one, the Rue offered better returns.

"Your contract is coming up, and you haven't renewed. Seems to me like you don't want to be here."

Kate's lips twisted. She didn't want to be here — she only joined the Rue for a consistent paycheck. Signing on for the next five years, which was the only contract Mullen offered after the initial trial year was up, when she meant to have a ship of her own was a form of self-sabotage she wouldn't undertake. No one broke pirate contracts — you try to leave, and the crew broke you.

"I'm weighing all my options," Kate said.

"Then weigh this one: if you mess up one more time, you're off the ship, Kate," Captain Mullen said. "And to be perfectly clear, that means no more night work off-ship. No more side-jobs if you're not on leave. A single instance here that you haven't pulled your full weight, and you're gone. You lose your place on the Rue, and we leave you at the nearest port. Are we clear?"

Kate ground her teeth as she bit back her retorts to allow only one word out. "Clear."

"And, Kate, you have an appointment with the cat when your watch ends. I think twenty lashes should make the point."

Kate groaned but knew better than to protest. She did that once and saw the lashes double, then triple. With a twenty in her future, she pinched her lips shut. "Yes, Captain."

"Now get to your watch."

Kate stormed away from the captain with as much malice as she could muster. Twenty lashes before her job tomorrow. She'd need some of Riesl's cat cure to make it, and that didn't come cheap. Already the coins in her pocket felt lighter.

"Black Kate," Riesl said when Kate climbed into the watch nest. Riesl, the only dvegar on board the ship, was as broad as she was tall. If Kate had to pick a favorite crewmate, Riesl would be it, straightforward in a way the rest of the world should be. Kate always knew what Riesl wanted, and Riesl knew Kate wouldn't do anything that didn't benefit her.

"Riesl."

"You're late."

"I was busy," Kate said.

"You're not usually late."

Kate sighed. "Some idiot stabbed himself in the leg."

"But not enough for a sympathy kill?"

"Not well enough."

"I heard the captain," she said. "Sounds like you're out of luck for tomorrow."

"No, I'm going to go. I'll work it out," Kate said.

"That'll cost you."

"I know."

"And I heard you've a date with the daughter. You'll be wanting some cat's cure, then?"

Riesl's eagerness to take advantage of the situation left Kate sharp, but she needed both Riesl's silence and the salve. "How much?"

"I'll take a handful of your haul from tonight. My handful, mind."

It was robbery, but Kate had no choice but to pay it. Riesl was the one person on board Kate actually trusted to keep her word. Kate emptied her pocket on the ground and watched Riesl lean down to take her her handful, all but seven tridevil glass coins. Tears pricked Kate's eyes. She was so tired. Had had enough of working so hard to get ahead, to get out from under others, only to come out like this. One way or another.

Kate grabbed the remaining coins and shoved them in her pocket. At least she had a good job lined up for tomorrow. She would make up for the loss then.

Black Kate sets sail October 13, 2026.